I0685804

A Deadly Mistake

A Lipton St Faith Mystery

A Deadly Mistake

KEITH FINNEY

LUME BOOKS

LUME BOOKS

Published in 2022 by Lume Books

Copyright © Keith Finney 2022

The right of Keith Finney to be identified as the author of this work
has been asserted by them in accordance with the Copyright, Design
and Patents Act, 1988.

All rights reserved. No part of this publication may be
reproduced, stored in a retrieval system, or transmitted in
photocopying, recording or otherwise, without the prior
permission of the copyright owner.

ISBN 978-1-83901-224-2

Typeset using Atomik ePublisher from Easypress Technologies

www.lumebooks.co.uk

For Joan

Chapter One: A Fateful Event

A light drizzle fell lazily across the Norfolk village of Lipton St Faith. Vicar's daughter Anna Grix and American Lieutenant Eddie Elsner chatted as they hurried with other parishioners to Sunday Morning Worship at Lipton's 900-year-old Norman church.

Late autumn had been kind as 1941 drew to a close. Now, as they celebrated the first Sunday of Advent, the weather had turned as a bitter dampness hung in the heavy air.

'The thirtieth of November already, where has the time gone?' said Anna as she waved at one of several evacuees billeted in the village.

'Let's hope 1942 brings better news for the war effort. You guys have had it rough for quite a while now. Surely 1942 has to bring better days,' said Lieutenant Elsner, who'd first come across Anna when he accidentally knocked her off a bicycle with his jeep several months earlier. After their unorthodox introduction, the pair had developed a firm friendship based on their differences and joint curiosity about solving murders.

'Do come along, Vinny, or we'll be late.' The soft voice dispensing a disarming rebuke to a small boy just short of his tenth birthday belonged to Anna's mother, Helen.

1

'Don't want to go in, it's all candles and stupid hymns.' Vinny, a Liverpool evacuee, had landed in the Grix household through a circuitous route in the late summer via North Wales and now found himself inveigled into a loving host family with the vicar serving as its titular head under the firm grip of Helen, and a close-knit village in which everyone seemed to know everyone else's business.

'I thought you liked church. What's changed?'

The little boy pulled a rubber band from a pocket in his short khaki trousers and began stretching it between two fingers as he kicked some loose gravel from the pathway. 'I want to see me ma, it's been ages.'

As Helen comforted the usually chipper Scouser, her daughter looked on with the hint of concern. 'It's easy to forget what these little ones are going through when you normally see them mucking around in the village.'

Anna thought her concerned tone had missed the mark as her companion straightened his immaculate uniform and removed his hat, ready to enter the ancient place of worship.

'Eddie.'

'Yes, I heard. I guess Christmas coming isn't helping, but he's a brave little man. He'll be fine,' whispered the American as they crossed the threshold from the damp exterior of the church to its dry, but cold, interior.

A kerfuffle from behind interrupted their exchange. Anna turned to see a policeman attempting to push his way through a throng of parishioners who now blocked the entrance to the flintstone-faced church.

'Morning, you two. I need a quick word before you go in.' Village bobby Tom Bradshaw drew the ire of several villagers as he impeded their progress to get out of the drizzle.

Better clear the way before we cause a riot, thought Anna.

Following much tutting and one or two comments that a vicar's daughter should know better than to delay their efforts to hear the Gospel, Anna worked herself clear and pulled Eddie from the small crowd.

'What's so urgent, Tom? Oh, and by the way, congratulations again on having your promotion to sergeant confirmed,' said Anna.

Tom rested a finger on his newly sewn-on stripes. 'Oh, you mean these!'

Eddie replaced his military cap to keep the worst of the intensifying drizzle from his Brylcreemed hair. 'Yes, well deserved, Tom. Especially since Anna got you suspended before you turned that murder case around.'

'Don't be so cheeky, you. I thought we'd knocked those sharp American corners from your shoulders. I can see now we have more work to do with you.' Anna smiled as she rebuked the lieutenant, while noticing Tom looking urgently at his wristwatch. 'OK, what's so important you almost got us thrown out of my father's church?'

Tom looked up at the Regency clock that sat in the squat Norman church tower and compared it to the time on his own watch. 'There's been a car accident a few miles outside the village. Sounds a bad 'un. The ambulance crew are already on scene, but guess what?' Tom waited for a response before continuing. 'Inspector Spillers said I can lead on the investigation. What do you think of that? My first big case.'

Sergeant Bradshaw turned on his heels and made his way to an old police car parked next to the church Lychgate. Stopping for a second under cover of the thatched roof of the old structure, Tom looked back at his two friends. 'Tell Helen I should still be in time for Sunday lunch, so to keep some of her lovely spuds ready for me.'

Anna waved the policeman off and raised her eyebrows as she turned back to Eddie. 'A little over-excited, don't you think?'

'He won't be when he sees what I suspect is in that car. Once seen, it's not something he'll easily forget.'

By the time the pair made their way back into church, Anna's father was well into his opening address.

Oops, he's seen us, she thought.

Anna knew he noticed every detail of what his congregation got up to in church when addressing them. Concentrating on the tiled floor, she tiptoed down the aisle in the full knowledge many disapproving eyes followed her and Eddie's every embarrassed step.

'I welcome you as we celebrate the first Sunday of Advent, though I know what ought to be a joyous occasion for the country, and us as individuals is, once again, overshadowed by the evil forces attempting to destroy our way of life.'

Anna scanned the almost full church for somwhere to sit, before pulling Eddie into a pew immediately behind Helen and young Vinny.

Contented that her father's solemn words had distracted the gossip-prone members of the congregation from her late entrance, Anna looked on fondly as Vinny distracted himself with his elastic band and bits of paper, trying his best to use the stretchy material as a crossbow to shoot projectiles at a tall brass candlestick in a small Lady Chapel to his right.

The vicar's gentle but penetrative voice resonated around the building's solid interior as he spoke. 'Let us remember the poor souls of the Indo-China region, whatever their belief, as Japanese forces continue to threaten them. Also, our brothers and sisters in Singapore as they face the peril of a possible invasion.

Anna's attention returned to Vinny as her mother stopped the youngster letting off another paper salvo by confiscating the elastic band.

After scowling at Helen, Vinny turned to Anna for support. 'Behave yourself, young man or no football later.' Her whispered tone gave the boy little hope of regaining ownership of his prized crossbow. Instead, he turned to his front and began scraping the diamond-shaped glazed tile floor with the heels of his newly cleaned shoes.

Forty minutes later the service ended with an uplifting organ chorus, which served as Vinny's signal to make for the door. Helen tried but failed to grab the boy before turning to her daughter. 'I'd better get back before that scamp ruins his Sunday best digging in his vegetable patch again.' Helen pointed to a wall clock. 'Don't forget, I need you back sharpish this week. We have a special visitor coming and there are potatoes to get ready.'

Eddie turned to Anna. 'Well, that's you told.'

'And the same goes for you, lieutenant. There's the rest of the veg to sort out, so hop to it, both of you.'

Anna pointed a finger at her companion and smirked as her mother got to her feet.

'And whatever you do, don't get caught by Beatrice Flowers. She's been bending your father's ear about how noisy the church bells are again. You wouldn't think they've rung every Sunday morning for half a millennium, would you?'

Anna could tell it wasn't a question her mother expected an answer to. Despite her best efforts, as soon as she and Eddie cleared the entrance to the church, Beatrice pounced, having already pinned her father against the flint face of the church as other congregants attempted to wish the vicar well.

As Anna attempted a rescue, she noticed Beatrice had grabbed Betty Simpson, widowed landlady of The King's Head public house, and began complaining about the evils of drink.

Mine is the greater cause, thought Anna as she extracted her father from Beatrice's interrogation. Not least, she knew the doughty woman took no prisoners with her hard-won success.

'You know what, Beatrice Flowers, you're the best thing in this village for my pub because you drive so many of the locals to drink.'

Anna smiled as she grabbed Eddie by the arm. 'I think we can leave Betty to her bête noire, or business asset, depending on which side of the fence you sit regarding warm beer and the occasional whisky!'

The vicarage kitchen rang to the sound of Vinny's protests at being washed at the large Belfast sink as Anna, her father, and Eddie entered.

'What's all this din?' exclaimed Anna as she watched a greyish wave of water overflow the sink and splash onto the otherwise spotless tiled floor, save for a trail of mud leading from the vestibule to the sink.

'I don't like water,' protested the shirtless young Scouser as he resisted all attempts by Helen to probe the boy's ears with the corner of a small hand towel, while taking a firm grip of his arm with her free hand.

'That's got to be the understatement of the year, young man. I should say King Canute had more of a liking for the stuff than you. You'll get washed whether you like it. I told you not to go digging in your Sunday best. Look at the state of your shoes.'

Anna smiled as she looked on the scene of the boy flailing about, while studiously not looking at his muddy shoes that rested in disgrace on an old newspaper at the foot of the AGA, a steady plume of steam rising from the soaking leather on which earth had already dried into a thick crust.

'I doubt he's left any soil in the back garden. Look at this lot.' Helen waved the hand towel around.

'Well,' said the vicar, 'things seem under control here, so I'll pop into my office and catch up on some paperwork.'

'The Sunday papers, you mean,' said Helen as she eyed her husband's quick exit with suspicion.

Vinny continued his plucky resistance to any thought of having a clean face.

'Here, let me take over. I expect he'll need a Hershey's bar after his wash... that's *if* he's a good soldier and follows orders. Do we understand each other, Vinny?' Eddie relieved Helen of the hand towel as the young man immediately ceased all resistance.

'I will for a full bar, not half a one like last time.'

Anna pointed a finger at Vinny. 'I don't think you're in any position to negotiate, young man. Superior forces have you surrounded, so I should take whatever you're offered.'

The young boy paused for a moment before replying. 'Suppose so.'

Eddie tickled his charge with the towel. 'There's no "I suppose so" about it, soldier. Now get a clean shirt from your bedroom and apologise to Helen for mucking up her kitchen and we'll see what the chocolate fairy brings you after lunch.'

As the lieutenant pointed Vinny toward the stairs through the open door of the kitchen, Anna strolled over to the sink, sighed as she observed the grimy water and pulled a tired-looking rubber bung from the plug hole and consigned the filthy remains of Vinny's excavations to the drains.

'Right, now I can start on the potatoes,' said Anna as she tidied the beechwood drainer and deposited a pile of large Maris Pipers on its pinkish-grey fluted surface. 'I've got the sink clean and here we go again. Those Land Girls do an outstanding job picking the crops, but they don't half leave a lot of soil on the potatoes.'

'Perhaps they get paid by weight. A bit of soil here and there soon adds up,' responded Eddie as he strolled to the larder to fetch a selection of autumn cabbage, swede, and parsnips, before encroaching on part of Anna's workspace to prep the home-grown produce.

'You mentioned a visitor coming for lunch earlier, Mum. Who is it?'

'Fanny Coulson. A little bird tells me she's got a soft spot for Tom Bradshaw and now he's a sergeant, he's quite a catch,' replied Helen as she peered into the open oven of the AGA to check if it was hot enough to use.

'Mother,' cried Anna. 'You're incorrigible. Does Tom know about this?'

'Not at all. What's it got to do with him? Honestly, Anna. You are naive for twenty-six. Half the time men don't know what they want, and so we must help them. Isn't that right, Eddie?'

The American looked back at the women from under his left arm as he struggled to chop a swede. 'Don't drag me into this, Helen. I have enough to manage with your wilful daughter.'

'At least I know how to cut a swede.' She pointed to a long, slim knife with a serrated edge resting on the kitchen table. 'And as for you, Mum, I'm not naive at all. All I'm saying is that it'll come as a bit of a shock to Tom that you're in the match-making business.'

Helen dismissed her daughter's comment with a wave of her hand as she took a second look into the oven, smiled contentedly, and shut the heavy enamelled door to keep the heat in.

Vinny re-entered the kitchen wearing a puzzled look. 'What does naive mean?'

Helen looked on disapprovingly. 'The opposite of you, young man. I thought Eddie told you to get a clean shirt?'

The boy looked at one of his sleeves. 'It's clean.'

Helen shook her head. 'No, it's not, I put that in the wash basket after school on Friday ready for washing tomorrow.'

Vinny inspected one of his cuffs. 'Looks clean to me and it'll save you some washing, so that's a good thing, isn't it? What with soap suds being scarce? I heard you saying that to a woman the other day.'

8

Anna turned to her mother. 'I think you've met your match this time, Mum. Out of the mouth of babes, eh?'

The boy followed Helen's pointed finger instruction to sit at the table. 'I'll give you soap suds, Vincent O'Conner. You sit there and stay out of trouble.'

'But—'

'But nothing, my young lad,' replied Helen.

Anna looked to Eddie for a solution to the boy's unhappy situation.

'All right, soldier. If it's OK with Helen, I'll take you for a quick game of soccer ball on the Green.'

Vinny's eyes lit up as he looked pleadingly at his surrogate mother.

Helen glanced at an old wall clock. 'You have forty-five minutes before lunch is on this table. If you're not back in time, we start without you, and you can make do with bread and dripping... that goes for both of you. Understand?'

Eddie gave a mock salute as the young boy sprang to his feet, launched himself across the kitchen to the back door and was almost out before turning to offer a last word. 'He means football. There's no such thing as a soccer ball, at least not in a proper country.'

The lieutenant winked at the two women as he followed Vinny out of the door, closing it softly behind him.

'Do you know, it makes me think which one is the kid and who's the adult in that relationship.'

Helen moved towards her daughter to offer the loving touch of a mother's hand on Anna's shoulder. 'They adore one another—it'll be a sad day when we all go our separate ways.'

What? thought Anna.

'What do you mean, Mum?'

Helen rubbed her daughter's shoulder. 'Don't forget, we only have Vinny while it's too dangerous for him to go back to Liverpool. As for Eddie, they could post him somewhere else. Best not to get too close to either of them or you'll get hurt. Do you understand what I'm saying?'

Anna fell silent.

Why is she saying that?

The moment passed as a quiet tap on the front door of the vicarage alerted its occupants to their lunch guest.

Shown into the kitchen by Helen, Fanny Coulson stood motionless in the centre of the room, looking at Anna.

Poor thing, we must mortify her.

Stretching out a hand in greeting, Anna welcomed the stranger with a warm smile. 'That's a lovely coat. How did you save up enough clothing coupons for it?'

Fanny blushed.

Oops, didn't mean to make her feel uncomfortable.

'I mean,' Anna quickly added, 'You know, what with everything, and—'

'I think you've dug that hole deep enough, don't you? Fanny, let me introduce you to my undiplomatic daughter, Anna.'

I can feel myself blushing. Mum always does that.

Fanny smiled. 'It's OK, I know what Anna means, but it's not new. I like to make my stuff. You know, look at a picture in the papers, make the patterns. It's easy.'

'How clever of you, Fanny, which is more than can be said for my daughter, who thinks we use sewing needles for pricking splinters from fingers and nothing more. You're a bit early, but that's no bad thing. You can help set the lunch things before you sit yourself down at the table.'

Before Anna could react, her father came into the kitchen, his head tilted back in an exaggerated gesture of sniffing the air.

'Lunch smells wonderful, my dear... oh, hello, you must be Miss Coulson?'

The visitor got to her feet and smiled. 'It's Fanny, please.'

'Of course,' replied the vicar. 'Fanny it shall be.'

Anna quietly studied the newcomer as their guest retook her seat.

I reckon she's about twenty-five.

'You work at that garage on the Norwich Road, don't you? Now, what's it called?'

'You mean Coulson's?'

'Yes, that's... ah, I see, your family own it. I apologise. Now it all makes sense.'

The visitor giggled as she leaned towards Anna. 'It's fine. The garage belongs to my uncle. I help when he's busy. Have done since being a youngster. If you want to know anything about spark plugs or distributor caps, I'm your girl. But my proper job is working as a police driver. They reckoned my knowledge of cars might come in handy if one breaks down when I'm driving one of their bigwigs about the place. The trouble is it's boring with all the waiting around and suchlike.'

This girl has her head screwed on the right way, that's for sure, thought Anna.

'I knew it,' exclaimed Helen. 'Those boys are going to be late for lunch. Be a darling and round them up for me, will you?'

'Want any help?' asked Fanny.

'No need,' quipped Anna. 'One of us getting soaking wet tracking two idiotic boys down is enough, but thanks for the offer.'

Strolling down the near-deserted high street, Anna pulled her heavy coat closed against a stiffening east wind. A minute later, she spotted her quarries. She could hear Vinny's loud protest that his opposition was being unfair, since he was bigger and heavier.

Eddie's response amounted to lifting the youngster clear off the ground with a single sweep and gathering Vinny under his arm and running down the field with him, making the boy laugh.

Perhaps Mum has a point, thought Anna as she witnessed the two laugh.

'Listen, you two are in trouble if you don't get your skates on. Remember what my mother said, it'll be bread and dripping instead of roast potatoes and the last of the meat ration until Wednesday if you hang about here.'

Taking the hint, Eddie gathered up the laced leather football made all the heavier from skidding across the wet surface of the village green. Vinny followed without further protest.

As they drew next to the police station, Anna caught sight of Tom standing on the top step of the entrance, looking into thin air. 'Everything OK?'

She watched as the policeman looked toward Vinny, then at her. Picking up on his cue, she gained the boy's attention. 'Run on ahead, will you, Vinny? Tell them we'll be along in a minute—and don't eat all the potatoes, right?'

'Depends on whether they're roast spuds or boiled. If it's roasties, you've no chance.' With that, the boy took off at speed, leaving the three adults to swap concerned glances.

'You look pale, Tom,' said Eddie as he neared his friend.

'That wasn't at all pleasant. He was still in there when I arrived. I've seen nothing like it. What an awful way to pop your clogs.'

Anna climbed three low steps so she could be closer to the sergeant. 'Chin up, Tom, it'll be OK.' She bumped shoulders as if they were two schoolchildren trying to console one another, but not quite sure what to do.

'Listen, I'll be up in a minute. I've got to update Inspector Spillers. It's routine procedure, but I want to get it done now.'

Anna realised Tom needed a few minutes alone and gestured to Eddie that they should make their way back to the vicarage. 'Don't be long.'

Tom Bradshaw headed back into the station without responding, leaving his two friends with their own thoughts.

'I haven't seen him like that before. Don't you think it's odd for a policeman to get so upset over something he must have come across before?' commented Eddie as they began the short walk back home.

'He almost lost his father in a car crash. The man was terribly injured and took a long time to recover. I guess even a bobby has feelings. Too close to home, perhaps.'

'Ah, now I get it. Poor guy,' said Eddie. 'It makes sense now, you know, the car crash bringing home some awful memories for the fella.'

The atmosphere back in the kitchen as Anna and Eddie arrived was light-hearted and chatty as Vinny took centre stage in entertaining Fanny with his school-boy jokes, which were only occasionally censored by the vicar.

Helen had already plated their meagre ration of meat and encouraged the newly arrived pair to dig into the roast potatoes and vegetables.

'See, I've been good,' said Vinny. 'I've left you some roasties. You said it was a full Hershey bar, didn't you, Eddie?'

'You're a one,' said Anna as she winked at the youngster.

Thank heavens he doesn't have to know what's going on, thought Anna.

The Scouser's antics had also brought Fanny out of her shell by commenting that she, too, had a much younger brother and he behaved the same way.

As the kitchen door once again opened, the atmosphere subtly changed as Tom's ashen face appeared around the doorjamb.

Heavens, he still looks awful.

The vicar sprang up from his seat and walked over to Tom. With his back to the others, Anna could hear him saying a few words to the policeman. She could see that her father had placed an open palm on Tom's cheek before moving it out of sight. She guessed from the fact that Tom had closed his eyes, that her father had given her troubled friend a blessing.

'Come along in, Tom, and sit yourself down,' said Helen. 'We've saved plenty for you. Even Vinny has been a good boy and donated you one of his roast potatoes.' Helen's light-hearted touch eased the situation and allowed Tom to at least try to enter the spirit of things.

'Good lad, Vinny. I owe you one. I'm starving.' Tom rubbed his stomach and licked his lips to exaggerate his attempt to humour his fellow diners.

You're a brave man, Tom Bradshaw, thought Anna.

Anna took the initiative and introduced the new arrival to Fanny, who he'd been giving an inquisitive look for several seconds.

'Mum tells me you two work for the same organisation, so she thought you should meet.' Anna gave Helen a sideways glance to check her reaction to a deliberate act of school-girl forwardness. 'I think she intends setting up a dating agency.'

Her father coughed. 'What? Young people today, I don't know. Then again, I suppose it's the war that does it.'

'What's a dating agency?'

Helen took up the cudgel. 'Oh, nothing much, just a way of people who don't know one another but who might have things in common to meet.'

Vinny shrugged his shoulders as he loaded a final roast potato onto his fork. 'Oh that. I heard me Ma telling me Aunt Lilly once about one of them places down an ally by the Grafton Rooms. Can't see the point if you ask me.'

The room fell silent with forks frozen between plate and mouth, except for Eddie, who wore a confused look. A quiet giggle filled the room, much to Vinny's bafflement.

'Yes, yes,' commented the vicar. 'Never you mind about all that. I think you can give me a hand to clean the bicycles, young man.'

'But I haven't had me rice pudding yet?'

'You shouldn't have been late from playing football, should you? It meant I was late putting it in the AGA, so it'll be twenty-minutes yet. That's more than enough time for you to get mucky again. Now off you go.'

Thank heavens we sidestepped talk of lively alleyways next to dance halls in the blackout.

Keen to change the subject, Anna turned to Fanny, who still looked a little flushed from Vinny's tale of Liverpool. 'Surely you two must have come across each other?'

Enjoying Tom's blush, she invited him to respond by raising her eyebrows at him.

'Er, well, I suppose, er—'

Fanny's shyness seemed to disappear as she smiled at Tom. 'Don't you remember us talking about the weather the other week?'

Anna fixed her gaze on Tom as he struggled to put two sensible words together.

'Oh, yes, I remember now. It's a small world, isn't it?'

Is that the best you can do? thought Anna.

'Fanny's uncle owns the garage on the Norwich Road. If I were you, I'd keep in her good books, so she gives your dad extra petrol for that old banger he drives.'

Tom gave Anna a look of horror. 'Oh, I couldn't do that, what with the coupons and everything. Dad is strict about the rules, and I'm a policeman, you know.'

Fanny joined Anna in the jape. 'Not any old policeman, but a shiny new sergeant.'

Both women fixed their gaze on the blushing policeman as his cheeks reddened by the second.

I like you, thought Anna as she switched her attention to Fanny.

'Your stripes are very fetching, Tom. Quite dashing, in fact.'

Oh yes. That's how it is, mused Anna.

A knock on the front door gave Tom respite from the female onslaught.

'Of course, Inspector. You won't come in? No, OK, I'll get him for you.'

Mention of his superior snapped Tom out of any remaining feelings of self-consciousness he'd been experiencing.

As Tom raced for the door, the others strained to hear. A minute later a serious-looking Tom wandered back into the kitchen, a sweet smell of cooked rice pudding now pervading the air.

'The Inspector's given me the car accident case and says I can let you and Eddie tag along. He said to remember if we make a mess of it, I'll end up back as a beat bobby.'

Chapter Two: Who Was He?

Anna pulled Tom's leg about abandoning Fanny as the group of friends, old and new, stood outside the back door to the vicarage kitchen. 'You've only recently met the girl and you're rushing off back to work. What kind of chap are you?'

Her playful tone seemed to be lost on the new sergeant as he blushed again. 'Fanny. You know what it's like. Perhaps we can meet up for a cup of tea. I—'

'Tom, I've only known Anna for an hour, but even I know she's teasing you. You can treat me to lunch at the cafe next to my uncle's place on Tuesday to make up. I'm only driving in the morning, so I'll be free from about one o'clock.'

Wow, Fanny can get a move on when she's keen, thought Anna.

Fanny's sudden boldness put Tom on the spot, causing him to glance at the other two as if they might suggest what he could do.

'I think the answer you're looking for is "That's a great idea, Fanny."' Anna grinned as she moved her attention from the policeman to Fanny and back again.

'Er… yes, I suppose, well… I mean, that's if nothing comes up that gets in the way. You know, police work.'

Anna shook her head in mock disbelief. 'Romantic, isn't he?' Her words meant for Fanny.

'I'll settle for that, but the bully beef stew is on you, Tom Bradshaw.'

Tom gave a weak smile as he looked over Anna's shoulder towards the quiet road into the village centre. 'That's settled. Right, I'd better nip to the police station and pick up the squad car.'

'Haven't you forgotten something?' quizzed Anna as the sergeant moved off. She watched as he made an awkward move toward Fanny.

'Er... sorry, Fanny, I... well,' spluttered Tom as he mistimed his movement and instead of planting a light peck on her forehead, made passing contact with the top of an ear. The object of his affection giggled as she turned her head away. 'Blimey, that's different. Come here and do it proper-like.' In an instant, Fanny pressed her lips to his. This time, Tom shied away and began fidgeting with his wristwatch. 'Goodness, you've gone bright red in the gills,' chuckled Fanny.

The sergeant blushed as three grinning faces made a few seconds of botched affection on his part feel like hours.

Why is Tom looking at me like that? he should concentrate on Fanny, thought Anna.

'What about exchanging telephone numbers, you know, in case something comes up to spoil your date?' said Anna, perfectly aware of what she was doing.

She sensed Eddie shuffling nervously on his feet at mention of a date. 'What's up with you?'

The American flicked a clod of mud from the garden pathway, a remnant of his football escapade with Vinny. 'Talk of dates makes me nervous.' Eddie gave the mud a final flick, and off it flew into a patch of nearby cabbage.

Is he trying to tell me something? thought Anna.

18

Fanny scribbled her works and uncle's garage telephone numbers onto a scrap of paper she retrieved from her heavy coat pocket. Tom withdrew his police pad, before thinking better of using official stationery for personal matters.

'Excellent choice, Tom,' said Eddie, handing over an empty Hershey bar wrapper. 'I doubt your boss will believe anything you say about the dog eating your notes when he asks to see them.'

Tom frowned as he took the paper from Eddie, dabbed the tip of his pencil on his tongue and jotted down a number. Notes exchanged, Fanny said her goodbyes, giving Tom a last, lingering look long enough for the others to notice.

'She's keen on you,' said Eddie. 'I'd watch out if I were you.'

Tom blushed as he slipped his standard issue police pencil back into his breast pocket and took his time in fastening the silver button closed.

'I don't know what you're talking about. I've only just met her, and it's only a cup of tea with her. Anyway, I'm too busy to get involved with anyone.'

His eyes tell me different, thought Anna. 'Oh no it's not. Beef-bully stew makes for a meal out, even if it's likely to be the last of the tinned rations from the Great War.'

'Get away with you,' replied Tom. 'You say some daft things for an intelligent woman.' Tom's look lingered on Anna.

A compliment? she thought.

'I'll be back with the car in a minute. Norwich Headquarters have given us one of their surplus Wosley Wasp saloons. It's a 1935 model, but Inspector Spillers says it's quite fast.'

'Surplus? You mean clapped out.' Anna's barbed comment struck home.

'Not at all, it's—'

'Don't fall for it again, Tom,' said Eddie with a smile broadening across his features. 'We'll follow you on. I've recently bought a car. Looks great, doesn't she?'

Anna glanced at the sleek red sports car a few yards up the narrow road.

Why do men always call cars "her", or "she"? Suppose they still think they own us, too, thought Anna.

'She's a 1939 MG Midget. Look at the soft-top, it'll be great in the summer. I'd give you a lift, but as you can see, it only has two seats.'

Give me strength, thought Anna.

'When you two are finished, we have the minor matter of a car crash to investigate.'

Anna's plea failed to tease the two men away from matters mechanical. 'The army asked for its Jeep back, so I picked this up for £200. It's exceedingly rare, you know, and is one of only 379 made before the MG factories switched to war production.'

One more minute and I'll let his stupid tyres down, she thought.

The men continued to drool over every nook and cranny of the sports car, oblivious to Anna's growing annoyance.

'It has a 1250cc engine, you know.'

'I bet it goes like the wind,' replied Tom, his admiration clear.

'Right, that's it,' said Anna in a tone leaving neither of the men in doubt as to her mood. 'Tom, you get your old police banger. We'll wait here, then follow you to the crash site. That's if our American friend can start his toy car.'

Her point made, Anna watched Tom scurry down the high street while Eddie opened a small passenger door without making further comment.

'How am I supposed to get in this thing? It's tiny.'

'Sports-styled, not tiny,' replied Eddie as his companion tutted, bent forward and shuffled into the red leather passenger seat of the sleeping beast.

As Eddie folded his six-foot frame almost double to shimmy into the driver's seat, he lurched toward Anna, knocking her against the condensing window of the car's canopy.

Get any nearer and you'll be in my lap.

'Oops, I didn't mean to do that. It's snug in here, isn't it?'

And you can wipe that cheeky smile off your face, thought Anna.

'You keep your mind on the road, lieutenant,' said Anna as Tom drove past at a sedate pace, leaving Eddie plenty of time to start the MG and catch the police car up.

Within two minutes, both cars were out into a sedate Norfolk countryside about to go into hibernation for the winter. A cold dampness clung in the air, causing droplets of water to obscure the impossibly small windscreen.

'Do the wipers work?'

'Of course they do,' replied Eddie as he flicked a switch.

'I shouldn't bother,' said Anna. 'it's less clear now than before you turned the wretched things on.'

The American ignored his companion's remark and instead changed the subject. 'The case is an enormous responsibility for Tom, isn't it?'

I clock what you're up to, Eddie Elsner, thought Anna.

'Inspector Spillers has seen something in our Tom and taken him under his wing. The thing is, we've seen Spillers turn on a sixpence before, so we'd better make sure we look after Tom.'

'So, you mean no going off on your own to do a bit of private investigating?'

'You mean "us"?'

'No, Anna. I mean, you!'

* * *

21

'Thank heavens we're here, any slower and we could've walked.'

'Don't be catty,' replied Anna. 'You heard how proud Tom is to have use of the police car.'

'I'm not being catty; did you see that blue muck coming out of the exhaust? That's why I held back, or we'd be unconscious now.'

The conversation tailed off as Bradshaw slowed to a stop.

Now parked behind Tom's car, the MG's occupants huffed and puffed as they extracted themselves from the low-sitting sports car and watched the sergeant's motionless figure survey the sad scene.

'At least the ambulance crew got the driver out. I suppose they'll be at the cottage hospital now,' remarked Anna.

'You can see he's still shook up,' said Eddie. 'Just Tom's luck. His first case in charge involves a death. Come on, he's looking at us.'

Chin up, Tom. thought Anna.

'What's your first move, Tom?' asked Anna, keen to break the sombre mood.

'Well, we don't know if the car suffered a mechanical fault, you know, failed brakes or steering, or if the driver misjudged the road. Perhaps a roe deer jumped from the hedge, they can be a nuisance at this time of the year.'

'You're telling me,' said Eddie. 'They might not be as big as the moose back home, but panic when one of those little critters appears out of thin air and whatever you're driving is likely to end up in a hedge… or worse.'

His companions fixed their gaze on him. 'What? All I'm saying is give me a Nazi anytime, at least they like making a noise.'

I despair of Americans sometimes, thought Anna.

She noted with pleasure that Tom ignored Eddie's remark.

'The other thing I need to do is identify the victim; so far we've found nothing to tell us who he is… I mean, was.'

22

While Tom spoke, the lieutenant approached the rear of the car and stood, feet slightly apart, looking attentively at the boot. 'No numberplate.'

Sergeant Bradshaw recorded the finding in his police notebook and walked gingerly around to the front of the vehicle. Or at least as far around as the buried bonnet allowed. 'You know what, the front plate is missing, too. That can't be right?' Tom took a few seconds to check that the licence plate hadn't ended up a little further away from the stricken vehicle. 'Nope, no sign of it.'

'Does that mean he drove the car without licence plates?' said Anna.

'Risky, if that's what he did,' replied Tom. 'Our lads would've been on him like a shot. You know, black marketeers and all that.'

'Or someone deliberately removed them to hide the vehicle's identity. If that's what happened, the question is, why?' said Eddie.

Anna frowned. 'What if the innocent explanation is he only recently bought the car? Perhaps it'd been rusting in a barn for years and didn't have any plates. That might explain why he crashed. You know, awful state of repair and all that.'

'And the not so innocent explanation?' responded Eddie. 'What better way to make someone disappear by staging an accident? I mean, it's a bit too convenient, don't you think? A man dies and any evidence that might identify him is removed from the car?'

'Don't you think we're getting ahead of ourselves?' said Anna. 'I know you want to do a good job, but Inspector Spillers probably thinks this is a run-of-the-mill car accident, not a murder.'

The sergeant moved a few steps away from the damaged car to study the sad scene. 'The inspector is always telling us to follow the evidence and not make assumptions, so that's what I'll do.'

Anna took his words as an invitation. 'That's what we shall do. Who's up for a trip to the mortuary?'

Eddie made good time in covering the fifteen miles to the entrance of the cottage hospital. 'The sight of that's enough to put anyone off wanting to go in.'

'That's what it's designed to do,' replied Anna.

'What do you mean?'

She laughed. 'The Victorians built them as workhouses, which popped up all over the country in the eighteen-hundreds. Not nice places. They supposedly gave relief to the poor of each Parish but tried their hardest to keep people out by making them so unpleasant.'

'Charming,' replied Eddie as he drove through the rusted open wrought iron gates and under a decorative metal head frame that held the gate jambs solid, and which read "In God We Trust".

Driving slowly down the side of the front range, Eddie brought the car to a stop in a location he'd visited with Anna once before. 'Still looks the same.'

'What did you expect, the mortuary has stood here since 1865?' Tutting at his idle remark, she opened the tiny door of the MG and once again struggled to free herself from the red convertible.

'All I'm saying is,' said Eddie as he unfolded himself and placed a hand on the soft-top to steady his step, 'that it looks the same as last time? You know, same crumpled curtains and dead flowers.'

She dismissed his explanation and looked back to the entrance to see Tom's car nearing, closely followed by a cloud of blue-grey smoke from the straining exhaust.

'I think that's the second death trap we're seeing today.'

Anna nudged Eddie. 'Stop it.'

Seconds later, the old Wolsey stuttered to a stop and out stepped Tom, who Anna noted was sweating from the forehead. 'It's not that warm, are you ill?'

The sergeant mopped his brow. 'A bit of a problem with the radiator, I think. She's running hot.'

There he goes again with "She" fumed Anna.

A solid wooden door opened behind them. 'I thought I heard someone. Come on in, I've been expecting the police, but what are you two doing here? Up to your whodunnit stuff again, are we?'

Anna smiled at her old school friend, Irene Little. 'Nice to see you again, Irene. Yes, that's us, disrupting police enquiries again.' The two women exchanged friendly pecks and a light hug.

'Come on in. I have everything ready.'

Passing through the wide doorway designed to allow a hospital trolly through, the sombre group entered a small, white tiled room devoid of furnishing except for a body-sized slate pedestal slab, solitary spindle chair and an ancient wooden filing cabinet. Against a second wall stood a thin metal-framed glass cabinet full of the tools of Irene's important trade.

'I'll bring him to you.' All stood fixed to the spot as Irene solemnly depressed a metal handle on one of two square hatch doors almost flush with the wall. Swinging the door aside, Irene reached in and gave a sliding mechanism a good tug.

'Can you manage?' asked Eddie.

Irene half-turned and smiled. 'You get used to it. I'm fine thanks.' She turned her full attention to a pristine white cotton sheet which covered the cadaver from head to foot. 'It's alright, I'll be gentle with you. Some people are here to see you. They want to find out what happened. Ok?'

What a dignified way to treat the departed, thought Anna.

The technician expertly pulled a heavy sliding-shelf along its rollers onto the slate slab. Detaching the structure from its anchor points, Irene quietly closed the cabinet door flush to the wall and checked all was in order with the shroud.

25

'He will appear as if he's asleep,' said Irene. She continued her conversation with the dead man as she folded down the sheet from his head and shoulders. 'I won't hurt you and this shouldn't take long. Is that alright?'

Waiting for a reply that Anna knew wouldn't come, she watched as Irene lay the covering cloth just above the victim's midriff.

'As you say, Irene, it's as if he's just fallen asleep. So sad.'

Irene turned her attention back to the body. 'Come on, now, help these ladies and gentlemen find out what happened to you. Did someone hurt you?'

I could cry.

'Tell me,' said Tom, 'Was anything found on him, or in his clothes. A wallet, perhaps?'

The technician shook her head. 'Not that I'm aware of.' She gave the corpse a compassionate glance. 'So sad don't you think, you know, there he rests without a name to be called by, or anything we can use to tell his wife what's happened.' Irene sighed as she lifted the sheet to re-cover the body.

'Wife?' responded Anna as she gave Irene a quizzical look.

The technician lowered the sheet and folded it to one side, allowing the other three to view the dead man's left lower arm and hand. 'The poor man must have lost his ring finger during the accident.'

Her voice tailed off as she pointed to the hand.

Tom stepped forward to take a closer look. 'That's if he was married, of course. All the same, there's something that concerns me.'

Anna moved closer and grimaced at the grisly sight. 'What do you mean?'

The sergeant gestured to a torn edge of flesh. 'It might have happened when he crashed, except we found nothing at the scene and look, the rest of the hand is undamaged. For my money that finger has been removed, and in a hurry too.'

Eddie moved around the body, so he too now had a clear view. 'That's a heck of a leap you're making, Tom.'

'Have you another explanation that makes any sense?' responded Tom.

As the seconds passed, Eddie slowly shook his head while brushing the tip of his nose with a knuckle. 'When you put it like that... I guess, well, no, I haven't. It sounds so farfetched. I mean, what are we talking about here; an angry wife, or jilted lover?'

Neither of Eddie's companions offered further explanation of how, or why, the finger became detached from the man's body. Instead, the room settled into a reflective silence, which, in time, Irene ended. Moving gently between Tom and Anna, the technician began to re-cover the body. 'I think it's time we let you rest a little.' The others quietly stepped back to a respectful distance to allow Irene to complete her duties. 'That's it. Let's get you covered and give you some privacy, eh?'

Anna kissed a small silver cross that hung from a delicate chain around her neck as Eddie bowed his head. He leaned forward a few inches as Irene began her preparations to move the body back to its temporary resting place.

'Is something the matter?' asked Tom while looking earnestly at Eddie.

'It's just... Irene, I'm so sorry, but can I...' Eddie took a step forward. Anna stepped to her right. *He's seen something.*

The technician neatly placed the white sheet under the dead man's chin and looked at his closed eyes. 'I'm sorry to keep you from your rest. It won't be long. I promise you.' With that, she stepped back while urging Eddie to be as quick as he could.

The lieutenant bent over the deceased man's upper torso and inspected his right earlobe. 'What is it?' asked Anna as she attempted to check what he appeared so engrossed in.

Eddie straightened up before looking at his watch without answering Anna's question.

'Oi, I'm talking to you,' she said, nudging the lieutenant for good measure before remembering where she was and nodding at Irene as a token of contrition.

'Oh, nothing. It's just… well, I glimpsed a minor wound on his ear, and it intrigued me, that's all.'

Before Anna had a chance to delve further, Eddie flicked his left wrist to expose his watch. 'Oh, no, I've just remembered that I have to telephone my boss, or I'll be for it. Sorry, got to go.'

Anna gave Eddie a quizzical look, before looking at the body and noticing a neatly cut crescent in the dead man's earlobe.

What's Eddie found so interesting about that old ear injury? thought Anna.

Turning her attention back to the American, she was about to speak when he beat her to it.

'Sorry, I have to go, or I'll be in big trouble. Tell you what, I'll leave you two here. I'm sure Tom will give you a lift back to the village.'

As the lieutenant made his way back to the mortuary entrance and scurried through the door, Anna apologised to Irene, who was busy closing the heavy metal door to the body store, for the abrupt end to proceedings.

He's up to something, thought Anna as Eddie disappeared.

Chapter Three: Pastures Old

Anna continued to puzzle about Eddie's demeanour, which she thought out of character, as she and Tom left Irene to her duties and strolled back to the Wolseley police car.

Tom tugged at the front passenger door to lever it open, allowing his passenger to pass into the spacious interior of the well-used car and completed the same manoeuvre with his own, more troublesome door.

'Five o'clock already. It's been a busy Sunday, don't you think?'

'More for you than me. At least I'm not responsible for sorting out this mess, poor man.' Anna frowned as she spoke, while watching Tom adjust his seat and rear mirror before turning the ignition key.

Why does he need to do that? He only got out of it half-an-hour ago, thought Anna.

Turning the heavy steering wheel, Anna's companion coaxed the lumbering car away from its parked position and out on to the quiet country road, complete with high hedges and field drainage ditches on each side. 'What do you think of Eddie's sudden departure?'

She hesitated before answering, her own thoughts having yielded no sense to the matter. 'It's not like him to forget stuff like that. It's not in his nature, but what the matter is, I don't know. He won't say anything until he's good and ready. You men are a stubborn lot.'

Tom coughed a laugh. 'What have I got to do with anything? Don't tar us all with the same brush. Anyway, it's you two we're talking about.'

'Are we?'

'Aren't we?'

I'm not sure anymore, thought Anna.

'You should talk. What about that silliness with Fanny? Why is going for a cup of tea with a girl such a big thing?'

Tom fought with the clutch to force the car into third gear as it gathered pace on a straight but bumpy stretch of road. 'There you go again, trying to change the subject.'

Oh, for Heaven's sake, she thought.

Anna unbuttoned her heavy coat and leaned forward to clear her bit of the tiny windscreen of condensation with her hanky. 'One matchmaker in the family circle is enough. Don't you start, too, Mr Bradshaw.'

The sergeant let out a throaty laugh. 'I must be in trouble. But come on, Anna. You and Eddie have been in each other's pockets for months now. Are you trying to tell me you don't have any feelings for the man... because your reactions often tell me something else?'

'No, I don't. I have no feeling for Eddie Elsner at all. Get it?'

Anna's sudden outburst brought the conversion to an abrupt halt. She could feel her companion observing her, which added to the awkwardness she already felt.

Why did I say that? thought Anna.

Both seemed happy to allow the moment to pass as Tom wound down his side window a few inches, trying to balance the need to clear his line of view and keep as much cold air out of the car as possible. 'Inspector Spillers won't let me carry an oil burner to keep warm like we use in Dad's car. Letting fresh air in is the only way I'll keep the window clear of condensation.'

Anna allowed her friend's words to pass without comment as she continued to ponder her unexpected reaction concerning Eddie.

He'll go home at the end of the war. What's the point? she thought.

'Oh, yes, it's breezy, isn't it?' said Anna. After a few seconds of silence, she glanced at him. 'Why are you wearing that inane grin, Tom Bradshaw? What did I say?'

He pointed to the open window with his left hand while gripping the steering wheel with his right to keep the heavy car in a straight line. 'You're in a world of your own.'

Dismissing the comment, Anna struck back by turning the conversation around to Fanny again. 'She seems like a nice girl, don't you think?'

'Who is?' replied Tom.

'Do you mean you have more than one girl on the go? Sly devil.' She allowed a smile to lift her features.

'That's better. The smile, I mean, not accusing me of chasing the ladies. In fact, and as you know full well, I'm not courting anyone,' replied Tom.

The brief exchange changed the mood between the pair as their long friendship shone through.

'As for Fanny, yes, she seems nice enough. A bit too forward for me, mind, but I suppose girls know what they want these days.'

Anna roared with laughter. 'You sound like my father, not a twenty-six-year-old full-blooded male. Do you feel threatened?'

'Threatened? What's that supposed to mean?'

'Tom Bradshaw, you know what I mean. Blokes are so stupid. Fanny isn't some fluffy cat, you know. She saw you looking at her. We all did. That's why she took control.'

31

Tom shook his head as if trying to dislodge a troublesome irritation from his ear. 'You talk in riddles. You lot are all the same.'

'Not that old cliche. Just tell me this, Mr Policeman. Do you like her?'

Tom pressed the clutch and grabbed the gearstick, ready to do battle again as he guided the car around a tricky bend in the road. 'Sergeant, if you don't mind, Miss Grix. As for Fanny, I suppose she's alright, but I've only just met her. Anyway, why are you so curious?'

Why am I? thought Anna.

Anna traced the shape of a simple house with smoke climbing from its chimney on the passenger door's window as she investigated the blackness of the early evening. 'I want to see you happy, that's all. What with the war and everything, not least the type of day you've had, well, you deserve to have someone special in your life?'

A few seconds of silence fell before Tom responded. 'I could say the same of you, you know.'

She turned to see Tom giving her the sort of look she hadn't noticed before. 'But, Tom, we're old mates, the best of friends… I—'

'Don't say another word. You've misunderstood what I meant. And you say men are the nonsensical ones.'

Why did that hurt? thought Anna.

'Anyway,' continued Tom, 'I'm sure Fanny has many admirers. She's an attractive girl, and clever with it. Why should she be interested in me?'

'Because you're a good man, Tom Bradshaw, and any girl would be lucky to land you.'

Tom laughed again. 'Oh, yes, what are you after?'

The levity of their exchange did little to mask the looks being exchanged.

He says one thing, but his look tells me something else. I'm confused, thought Anna.

A car horn blasted the intimate moment away.

'Watch out,' cried Anna as she leaned towards the windscreen, trying to see the approaching vehicle.

'Stupid dimmed lights. They're more dangerous than the Luftwaffe,' roared Tom as he took evasive action to squeeze past the other car without touching. 'A brave man, that, shaking his fist at a police officer.'

Anna gave a sigh as the danger passed. 'Well, I suppose you were on his side of the road. Oh, look, we're almost back home.'

A few minutes later, Tom parked the car outside the vicarage, at which point the pair exchanged a lingering look.

'Well,' said Tom, now breaking eye contact. 'I'd better update Inspector Spillers… I doubt he'll leave me in charge of the investigation when I tell him about the number plates. See you tomorrow to catch up on things?'

Anna gave Tom a gentle smile. 'Sure thing.' Leaving the car and walking the few yards to the garden gate, Anna waved Tom off as he made for the police station.

Where is everyone? pondered Anna as she closed the front door and wandered down the deserted vestibule of the Victorian vicarage. She glanced at a grandfather clock that had stood at the foot of the stairs for as long as she could remember. *Ah, I know where he'll be.*

Giving a single tap on the pine-panelled door, she popped her head around the doorjamb of her father's office to see him sat at his desk, studying a dense text. 'Hello, you. Where is everyone?'

Her father looked up from his book and offered Anna a fatherly smile. 'Quiet, isn't it? Wonderful, but don't tell your mother I said that. She's taken young Vinny to see Tilly Smith for ten minutes before bath and bed ready for school tomorrow. I think those two have a soft spot for one another.'

'Seems to be a lot of it going about,' chuckled Anna, to the bemusement of her father. 'Then again, given what those two have been through, it's no wonder they're kindred spirits. Never mind me, Dad, it's been that sort of day.'

'Oh, er, I see. Well, your tea is in the AGA. Mum's left you a nice bit of bubble and squeak.' Charles took a second look at his daughter. 'Are you alright? You look a little flushed?'

Anna pressed an open palm to her cheek. 'No, I don't think so. Food will sort me out, I'm starving.'

Charles studied his daughter once more, shut his heavy book, and leaned forward in his chair so that his elbows rested on the paper-strewn desktop. 'You know, even after experiencing all the suffering I saw in the Great War, and years of giving pastoral care to the dying and bereaved, it still takes its toll. I imagine you have seen things today that no one wishes to experience.'

You have a way with words, father, thought Anna as she allowed her head to lower so that she could fix her gaze on the coconut matting of her father's office.

'As you know, I put my faith in God as friends and strangers alike return to His grace and peace.'

'That's OK for you, Dad, you're a vicar. The rest of us don't have that kind of strength.'

Anna's father smiled as he rose from his chair, walked the few paces around his desk to reach his daughter, and lifted her chin with a finger. 'It's not strength, Anna. It's belief based on the realities of life and death. We all suffer pain and disappointment, the same way we each get to enjoy happiness and the love of others. It's a case of how

34

we deal with our journey that matters. You're much stronger than you think, young lady. Believe me when I say time and experience will show this in abundance. You'll be fine.'

Charles tapped his daughter's chin with a finger while offering a warm smile of fatherly devotion.

'I love you, Dad.'

'The question is, Anna, do you love your bubble and squeak more, because if you don't lift it from the AGA soon, it'll be dust.'

As she turned to leave, she watched her father as he returned to his chair.

'And what about you? No one ever checks you're doing OK because, well, I guess, people expect their vicar to be the strong one.'

Charles allowed himself a faint smile as he picked up an addressed envelope.

'What's that?'

'I spoke of caring for the bereaved. Well, this letter is for one such parishioner.'

'Do I know them?'

The vicar shook his head. 'No, at least not now. There was a time when this lady and her husband were stalwarts of the church and our little community… alas.'

'What, did they move away?'

Charles sat back in his chair and rubbed his tired eyes. 'Their only child, a boy, killed in a car accident. Six he was, and a happy little soul.'

Anna stepped back into the room from the doorway and sat on the arm of a two-seater brown cloth sofa. 'How awful for them.'

The vicar nodded as he gave his eyes a second rub. 'Worse than that, my dear, the father ran his own son over. A pure accident with tragic consequences.'

'I don't understand?' Anna stood and moved to her father, whose mood darkened as each second passed.

'This lady's husband committed suicide last week. Some said it was always coming. He'd tried once or twice before, but we all hoped for the best. I guess it all got too much. And in the depths of utter despair, he killed himself. Who can say what each of us might do given the same circumstances?'

Anna leaned over her father. Now it was her time to offer comfort. 'You won't do anything daft, will you?'

The vicar put a hand to his daughter's arm, which rested around his neck and shoulders. 'No, dear. I know I've had my moments, but no, if not singing from the roof tops, I'm fine. But there is something you can do for me.'

'Anything, Dad.'

He caressed her arm again. 'You're a dutiful daughter to your old father. This lady does not know my letter is coming, and it's most unlikely she will open the door to me. But perhaps she may be more responsive to you. She's unlikely to recognise you and will assume you're a stranger calling on some pretext or other.'

Anna took the letter from her father and scanned the address. 'It's not that far by bike. Do I need to take it tonight?'

Anna's urgency caused her father to break free of his daughter's tender embrace. 'No. Any time over the next day or two will be fine. There is a lot to sort out. That's if the lady will allow me to help, of which I'm uncertain.'

Anna frowned. 'I'm uncertain what you mean. There's always a lot to do organising a funeral, why…'

Oh, no, thought Anna.

'Suicide is a sin in the eyes of the church, isn't it? Are you saying you'll refuse to bury him in consecrated ground? How can you, Dad?'

'It's also a criminal act. But no, how could you think such a thing of me? You know my views; we are all the children of God without exception or prejudice.'

That was wrong of me.

Anna placed a gentle kiss on his forehead. 'It's… well, I don't know. I'm all over the place today.'

'I know, my dear. However, the fact is that the church won't allow me to bury this man in the same grave as that of his son, and where his wife will rest. My conscience tells me different. I'll bury him with his son in this graveyard, no matter what the consequences. Except that his widow does not yet know this.'

Anna gave her father a more fulsome kiss. 'Hence the letter?'

'Precisely.'

'Father, I'm so proud of you. We are all so lucky to have you looking after us.'

The vicar pooh-poohed his daughter's tender words as he raised his nose into the air with an exaggerated movement of his head. 'Now, what about that bubble and squeak?'

Before Anna could respond, the intimate moment between father and daughter ended as the giggle of an excited young boy filled the air.

'They're back. Best say hello to them both before your mother whips the lad upstairs.'

As Anna entered the long, narrow vestibule, the sight of Vinny charging towards her presented itself. In seconds, he'd collided with his target and wrapped his arms around Anna's lower waist.

'I love you.'

Neither expected Vinny to show such affection, which led to the exchange of a glance of joy tinged with sadness of reality.

'Oh yes,' replied Anna, 'And why am I in favour?'

The little boy looked up, his eyes twinkling with delight. 'Cos you're my big sister, like. Even if you're a soppy girl.'

Anna watched a tear well up in her mother's eyes while giving Vinny's hair a vigorous rub.

'Come on, my lad. Up the apples and pairs. It's bath, cocoa and bed for you.'

After exchanging a last glance with her mother, Anna passed into the kitchen, retrieved her tea from the AGA, and sat alone at the kitchen table.

In the tiny hamlet of Three-Mile-Bottom, Lieutenant Eddie Elsner let himself into his billet to be met with a cheery smile from his landlady, Hilda Cross. Her husband, Albert, acknowledged the lieutenant's arrival by removing his pipe and lifting it a little as he sat in his favourite chair next to a roaring open fire.

'Have you had tea, Eddie? I know what you're like for missing meals,' asked Hilda as she smoothed her coloured apron against her rounded frame and pointed at her husband. 'Don't you dare.'

Eddie looked over at Albert to see him leaning towards the glowing coals, as if frozen in time, following his wife's timely rebuke.

'I've told you before. No spitting in that when we have company. I saw what you were about to do. Now get a hanky like a normal person.'

Eddie thought the better part of valour was to hold his council and act as if nothing had happened as Albert retreated into the safety of his newspaper, removing an old handkerchief from his trouser pocket.

'No, I haven't had tea, but I'm not hungry.'

'Nonsense,' replied Hilda as she gave Albert a final withering glance. 'I've some tinned SPAM. It won't take long to heat and I've some spuds coming to the boil.'

Eddie knew there was no point is attempting to dissuade Hilda from her constant endeavour to feed him up. Instead, he smiled, gave a nod of thanks, and slumped into his usual chair opposite Albert.

'That bad?' whispered the husband as he peeped at the lodger over his newspaper.

'You don't want to know,' sighed Eddie as he rested back and lost himself in the comforting warmth of the fire. After a few seconds, he gathered his thoughts and looked over to where the telephone rested behind the front door by the small bay window of the cottage. He knew Hilda and Albert were wary of the contraption, so few private households had one fitted, but he was grateful they'd allowed his military command to install it for him.

'I wonder,' said the lieutenant. 'Er, the phone, I, er—'

'Come on you, and you can bring your pipe into my kitchen as a special treat.'

Albert obeyed his wife's command as she pointed to the small cooking area at the back of the cottage.

'Eddie must have an important call to make, so let's give the man some privacy.'

'Sorry to be a nuisance and thanks. It'll only take a minute.'

'Don't you worry about that. By the time you've finished, I'll have your tea ready.' Hilda ushered Albert to the small room and closed a narrow brown painted pine door behind them.

I hope he's there, thought Eddie.

Dialling the local exchange, he asked for a London number. When the telephone connected, Eddie gave a perfunctory greeting without using names or rank and said, "Now".

He pressed a button on the black Bakelite telephone base and waited for a verbal confirmation that the other party had done the same.

'On scramble,' said a clear, authoritative voice.

'Apologies for disturbing your Sunday evening, General, but there's something I need to brief you on, and it can't wait.'

Eddie listened to his superior's response. 'That's kind of you, sir.'

The lieutenant briefed his general on concerns he had about the dead man. 'So, you can see why I'm requesting permission to visit Bletchley Park?'

Again, he listened to his senior officer. 'Yes, yes, sir, I understand how sensitive these matters are, but the fact is, it's only by checking with certain people and my old records that I can say for sure whether I'm right, or I've made two and two make five.'

Eddie listened to his superior's decision and instructions. 'Yes, sir. By train, of course, and yes, I'll wear civilian clothes and make sure I'm not followed.'

The sound of the telephone ringing as Eddie replaced the handset served as the all-clear signal to Hilda, who opened the kitchen door and prodded her husband to take Eddie his meal.

'You sit yourself down and get tucked into that. I'll bring you a nice big mug of tea.'

The lieutenant needed no further invitation to settle himself back into his chair as Albert rested a wooden knee-tray on Eddie's lap. 'Looks good, that does.'

'Do you want some? There's plenty,' replied Eddie.

'Get away with yourself, I've had mine, now go on, get it down you, lad.'

Something tells me I've got the lion's share, thought Eddie.

Twenty-minutes passed in pleasant chit-chat as Eddie devoured his meal and washed it down with Hilda's special strong tea brew.

'And what about those two pastors? Arguing, I ask you,' Hilda's mention of the incident among a rapid stream of other gossip failed to draw Eddie's attention. Instead, his thoughts were on Anna.

I'd better ring, but not from here.

'Do you know what? I think I fancy some fresh air and a pint across the road.'

He noticed Albert spring to life, tapping his pipe on the fire hearth to empty the burnt tobacco.

'You're not going anywhere, Albert Grossman. I've some wool to wind, so I need both your hands. You sit yourself there and there might be a slice of apple pie in it for you.'

Albert shrugged his shoulders and settled back into his chair while looking at Eddie.

'I'll only be an hour, busy day tomorrow.' Without further comment, Eddie grabbed his winter coat from the stand where he'd deposited it earlier and disappeared into the chilly night air.

Pausing at the front gate to the small cottage, Eddie scanned the deserted lane of Three-Mile-Bottom before turning his attention to the pub across the road, blackout curtains making the medieval hostelry look deserted.

Instead of doing what he'd told Hilda, Eddie moved his attention to his right. On the edge of the hamlet stood a solitary public telephone box, its usual candescent light removed for the duration of the war.

It seemed to take ages for the call to connect before Eddie heard a familiar voice and spoke. Pressing button 'A,' he allowed a coin to drop into the machine. 'Anna, listen, it's me… No, I can't say much, but something has come up. Nothing to worry about… what? No, I can't tell you. Listen, I'll be away for a day or two. See you when I get back, yes? Got to go, Anna, I've run out of money.'

The lieutenant replaced the handset and gathered three one-penny coins from a metal shelf.

Chapter Four: The Widow

Muted frustration pervaded the vicarage as Helen and her daughter attempted in vain to hurry Vinny along to make school on time.

The vicar remained steadfastly ensconced behind his desk on the pretext of checking a final draught of a letter to the bishop.

'It's funny how your father always seems to have important work to do instead of helping to get Vinny ready for school.'

'Perhaps it has something to do with the male of the species,' replied Anna as she spun the young Scouser around with a palm to the top of his head of unruly hair. 'You know, pathological distrust of clean water and hours behind a school desk.'

The two women exchanged a twinkling smile as Anna's mother gave her daughter a light-hearted admonishment for pigeonholing a large proportion of the world's population.

'Get a move on, Vinny. I told you to put your homework away carefully. What I didn't say was hide it so securely it takes on its own life as holding a torch up to the search for Tutankhamun's tomb.'

Helen's reference to Egyptian history baffled the young lad. 'Who's he when he's at home? I don't know no Greek fella. What's a torch got to do with anything?'

'Oh, never mind, it's half-past-eight already, so let's not complicate matters. Get your shoes on, please, while Anna wets that unruly hair of yours again.'

Mention of water sent Vinny scurrying into the vestibule to retrieve his footwear and stay well out of the way of the kitchen sink. 'Got it,' shouted Vinny triumphantly. 'I put my drawing of my vegetable patch in one of my shoes so I wouldn't forget to take it to school. See, I told you I knew where I'd put my homework.'

A second, exasperated glance flew between mother and daughter as Helen made her way towards the front door.

'Do you want me to drop Vinny off, Mum? I need to check how a couple of new evacuees are settling in at the school, so it's no trouble?'

'Oh, that will be wonderful, Anna. It means I can get an early start in the thrift shop. There's a pile of donated clothes I need to sort and price up. Alice and Flo are both busy today, so can't help.'

Arrangements completed, Anna made sure Vinny had his shoes on the correct feet, dampened down a tuft of hair from his crown with a wet finger and opened the front door, ready for their brief journey to school. 'Stand straight, let's check you're ready for the parade before anyone else sees you.'

Vinny frowned as he tried to duck Anna's persistent primping and preening. 'I can't see me hair, so I don't care.'

Anna frowned 'No, but I do, young man. Now, get your duffle coat on. You might want your hat and mittens. There's a crisp breeze blowing.'

Vinny popped his head out of the front door to take in the temperature and shook his head. 'Nah, only soft lads wear woolly hats, and you can keep them mitten things. They're for girls.'

Anna sighed and gave up the fight. 'On we go, young man. Come on, no dawdling or we'll be late.'

In an instant Vinny was off, having caught sight of his best friend, Jimmy, several yards ahead.

'They're all the same, aren't they?' said the other boy's mother as she turned to greet Anna.

'Ferrets in a sack, more like. How are things? Heard from your husband lately?'

The woman shrugged her shoulders as she turned her attention back to the two boys running ahead to make sure they weren't up to any mischief. 'I get the occasional postcard via the Red Cross, but everything's censored from the Prisoner of War camp he's in, so he doesn't say much.'

'Can't be easy for you, or Jimmy?'

'We have our little code words, so I know he's coping, though if he doesn't stop winding those German guards up, I'm not sure it'll go on that way.'

'Oh, hi, Charlotte,' said Anna as one of the mothers overtook them with her daughter.

'Morning, you two. Sorry, I'm in a bit of a hurry. They're sending me to Lawrence and Scott's factory in Norwich, so got to rush.'

Poor woman, I bet she wishes it'd been the Land Army instead, thought Anna.

'See what I mean. At least my man is safe in a prison camp, not waiting to be blown up on night-shift doing war work in Norwich.'

Anna offered an awkward smile. 'How long has it been now?'

Jimmy's mother responded without missing a beat, 'Stupid man, he missed the boat. Was no good at keeping time, so instead of joining his regiment for evacuation from Dunkirk, a German officer caught him in a barn drinking vino with two locals. Drunk as a lord, apparently.'

'Wow, lucky they did not shoot him.'

'Him? You must be joking. Fall in a muddy pond, he could still come up shining like a silver penny. Anyway, he probably offered to share his wine with the German.'

The two women chuckled as they reached the school gates, which thronged with mothers and children coming and going.

'Listen, I can't stop. Can you see my Jimmy in? I've heard a rumour they're getting some extra flour in at the bakers. I missed out last time, so I want to get in line sharpish.'

Anna made for the police station after having waved off her friend and seen the two boys into school and checking up on the new evacuees. Entering the small reception of the small Victorian building, she noticed a raised voice.

'You might be the same rank as me now, my lad, but I've got a lot of years' service on you—you don't know it all yet.'

What's wrong with Dick Ilford? He's usually so calm?

Anna watched Tom Bradshaw rolling his eyes without his old boss catching him.

'Yes, sarge, I'll check to see if anyone in the village has seen Mrs Clifford's Thomas.'

'But she hasn't got a son by that name,' said Anna, unable to contain her confusion on a subject she knew to be none of her business.

The desk sergeant slowly shook his head. 'And don't you start, Anna Grix. It's her cat we're talking about.'

'What's all this about cats?' commented Inspector Spillers as he came out of his office with an empty cup and saucer in hand. 'Has His Majesty's Constabulary of Police got nothing better to do than track down clapped out felines?'

'Don't let Mrs Clifford hear you talk about her cat like that, governor. I'm sick and tired of her, as if I haven't enough to do.'

Anna scanned the empty desktop of the high reception desk,

devoid of anything other than a closed, dusty day-report ledger and a half-full cream-coloured mug of tea.

'So I see, sergeant,' said Spillers, his tone tinged with a note of scepticism. 'I'm glad you've called in, Miss Grix. May I have a word? You too, Bradshaw, in my office, now. Oh, and you can take this, Sergeant Ilford.' He handed his subordinate the empty cup and saucer. 'Two sugar's this time and I don't care if there's a shortage, you can lend me some of yours.'

As the desk sergeant moved off to the kitchen while mumbling under his breath, Anna and Tom followed Spillers and sat as directed.

I wish the man would put some flowers, or at least more pictures, in. It looks like a courtroom with the king looking down on us.

'I'll get straight to the point, Bradshaw. Because of your update last night, and doing one or two checks, I'm treating the car accident as suspicious. I no longer think it necessarily a simple, if tragic, motor vehicle accident.'

Anna noticed Tom lean back in his chair, his head dropping. 'Does that mean you don't want me to—'

'You know better than to interrupt your superior, sergeant.'

'Inspector, it's just—'

'There you go again. Now, where was I? Oh, yes, I remember. Therefore, I'm ordering you to continue with your investigations.'

Tom straightened up in an instant. 'You mean—'

'I mean, Sergeant Bradshaw, that the responsibility to sort this matter out remains with you. Do you understand?'

Good for you, Tom.

Anna gave her friend a wide smile before Inspector Spillers brought her back to earth with a caution.

'Which means Miss Grix here needs to behave herself and help, not hinder, your investigation. Do you understand what I'm saying,

Anna? And that includes Lieutenant Elsner. Don't go leading him on, I'm sure he has quite enough to deal with now.'

Does the inspector know something I don't?

'Now, what's your next move, sergeant?'

Tom sat on the edge of his chair, leaning into the desk, eyes fixed firmly on his superior. 'Well, my priority is to identify the victim and discover what he was doing in the area. I've already spoken to Norwich and King's Lynn headquarters about any reports of stolen cars in the area. With a bit of luck, we'll discover the number plates and tie it all up soon.'

'Solving crimes isn't a matter of luck, Bradshaw. It's about good old-fashioned police work, do you understand?'

You walked into that one, Tom.

A sheepish-looking Tom Bradshaw visibly sank into his uniform. 'Yes, Inspector. All I mean is—'

'I know what you mean, son. Stick to the basics, and I know you'll be able to sort this mess out for me. Remember, somewhere a mother, girlfriend or wife is waiting for the man who met his end in that car. Our duty is to give them answers, yes?'

Who'd of thought Inspector Spillers has a soft side to him?

'You can count on me, sir.'

Anna felt the need to clear her throat.

'Oh, I mean, us, sir.'

Inspector Spillers threw the sergeant a weary look before turning his attention to some paperwork on his desk and dismissing Tom and Anna with a wave.

Outside the station, Tom asked Anna where the lieutenant was, and what Spillers may have meant. 'An odd thing to say, don't you think?'

'I thought the same. It tells me something's going on that neither Eddie, nor Spillers, is prepared to talk about.'

Tom glanced at his watch. 'Heck, I'm late for a meeting in Norwich to see if they've turned anything up. Do you want to tag along?'

'Oh, what, er, no, but thanks? I've an errand to do for Dad. Meet up later, OK?'

He's quite dashing in his sergeant stripes.

Eleven o'clock, shouldn't be too early to call.

Anna parked her old-fashioned bicycle, complete with wicker basket, against the low flintstone front wall of a brick in-filled oak framed cottage; its timbers turned silver through the centuries.

This must have been an incredible place at one time, she thought, pondering when the once grand gentleman farmer's home was split into the three cottages it contained now.

Still warm from peddling hard against a stiff breeze of intermittent drizzle, Anna undid the top three buttons of her heavy winter coat and approached the wood-plank front door.

I wonder if she'll talk to me?

Standing a few feet from the entrance for a few seconds, Anna eyed the front of the cottage up and down. As she widened her look, she noticed curtains from the cottages on either side of where she stood twitching, without being able to make out her observers.

Approaching the door, she gave three sharp taps on the dense timbers.

Come on, I'm sure you're there.

Waiting a few seconds, Anna gave the entrance door a second rap. This time she sensed movement through three small diamond-shaped leaded glass panels. Not enough to see the person behind the door, but enough to know her visit might yield at least some contact.

Slowly, almost imperceptibly at first, the aged oak door opened, its rusty wrought iron hinges making a squeaking sound that reminded Anna of a Boris Karloff horror film.

A few inches more and Anna caught sight of a sad looking woman dressed from head to toe in black, who she thought looked to be in her late fifties.

'Good morning. Mrs Flotman? My father's the vicar of Lipton St—'

'I know who Charles Grix is,' replied the woman in a cold, detached voice while looking the stranger up and down. 'And you want?'

Anna knew her response wasn't so much a question of interest, more one of distrust, even dislike. 'I'm sorry to intrude. I know it must be a hard time for you, but Dad wanted to make sure you were alright. You know, if you needed anything, and I have something for you.'

She fumbled in a pocket to retrieve her father's letter. The widow ignored the envelope, instead keeping her eyes fixed on her unwanted visitor.

The two women held each other in their gaze until Anna noticed a softening of the woman's demeanour.

'Your name is Anna, isn't it?'

'Yes, it is,' she replied in a soft, considered tone.

'I remember you as a wee lass.'

It was only then that Anna picked up on the woman's silk-soft Edinburgh lilt. The widow's words sang to a rhythm that entranced her.

'Dad says you used to be a regular at the church and helping in the village. He says it's time you had help.'

Mrs Flotman's faint smile vanished in an instant as she stiffened. 'I need charity from no one. Now, what do you want of me? To know how I found my husband hanging in his shed? You're like all the others.'

Anna took a step back; such was her shock at her sudden change in mood. 'No... not at all, and apologies if I caused offence. That's not my intention. Please, Mrs Flotman, let me explain why I'm here.'

She watched as the woman pondered on what to do next. Eventually

Mrs Flotman opened the door enough for Anna to squeeze through and enter the small sitting room.

'I don't suppose it can do any harm to listen, but remember, I don't need your money. I need nothing from anyone.'

Sensing the tension easing, Anna undid the rest of her coat buttons and looked towards the beech-framed sofa of a cottage suite.

'Oh, please sit. Would you like some tea, I'll... oh, I'm out of tea at the moment, but I'm expecting, well—'

'Mrs Flotman, it's not a problem, I'm fine.'

The woman looked at the red-tiled floor before taking a seat opposite her visitor. Silence followed as the woman gazed unseeingly into a small log fire that struggled to heat the room.

I know she wants to talk about her husband. I guess she doesn't know how to start.

'That's a lovely picture, Mrs Flotman.' Anna pointed to a faded photograph in a small, square silver frame sitting on the overmantel to the fireplace.

I hope I'm doing the right thing.

She could see the widow studying the familiar image. A young man and woman sat smiling on a fallen log, cuddling a small boy who sat between them.

'Three weeks after that picture, we lost our little boy. One second everything was the same, the next, well...'

Poor woman. She's desolate.

Anna leaned forward but sensed Mrs Flotman pulling away.

'It wasn't his fault, you know. They all said it was, and he never forgave himself, but he didn't know our little one was behind the car.'

How awful. I can't imagine. Yet they lived through it.

'My husband tried so hard to deal with things. Such a brave man, but deep down, I always knew what he'd do in the end. My

50

husband only ever wanted to be with our wee lad again. And now I'm left with this mess. What am I going to do? The police have been around and what about the burial?'

That's it, keep talking. It's now or never.

Anna once slipped a hand into her jacket pocket and pulled the envelope out. 'That's why I'm here, Mrs Flotman. It's from my father.'

The widow glanced at Anna's outstretched hand before turning away. 'I suppose he's telling me he can't or won't bury my man with his son. Didn't even have the courage to tell me himself.'

Anna pressed the letter into her hand. 'You don't understand. Please, read what my father has to say.'

After a few seconds of gazing uninterestedly at the pale envelope, Mrs Flotman shrugged her shoulders, read the handwritten address on the front, and tore a narrow strip from the top of the envelope.

The widow placed a hand over her mouth as if to stifle emotions she'd kept deep inside from the day her husband died.

Thank heavens for that, thought Anna as tears trickled down her host's face. *Now she understands.*

'I'm sorry for doubting your father. He always was a stickler for the rules, but he says he'll bury my husband in consecrated ground and reunite him with our little one at last.'

Anna held out a hand. This time the widow clasped it lightly within her own.

'But he'll get into trouble with the bishop for this. Why is he doing it? We don't deserve—'

'It's nothing to do with deserving anything, Mrs Flotman. Dad is always telling me he reports to only one superior, and he doesn't spend his time drinking sherry from a crystal decanter in a bishop's palace.'

'But—'

'But nothing, Mrs Flotman. Dad will take care of all the

arrangements if you'll allow him to. He will do nothing without your blessing. And don't worry about any expense. The village will gather around you, just as my father tells me your husband and you so often helped others in times of need. Now it's the village's turn to care for your needs.'

The tears flowed again, leading Anna to move from the sofa and kneel in front of the distraught woman. This time, she was not to be dissuaded from offering a comforting hug.

Minutes passed as the two women held tightly on to each other. Anna relaxed her grip as she sensed Mrs Flotman wished to speak.

'What's wrong?'

The woman looked back into the failing log fire. 'I don't know. Perhaps how fickle life is. Everything has changed. All the things we used to take for granted… all gone. Some have more money than ever, with all this factory work, yet nothing to spend it on in the shops. Young people doing things my mother would never have allowed me to get up to. Even the church argues between itself. How can that be?'

I'm confused?

'What do you mean, Mrs Flotman?'

The lady thumbed the letter before placing it on the rush carpet next to her wear-worn chair. 'The last time I saw my husband, he said he'd seen two vicars arguing in the street. Can you imagine two vicars? Well, it seemed to have upset him. He was already in one of his low moods, but I thought he'd shake it off like all the other times.'

'I'm still not with you, Mrs Flotman.'

Mrs Flotman fixed her stare on the visitor. 'Who knows, perhaps he thought if the clergy couldn't be civil to one another, that things had gone too far and there wasn't any hope left. All I know is he finished his usual late morning cup of tea and went to his shed like always. Only this time he didn't come back.'

Closing her coat against the driving drizzle, Anna gave Mrs Flotman a last wave before pulling her cycle from the wall and shaking it to remove as much water from its seat and frame as possible.

Noon. Best get back for lunch. I'm starving.

As she set off, Anna noticed two young women strolling arm-in-arm, leaning into one another and giggling as they walked.

One girl placed a hand to the back of her leg, a little below the hemline of her coat, to dislodge a rain drop.

Oops, thought Anna, *that's her gravy browning fake stocking seam gone for a burton. So much for the Glamour Hose look!*

As she passed the two dolled-up youngsters, Anna thought about alerting the one with a now smeared stocking line about her misfortune but concluded that ignorance was a sort of bliss.

I bet they're off to Norwich for a treat, bless them. Good luck, girls, at least someone's happy.

Passing the bus stop the girls seemed to head for, Anna heard the sputtering engine noises of a bus wending its way towards her position.

I don't think those girls are in any danger of missing that old thing, never mind make it to Norwich.

Thanking her lucky stars not to have taken the bus, Anna peddled furiously and made good time back to the vicarage. As she opened the garden gate, the sound of a police car bell took her attention, giving off its trill tone.

'Fancy some fish and chips in Winterton?' The familiar voice of Tom Bradshaw, together with his impish grin as he hung out of the driver's side window, melted any resistance Anna might've had.

'You're on, just a tick. I'll put my bike back in the stables and tell Dad what I'm up to.'

Tom contented himself by yet again investigating all that the old police car offered, much to the annoyance of a local who caught the full blast of the police bell as he walked past the car.

'I'm checking it works before I go on patrol. It's standard practice.'

The villager muttered something inaudible as he shuffled onward into the village.

'OK, let's get going. You'll have to pay because I'm out of cash until Thursday unless I can get a sub from Dad.'

Tom smiled as Anna climbed into the car. 'Don't worry, I've got five bob on me, so unless you want champagne with your cod and chips, we'll be fine.'

'I should be so lucky. Anyway, you weren't long in Norwich. Did they have anything interesting for you?'

Tom shook his head as he coaxed the police car into life and headed the ten miles to Winterton-on-Sea. 'Nothing other than a couple of lorries stolen, probably by black marketeers.'

The rest of the journey comprised two long-standing friends chatting away aimlessly. However, as they entered the tiny fishing village of Winterton, a woman waved frantically from the pavement.

Tom brought the car to a halt as fast as his inadequate brakes allowed. 'May I help, madam?' he said after winding his window down.

'A stranger. I've seen a stranger in the village coming and going from the cottage next to mine. It's been empty for years. What if they're a spy? You hear so much about fifth columnists these days, don't you?'

Tom recovered his police notebook from a breast pocket and took notes. 'Are you able to describe the man for me?'

The woman frowned. 'Man? Who said anything about a man? It's a woman I saw, a right hoity-toity sort, if you ask me. I've done my duty, so it's up to you now.'

Before Tom could respond, the woman turned on her low heels and made off into a maze of tiny lanes, soon disappearing.

'Hardly the stuff of Mata Hari, is it?' commented Anna. 'Come on, I want my fish and chips.'

Needing little encouragement, Tom eased the car forwards and parked fifty yards along the narrow sand-blown tarmac road until it sat next to the shop entrance.

It took less than fifteen minutes to polish off their meal as the pair gazed towards the sand dunes and beach beyond.

'I can't wait for the war to end. It's a lovely beach here.'

Tom turned to his companion. 'Judging by all that barbed wire and the training the army does here, I think it'll be a long time after hostilities cease until you get anywhere near the place.'

Having gone as far as permitted along the road, the pair turned back towards the village as Tom took Anna's empty newspaper chip wrappings and looked for somewhere to dispose of their rubbish. 'By the way, I forgot to ask. How did your errand go?'

Anna gave the briefest of details, making sure not to tell Tom anything that might compromise his position as an officer of the law in cases of suicide.

Tom laughed at mention of two ecclesiastics arguing. 'That'd be a first for me, arresting two vicars for a breach of the peace. Priceless!'

As Tom tossed their greasy paper into an open rubbish bin full of cold coal ashes, the sound of a now familiar voice filled the immediate vicinity.

'Here we go, round two,' said Tom as he fixed his gaze on the informant again.

'Too busy eating fish and chips to investigate spies, I see.'

The two friends giggled once the woman had walked past in a huff before making their way back to the police car and heading back to Lipton St Faith.

'Look at Dad,' laughed Anna as Tom brought the car to a stop outside the vicarage. 'Mum says he brought the trench coat back from France in 1918. It's still his favourite winter coat for gardening, although there's not much to dig up now. Perhaps he's keeping out of Mum's way.'

She exchanged smiles with Tom as she climbed from the police car, offered a glancing wave, and sauntered over to her father.

'I'm tidying the raised beds ready for a fresh crop. Anyway, I've had enough. It's too wet to dig. Let's grab a cup of tea, shall we?'

Neither got beyond the threshold of the back door before Helen demanded her husband withdrew in his muddy boots.

Several minutes later the vanquished vicar took his seat at the table, now shorn of all vestiges of soil. Anna took her usual chair opposite him.

'Lunch will be ready in two shakes of a lamb's tail. It's a cold table today.'

Anna breathed a sigh, knowing she wouldn't have to eat two hot meals in the space of an hour.

'Well, Anna?'

Anna looked at her father.

'Your visit. How did it go?'

'Oh, er…, Dad, I'm miles away. Yes, it went well. Your hunch was right, but it was sticky to begin with.'

She retold the details of her visit and raced along until she got to the part about the pastors. Anna watched as her father drained of colour. 'What's up, Dad? You look like you've seen a ghost?'

The vicar rubbed his forehead with two fingers. 'Nothing, I'm sure of it… only—'

'What, Dad? Is it something I've said that's upset you?'

'A coincidence, I'm sure, but the vicar of St Paul's rang me earlier. He expected a new curate to arrive yesterday. Would you believe it, the man didn't turn up, and still hasn't? I hope there's no connection between what you've told me and that young man.'

Chapter Five: A Golden Link

The coincidence of two men of the cloth involving themselves in an unseemly argument and a separate matter to do with a missing curate continued to trouble Anna as she left her father in the kitchen and wandered into the vestibule, heading for the vicarage telephone.

Perhaps I'm being daft, but there's something not sitting right with me about this lot. I've got to track Eddie down.

Reaching out for the black Bakelite handset, she dialled a familiar number, not expecting it to be answered.

I bet I'll need to bike around to Hilda's place. They won't want to answer "The lieutenant's" telephone.

She glanced at the grandfather clock, its long-case silvered pendulum swaying unendingly, as the floral-faced roundel showed two o'clock.

Anna knew that Lottie Longhorn, the elderly telephone operator who controlled the local post office switchboard, would listen in.

'Good afternoon Lottie,' announced Anna, knowing the firm greeting normally caused the operator to stop listening after the regulation five seconds and mind her own business, even though Lottie was only supposed to listen in to make sure any call she connected went through.

Come on, Hilda, don't make me ride all the way to Three-Mile-Bottom.

To her surprise and relief, Eddie's landlady answered her call.

'Yes, who's speaking?' said a hesitant voice, the line cracking more than usual.

'Hilda, it's me, Anna Grix. Is Eddie there?' she said without giving Hilda the chance to put the phone down again for fear of getting the lieutenant into trouble.

'Er, yes. I see. Who did you say is speaking?'

For heaven's sake, Hilda. Being careful is one thing, but you must recognise my voice?

At least that's what Anna wanted to say. Instead, she kept the thought to herself and tried another tactic. 'Don't worry, Hilda, I know it's a poor line. I'm only after that stupid man who ran me over the other month.'

'Ah, Anna. Why didn't you say?'

Good, she believes I'm who I say I am!

Turning to kiss her father on the cheek as he wandered past, opened the front door and vanished into the early afternoon, Anna pressed on.

'I apologise for ringing, but I need to speak to Eddie?'

The telephone fell silent again.

Come on, Hilda, don't clam up now.

Seconds passed before the landlady spoke. 'Er… no. Well, in fact, no, not at all. All he said was he'd be back soon. You know what he's like and I don't like to pry or anything like that.'

It's not like Eddie to be this secretive. I hope he's safe, but this isn't getting me anywhere.

'I see, Hilda. He is a curious chap, isn't he? What say we contact one another, whoever hears from the ridiculous man first?'

A further brief silence fell before Hilda responded. 'Well, I suppose… yes, that's the thing to do. And thank you for tipping me off about the lard. I'll get down to the butcher's straight away before he runs out again.'

What, thought Anna, before realising the obtuse comment represented Hilda's attempt at subterfuge.

Well, if that doesn't set the spies running after geese, nothing will.

A distinctive click rang in Anna's right ear, confirming Hilda had replaced the handset. As she replaced her own, Anna noticed the outline of a familiar figure through the stained-glass leaded light of the front door.

'Was that Eddie?' said Bradshaw within half-a-second of his host, offering her welcome.

'You've got good ears.'

'Part of the training for the job. The police hear everything, didn't you know?'

'I'll remember that next time it's your turn to buy the drinks. Come on in. And for the record, Hilda doesn't know where our American friend has gone. It's as if he's vanished into a puff of smoke. Has Inspector Spillers said anything to you about him?'

Tom shook his head as he crossed the vicarage threshold and cradled his police helmet under his right arm. 'He fends me off with some rubbish about Eddie not being his problem. It's odd.'

'You can say that again. So, what's next?' Anna led the sergeant into the vicarage lounge, a large, warm room filled with country furniture, a donated art deco radiogram, and several pictures of the family.

'Well, I've filed a report about the woman in Winterton-on-Sea. Not the one who told us, I mean…'

'Yes, Tom. I know who you mean.'

Oops, I didn't mean to sound sarcastic.

Tom gave Anna a second take before smiling. 'Who's in a foul mood?'

'Sorry, Tom. I deserved that,' she replied as she offered to put the kettle on.

'It's OK. What with everything that's going on, well, it's a right old funny time. Thanks for the offer of tea, but—'

'Did somebody mention tea? That will be wonderful. What a day I've had. So many donations, I think people are clearing out ready for the New Year.'

Helen's harassed tone filled the vestibule and passed through the open door of the lounge.

'You've no choice, now, Tom, you'd better sit yourself down.'

'You two are looking furtive. What are you up to?' Helen sped into the lounge as if her life depended on it.

'Slow down, Mum, you'll have a heart attack. Here, take a seat and entertain the good sergeant. I'll make the tea.'

Helen smiled as she removed a brightly coloured cotton headscarf, neatly folded it, and placed the fabric on her chair arm. 'It'll soon be time to collect the scallywag from school. Tea is just what I need before the hurricane that is Vinny lands in our midst.'

A few minutes later, Anna returned with three hot drinks sitting on a wood tray.

'What are you looking at? Have you lost a shilling and found a sixpence?'

Anna looked at the cups again, then at her mother. 'I've remembered. I told Mrs Flotman we'd buy and deliver some essential supplies. She refused at first, but I know she needs our help.'

'Poor woman. I'm sure the village shopkeepers will each chip something in. I'll have a word with them.'

Anna placed the tray on a small square table by her mother's chair. 'Thanks, Mum, you're a real trooper.'

'We'll see what a trooper I am after a couple of hours keeping Vinny entertained and out of mischief.'

Soon, Tom had finished his tea and stood.

'Got to go already?'

'I know it's a pain, Helen, I only popped in to say hello to Anna. I've a lot to catch up with.'

Anna pretended to choke on her drink. 'He's off to talk to a woman about a cat, that's what he's up to.'

'A what?' said Helen.

'Don't ask,' sighed Tom, as he unfolded his tall frame from a chair and sauntered into the vestibule.

'Got to go, too, Mum. I'll get changed and be back for tea.'

Helen's gaze moved from one to the other as the two adults breezed through the lounge doorway, shaking her head as if bemused by the burst of sudden activity.

From her bedroom window, Anna enjoyed a bird's-eye view down the village high street. As she scanned the near horizon, her eyes drifted towards the movement at the front gate. Tom had replaced his police helmet and stood tall, ready for his important interview with Mrs Clifford, owner of the missing cat.

He's quite handsome, thought Anna.

Her attention shifted to a gathering line of women standing outside the milliners.

Don't say there's a rush for cotton thread?

Leaving the street scene to its own devices, Anna quickly changed and started for the stairs when she heard the front door open, followed immediately by the vicarage telephone ringing.

Eddie, she thought.

'That was good timing, Dad.'

The vicar appeared flustered as he attempted to close the front door, open his damp coat, and simultaneously balance the telephone handset under his chin.

'Vicar Grix speaking. How may I be of service?'

Anna perched halfway down the stairs, leaning over the oak bannister rail. She motioned her father to say if the caller was Eddie.

Her attempt at charades to show a pilot, the Statue of Liberty and John Wayne, simply caused her father more confusion.

'Yes, yes, I'm still here.'

'Eddie. Is it Eddie?' said Anna impatiently.

The vicar shook his head and turned his back on Anna.

Rude thing, she thought.

She remained fixed to the spot, hearing only her father's cryptic responses to a conversation she couldn't engage in.

'Thank you for ringing. God go with you, James. I'm sure all will be well. If I hear anything, I'll call immediately.'

Anna slowly descended the remaining stairs and wandered over to her father, who still held the handset mid-air.

'Here, let me take that. Is everything alright, Dad?'

Anna's concerned tone caused Helen to wander into the vestibule. 'Something wrong?'

The vicar stood in silence for several seconds before turning to his wife. 'That was the vicar of St Paul's. His curate still hasn't turned up.'

'As you said yesterday, it's not the done thing, is it?' said Anna.

'No, you don't understand,' replied her father. 'The seminary told James the man left for the train station yesterday. They know this because he was running late, so the local butcher who'd been making a delivery volunteered to drop him off at the station. It seems the chap saw him purchase his ticket and run to the platform. After that, nothing.'

Helen straightened her husband's clerical collar after his fight with the telephone and overcoat. 'Come here, you scruffy man. What would your parishioners think if they saw you like that?'

The vicar tried in vain to escape his wife's clutches. 'Yes, alright, my dear. I'm sure you've made me look presentable once more, but I'm more concerned about that curate, it's just so odd.'

Anna warmed to her father's theme. 'Look, I've a couple of things I need to do this afternoon. After that, why don't we pay a visit to St Paul's to offer your vicar friend some support? You never know, by the time we get there, I bet the elusive young man and his mentor are sitting by a roaring fire enjoying a cup of tea.'

As Anna rode down the high street on her way to carry out a first visit on a prospective evacuee host family, she marvelled at the enthusiasm the young ones had for life as their mother's, actual or government sponsored, gathered up their charges and hurried off home.

With luck, they won't remember much about the war when they grow up.

The daylight was already failing, yet Anna looked forward to the luxury of a following wind to speed her journey when progress came to a halt. Hardly had she reached the village green when Beatrice Flowers demanded she stop. Her outstretched arm was not something Anna could avoid.

'What's the matter, Beatrice?' asked Anna as her attention became momentarily distracted by glimpsing a well-dressed woman with immaculate makeup and, despite the stiff breeze, perfectly coiffured hair staring at her. *That's odd. I wonder who she is?*

Turning back to the village gossip, Anna waited for the latest in a long line of barbed comments about her clothes, hair, or revealing too much flesh for the daughter of a vicar.

The villager chose not to answer immediately; instead she stood back and gestured with an angry finger toward Anna's billowing coat.

Feigning confusion about what the woman meant, Anna checked her coat for dirty marks or damage of some sort, then offered her accuser a shrug of her shoulders.

Beatrice pointed once again, this time waving her index finger as if mimicking the windscreen wiper of a car. 'And what, may I ask, is a vicar's daughter doing riding a bicycle in this weather and thus allowing her skirts to be blown to the four winds?'

I give up, thought Anna.

'Beatrice, I hardly—'

'What kind of example does this display show to the other young women in our village?'

Anna looked at her coat again before frowning at her accuser. 'It's the end of November. It's cold and windy and I'm wearing my mother's thick woollen stockings and a long tweed skirt. I doubt the combined weight and design of this get up allows anyone to see anything. Now I am late, so—'

The elderly woman refused to be dismissed so lightly. 'And what about your ankles? They're on show for all to see. What will the young men think about that?'

Anna couldn't help but giggle. 'Beatrice, anyone of an interesting age to me has already gone off to war. As for the younger ones, well, to them I expect I'm just another old spinster.'

Beatrice huffed. 'There's no need to be so disrespectful to your elders. I'm only looking after your best interests and that of the church.'

Give me strength. Anna thought better of arguing further about the matter and instead offered a disarming smile. 'I apologise, Beatrice. You are, of course, correct, and I promise to try harder. Now I must be going.'

Anna used her right foot to push the bicycle forward, then pedalled. She momentarily glanced to the other side of the high street to notice the well-dressed lady following her every move.

Why does she look so angry?

'But what about the car crash?' shouted Beatrice as Anna rode away.

Ah, so that's what this is about, thought Anna.

She stopped pedalling and brought the bicycle to a stop. 'Car crash, what car crash?' she responded, her voice raised to counter the wind and several feet which separated the two women.

Beatrice pulled herself up to her full four feet ten inches and crossed her arms, with some difficulty because of her own heavy coat, across her chest. 'Anna Grix, we villagers have seen you in the police car with your young gentleman, and—'

'My what?'

'As I say, I'm only saying what I've been told. Anyway, the dead man must be a stranger because I've not heard of anyone local getting hurt.'

'Beatrice, I don't know what you're—'

'Burnt to a crisp, they say. Drunk as a lord and crashed into a horse. Poor thing. What had the horse done to deserve that?'

She's fishing, thought Anna.

Leaving the spinster wearing a self-satisfied look, Anna lifted her foot from the road, pushing off. 'As you say, Beatrice, poor horse. Now, got to go, I'm late for my appointment... now.'

Beatrice's dogged attempt to elicit information caused Anna to think.

My journey takes me past the accident site. It's got to be worth another look. I've got time before it goes dark.

Ten minutes later, Anna stood looking over the desolate scene that had witnessed such a recent tragedy. All traces of the accident seemed to have disappeared, leaving Anna to shuffle around the small area for anything that might help explain what happened.

The police will have gone over this place with a fine-tooth comb. I'm wasting my time, she thought.

Turning to walk back to her bike, Anna unintentionally kicked a spray of small stones from under her foot. Her attention fell on a small flat-faced object that glistened as it tumbled forward several inches.

What's that?

The tiny item stood out from the drab, grey stones even though the light had almost gone.

Anna bent down and picked the metal object up between a finger and thumb.

It's a collar stud. Dad has one exactly like it.

'May I speak to Sergeant Bradshaw, please?' Anna tried to keep calm as she spoke into the handset of a public telephone and waited expectantly.

'He's not there, you say. Do you have any idea when he'll be back?'

She listened impatiently as the other party replied.

'He's still investigating the missing cat. Oh, I see… leave a message? No, that's kind of you, but I'll catch up with him later… Now, as I think about it, perhaps you might tell him I called. It's not urgent, but I'd like to speak to him when he has a minute… Perhaps he can call at the vicarage this evening? Yes, that's right, thank you, Sergeant Ilford.'

Anna winced as the policeman made light about Tom spending a cosy evening in her company.

How original, she thought.

'Something like that, sergeant. Thank you all the same.'

Not wishing to prolong the man's theme, Anna said a last goodbye and replaced the telephone handset.

Pushing the heavy telephone box door open with her shoulder, Anna glanced at her wristwatch.

It's too late to make my appointment now, I'll call in tomorrow and make my apologies.

The journey back to Lipton St Faith took longer than she expected because of the stiffening headwind, and she breathed a sigh as she finally placed her bike back into its allotted position in the old stable block of the vicarage.

I wonder if Dad can identify this? she thought, twiddling the stud between two fingers as she pushed the already half-open kitchen door.

'Close it to, will you? I often think young Vinny was born in a barn, not a terraced house in Liverpool.'

Anna found his words hard to hear, since the vicar had his head buried deep inside one of the AGA's two ovens.

She looked at Vinny, who was oblivious to events as he sat at the kitchen table devouring his latest comic book.

'Have things got that bad that you're attempting to do away with yourself in the oven? You know it's coal-fired, not gas?'

She immediately regretted her words.

Oh, no. Poor Mr Flotman.

'Only joking.'

As Charles Grix slid himself from the oven's blacked interior, he hit his head on one of two heavy cast iron hinges that held the open oven door in place. Rubbing the back-right corner of his scalp with an open hand, Charles sighed. 'Sometimes I wish I wasn't a vicar because there are occasions on which I'd like to blaspheme.'

As he got to his feet, he rubbed again and checked for signs of blood. Anna gave her father a comforting kiss, but only appeared to make the pain worse. 'Oh dear, I didn't mean to touch that.'

'What does blaspheme mean?' Vinny's out-of-the-blue remark, eyes still fixed firmly on his comic, lightened the moment.

'I'll tell you when you're twenty-one, young man.'

'No, you won't. You'll be dead by then,' replied Vinny, again without acknowledging the physical presence of either Anna or her father.

'Who's dead?' asked Helen as she breezed into the kitchen.

The vicar gave his head a third rub before responding to his wife. 'As Mark Twain said, "The reports of my death are greatly exaggerated", except this chap already has me six feet under. Isn't that correct, young man?' Anna's father pointed at the youngster, who steadfastly kept his eyes on his comic book.

Three adults giggling at the exchange did nothing to distract Vinny from his task. Instead, he shrugged his shoulders and flicked over to the next story.

'Can I have a word, Dad?' said Anna quietly, her smile suddenly fading.

Charles frowned. 'Everything alright?'

Anna pointed at Vinny with a single finger.

'Oh, yes, I see. Let's go through,' replied the vicar in a soft tone. 'By the way, wonderful wife, the AGA's fixed and, as you can see, I risked life and limb to make it so.' Charles placed a hand on his crown to emphasise his point.

'You may have fixed my AGA but ruined my tiled floor into the bargain. Look at all that soot.'

'You say the matter is urgent, Anna? Then we must proceed.' The vicar gave his wife a peck on the cheek and winked.

'Don't you try to soft-soap me, Charles Grix, now off with you both. I've got my work cut out.'

Not waiting for any further invitation to leave the messy kitchen, Anna led the way to her father's office.

'That was a close-run thing. I think I got away with it.'

Anna laughed as she perched on one corner of her father's twin pedestal desk. 'I wouldn't be so sure about that. There was no mention of supper later, so you're on bread and water rations for the week.'

Anna held out the tiny object she'd found at the crash site.

'What have you there?' replied Charles, having taken his daughter's jest in good spirits, and sunk into his chair.

Collecting the stud from Anna's open palm, the vicar examined the delicate object before placing it on top of a closed King James I Bible.

Without further comment, Charles hunched forward and opened the top left-hand draw of his desk. Reaching inside, he withdrew a small box covered in a delicate, red-grained leather.

'Do you recognise it, Dad?' Anna's voice conveyed a tinge of concern.

'I do,' replied her father as he opened the small box, smiled, and lifted out a small gold object. 'It's not one of mine. Where did you find it?'

'Do all pastors have them?'

Her father frowned. 'They're common among my colleagues, I suppose, not to mention middle-class men in general. Is there a problem?'

Anna's cheeks drained of colour. 'I think it's even more important that we visit your friend at St Paul's, don't you?'

Chapter Six: Woman in Black

St Paul's church lay a little under four-miles north of Lipton St Faith, which on this bright, calm Tuesday morning in early December took Anna and her father forty-minutes to cover on their bicycles.

'You'd never think there was a war on, would you?'

'It's difficult to forget, Dad, but I know what you mean,' replied Anna as they cycled side-by-side through the quiet Norfolk countryside.

Overhead, a skein of pink-footed geese chattered as they progressed from the coast towards their morning feeding spot inland to feast on sugar beet tops, wings flapping in unison; their siren call making no allowance for the sensitivities of other creatures, human or otherwise.

'They're noisy beggars, aren't they?' said the vicar, breathing harder as they peddled up a rare incline for such an otherwise flat area of England. 'Anyway, not long and we'll be at St Paul's. I'm ready for a nice cup of tea.'

Charles prediction proved accurate as the pair rounded a gentle bend on the narrow road, fields either side hidden behind dense hedging, the only clue to their position the flint round bell tower of their destination piercing the skyline a few hundred yards ahead.

Resting her bike on its stand on a strip of grass that flanked the narrow roadway, Anna took her father's cycle and leaned it against a low brick wall that surrounded the graveyard of the rural church as Charles bent forward to remove his bicycle clips, grunting as he did so. 'I'm getting too old for this malarky.'

'Get away with yourself,' laughed Anna. 'You've a few miles left in you yet.'

Exchanging a fond smile, the pair sauntered up a narrow path that wound its way through the picturesque scene which led to the church's main entrance.

Passing through an open door, its oak timbers bleached silver-grey from a millennium of winters, Anna became aware they were not alone. As the pair progressed into the main body of St Paul's, two figures gave life to the otherwise silent space.

Trust us to barge in at the wrong time, she thought.

One she recognised as the vicar, the other a woman dressed head to foot in black, she had no clue about.

'Best we withdraw,' whispered the vicar, as he brushed Anna's arm.

She reacted instantly, turning on her heels and following her father outside and into the bright morning. As they wandered among the mix of ancient and more recent headstones, Anna took notice of one particularly small cluster. 'Look, all 1919 or 1920.'

'The Spanish Flu, I'm afraid,' replied her father. 'We didn't escape it. No part of the country did. A horrible end to a decade of slaughter.'

I've touched a nerve.

'Dad, I didn't—'

'No need to apologise, Anna. They were desperate times and imagine the joy and grief of local families who were lucky enough to welcome their sons back from France, only to see them die of influenza months, or even weeks later. It took the young and fit more than the old ones, you know.'

Before Anna could react, her attention focused on movement at the church door. The woman dressed in black exited the ancient church, followed by her confessor.

Poor woman, thought Anna, as she watched the sad figure lift a shoulder-length black veil and dab her eyes with a delicate white handkerchief.

As parishioner and vicar walked slowly to the lych gate, the pastor acknowledged his visitor's presence with a respectful nod, before turning his attention back to the woman in black.

Minutes later, the vicar retraced his steps, this time offering Charles and his daughter a friendly wave.

'Lovely to see you both. You must be Anna. Your father has told me all about you.'

Why do parents do that?

'That sounds ominous,' replied Anna.

'Not at all, Charles is clearly immensely proud of you.'

Make this go away.

'Good morning, James. Isn't it delightful that a father can still embarrass his daughter by deploying a few simple words of praise?'

Will you both stop looking at me?

'That appeared a sad case, poor woman,' commented Charles as he dropped his voice a tone and extended a hand to the vicar.

'As you say,' replied James. 'Though as you'll testify yourself, not at all uncommon during these testing times. Now, tea, I think.'

He *lives on his own*, thought Anna as she followed James into the rectory, its sparse interior lacking for the want of care and attention.

'I'm not one to break a confidence, but we're both men of the cloth so use the same channel of communication do we not?' said James as he showed his visitors into a large sitting room devoid of even the slightest home comforts. 'It seems she promised her husband that if he died fighting for King and country, she'd do all she could to track down his estranged brother.'

'A sad set of circumstances, yet, I fear, not uncommon,' replied Charles as he sat on an ancient leather sofa, where he promptly slipped to forty-five degrees because of its lack of horsehair stuffing.

'Ah, I should have warned you about that.'

I can't wait to tell Mum about this.

'Did you recommend the Salvation Army?' replied Charles, brushing aside the peculiar angle at which he sat. 'They're fantastic at finding people.'

'I did, Charles. As you say, first rate at locating those that, for whatever reason, may not wish to be found. Ah, Mrs Walsh, so kind of you.'

A small, frail-looking woman wearing a tartan patterned cotton headscarf and fingerless gloves ambled into the large Victorian room holding a tray of tea that looked as though it might topple at any second. 'There's no sugar,' barked the woman.

Ouch, thought Anna.

'Is that so, Mrs Walsh? Well, we each must sacrifice for the greater war effort, must we not?'

That was sharp, thought Anna.

'If you say so. Right, I'll leave you to it Mr, I've your washing to do… again.'

James gave an embarrassed smile as he nodded. 'We won't detain you. Thank you so much for the tea, Mrs Walsh.'

The housekeeper muttered something Anna couldn't pick up, before walking in a tight circle to face the open door into the wide lobby and eventually disappearing into the bowels of the immense house.

'A delightful woman, so helpful… if a little too attached to the day-to-day routine of my long-standing and venerable predecessor,' said James as he took a gulp of his tea and bared his teeth at the strange taste. 'You'll remember him, I'm sure, Charles?'

Anna's father offered a wry smile. 'Ah, yes, Uriah, Witheridge-Soames.' Charles raised his eyebrows as he smiled and shook his head. 'The last of the Hell and damnation brigade was Uriah. I suppose your housekeeper hasn't got used to your modern way yet!'

James gave up on his tea and placed the cup and saucer on the broad arm of his upholstered chair. 'I've been here five years, Charles. This tells me I have no prospect of redemption as far as Mrs Walsh's concerned.'

The trio fell into a contemplative silence, during which Anna and her father wore a gentle smile, while James frowned as he lamented the delicate relationship with his housekeeper. Anna giggled as she watched her father venture on three occasions to drink his tea, abandoning each attempt as he caught the unusual aroma and colour of the concoction.

Time to move the conversation on, thought Anna.

'So, the curious case of the missing curate, James. Do you have a theory?' asked Anna.

Charles repositioned his cup and saucer so that they covered a small tear in the fabric of the chair arm. 'I'm afraid not, and to say I'm worried is an understatement. My only means of relating to the man is what I've gathered from the character reference his college sent and subsequent telephone conversation with the principal. Sidney Langham is twenty-five, has, as you would expect of a curate, a strong faith guided by a deeply held set of principles. All perfectly normal in the circumstances, wouldn't you agree? Except—'

'Recent events show he acted out of character,' interrupted Charles.

James sighed as he retrieved a brown manilla folder from a battered metal filing cabinet. 'As you say. It seems he had a tough childhood.' The vicar opened the folder and summarised its contents for his guests.

'His father died in WWI… some sort of shelling accident and, poor fellow, his mother died in Berlin around the time we declared war on Mr Hitler and all that detestable man stands for.'

'His continued faith is a most telling testament to the young man,' responded Charles as he finally gave up any pretence at drinking his tea.

'You mentioned a telephone call from the college principal. Did he offer any clue why Sidney asked to come here?' asked Anna as she drew closer to her host.

James flicked back and forth through several sheets of foolscap paper resting within the thin cardboard folder. 'None that I can recall… except now you've prompted me I recall him making a vague comment about how the change of location may… now, how did he put it?' James slowly closed the folder and placed it on top of the filing cabinet. 'Yes, I have it. He said a change in Mr Langham's surrounding was "sure to help the curate on his spiritual journey to find peace and fulfilment through service to others". I assumed at the time Sidney's superior meant thinking less of one's own struggles and more about the church's flock in these testing times… but now that I reflect on matters, perhaps young Sidney is carrying more of a burden than I have assumed.'

Anna stepped purposefully over to the filing cabinet and made to pick up the file, looking at James for approval, which he provided with a slight nod.

Charles retrieved his pipe from within a cavernous jacket pocket and began the ritual of packing the bowl with tobacco. Moving toward the open fireplace, he stooped forward to select a wood-taper from a highly polished brass container resting on the hearth and delicately offered the narrow strip of timber into the flames before using the glowing taper to light his pipe. 'Which rather begs the question of why send the young man to the relative remoteness of east Norfolk, rather than, say, Cambridge?'

James shook his head. 'No, no, you have it the wrong way around. I understand Sidney specifically asked to be sent here.'

Charles puffed into his pipe as if filling the airbag of a set of bagpipes in readiness to play a tune. 'That makes no sense… not unless he has connections with the area, or knows someone who lives here?'

James shook his head. 'None that I'm aware of and certainly, the college principal said nothing to that effect.'

Anna re-joined the conversation, having scanned Sidney's file, discovering nothing of use, before returning it to the filing cabinet. 'Dad, we need to talk about the car accident, don't you think?'

Mention of a crash caused James to drain of colour. 'Accident? What accident? Are you suggesting…?'

'Calm yourself, James,' said Charles in a low, reassuring tone. 'What Anna means is that a man was found unconscious in a car that had crashed into a hedge recently. I'm sure there's no connection to Sidney, but…'

'My curate was… is to travel by train, not car? I rang the police earlier this morning to report him missing. They were most polite, but I sense they have many other priorities than a young curate who's late for his new job. They mentioned nothing about an accident.'

Charles closed the few yards between himself and his host. 'Which rather confirms what I'm saying. It's most unlikely there is any connection between a curate late for his posting and the unfortunate soul who was in that car, isn't that right, Anna?'

She sensed her father's tone and responded accordingly. 'Sorry, James, that was unforgivable of me. I'm sure Dad is correct and there is no connection between the two events. Sidney is sure to turn up soon.'

He doesn't believe me for one second, thought Anna.

An awkward pause in the conversation followed, during which

Anna looked at her wristwatch for want of something to ease how self-conscious she suddenly felt, before realising her error. 'I'm sorry, I didn't mean to be impolite.'

Rather than cause further embarrassment, her unintended indiscretion broke the tenseness that pervaded the room.

'You've nothing to apologise for, Anna,' replied James. 'I'm sure we all have things to get on with. In my case that means keeping out of Mrs Walsh's way.'

'And I must be about parish business back in Lipton St Faith, where a certain Beatrice Flowers commands I must attend her to discuss too much ankle flesh being on show at Sunday service recently.'

James smiled knowingly. 'Your Miss Flowers is my Hilda Shawshank. What would we do without such diligent parishioners who, it seems, see it as their life's work to keep us all on the straight and narrow!'

Thank Heavens that's over, even if I'm no further on in understanding what's going on, thought Anna.

Pleasantries concluded, including a promise to each keep in touch concerning any developments about Sidney Langham, Anna and her father wished James goodbye and sauntered down the stone pathway from the vicarage back to their bicycles.

'And what is it that calls you so urgently?'

He's annoyed with me, thought Anna

'I need to catch up with someone I missed yesterday.'

'Tom?'

She smiled. 'No, not, Tom. In fact, he'll be getting ready for his lunch with Fanny as we speak.' Anna could see that her father looked confused. 'Remember, the woman mum invited to lunch the other day? I tell you what, I'd love to be a fly on the wall when they meet.'

'Oh, I see,' replied Charles. 'And have you heard from the lieutenant yet?'

Anna gazed into the distance and shrugged her shoulders.

'Hello, Mrs Ferris, I'm sorry I didn't get over yesterday.' Anna's smile broadened as she offered her apologies without going into the reasons for her non-appearance.

'Not to worry, Miss Grix, I was here all day, so no trouble at all.'

'Oh, please call me Anna.'

'Thank you,' she replied, showing Anna into the small house. 'And I'm Frances.'

'It's a lovely place you have here, Frances.'

The woman's smile broadened as she accepted her visitor's compliment. 'I like to keep everything clean and cosy, of course. A house must be a home, mustn't it? Now, will you have some lunch? You must be starving after your bike ride?'

'Oh, that's kind, but no thank you. The last thing I want to do is to take any of your rations. They're sparse enough as they are.'

Frances waved away Anna's concerns. 'Not at all. It's only a bit of warming broth. I've used the last of the pig's trotters for the stock and to give it a bit of body. It'll do you good with a slice of bread and dripping in this weather.'

I hate pig trotters, thought Anna.

Anna offered a disarming smile. 'That's generous of you, Frances, but my mother will have a cold plate waiting for me when I get back. If I don't eat it, she'll have my guts for garters for wasting food. You know what mums are like.'

'I suppose us mothers are all the same, aren't we?

'How's your new little chap getting on?'

Frances smiled as she sat on a chair arm.

'He'll be fine. We're still going through the tears at bedtime bit. The lad is homesick. It's only natural.'

I can't imagine what they all go through.

Anna ruffled in her shoulder bag for the boy's file. 'How's the—'

'Bed-wetting?' interrupted Frances. 'Still a bit of a problem, but the WRVS have been wonderful with extra bedding and a rubber sheet. I keep reassuring the poor little mite that it's quite natural.'

Anna made a note on the boy's file. 'I'm so glad you're handling it that way. What must he have gone through at home?'

Frances nodded as she stood and walked through to her tiny kitchen. 'Bombs falling all around him, I expect. Makes you wonder how any of them are sane, doesn't it? But he's safe with me, that's the chief thing. Now, are you sure you won't have some broth? You look as though you could do with feeding up.'

Please, no pig's trotters.

'No, I couldn't,' replied Anna as she followed Frances through to the kitchen. 'Are his parents keeping in touch?'

Frances wrapped a towel around her fingers and lifted a large cooking pot from a blackened oven that formed part of the fire range. 'I think they're doing their best, but what with all the air raids going on, it must be difficult to get letters off. It'll soon be Christmas, so we'll see what they manage. Is anything being arranged for the evacuees?'

Anna smiled and held a finger up. 'I have a plan,' she said with a twinkle in her eyes. 'My Dad doesn't know it yet, but he's going to be Father Christmas and we'll have a splendid do at the Memorial Hall in the village.'

Frances sighed as she pointed to a newspaper resting on top of a box of carrots. 'We need cheering up. Look at that lot. The Russians have them Nazi quislings on the run from that Rostov place, wherever that is. Serves 'em right as well. The trouble is, I suppose it means more will come our way now. And what are the Japanese up to? My Henry is out that way and I haven't had a letter for over a month now.'

80

It's easy to forget what the wives are going through.

Anna responded to Frances' finger pointing at a loaf of bread on the larder shelf, its thin fabric curtain doing little to hide its meagre bounty. 'All we can hope is that the Americans are keeping a close eye on things down there. As for the quislings, I doubt we have many.'

Frances huffed. 'Don't you believe it. My Henry says there are such people in every country. You know, waiting for the chance to gain an advantage by betraying their country.'

Is that the case in Britain? Surely not!

'I was talking to the postman only last week,' continued Frances. 'He says he's always seeing suspicious people on his rounds. He told me about one chap who asked him where the nearest pub was. It was a quarter-past-eight in the morning, for goodness' sake. Apparently when the postie said he'd have to wait, but it'd be worth it because they served a great pint of twos, he reckons the fella hadn't a clue what he was talking about.'

Probably means the man didn't come from Norfolk!

'And one of my neighbours said the ARP Warden told her the coal man reckoned he watched two nuns with suspicious habits. He reckons they kept wiping their noses with a handkerchief, then flicking it up and down like as if they was signalling to someone. You never know, do you? It might have been a submarine lurking off the coast of Great Yarmouth?'

Anna broke into laughter.

'What's the matter with you? Submarines are dangerous things,' said Frances in a hurt tone.

'Do you realise what you said?' replied Anna, a broad smile spreading across her cheeks. 'He was pulling your leg, you know, Nun, habit… like what they wear.'

Come on, Frances, catch up.

As it dawned on Anna's host that she'd had the rise taken out of her, she moaned. 'Wait until I get my hands on that coal man, I'll give him suspicious habits.'

Perhaps we're all getting too paranoid about strangers. What if I'm on the wrong track about the curate?

Paperwork was something Anna knew came with the job, whereas she much preferred to be dealing directly with host parents and evacuees, instead of completing the seemingly endless reports she had to submit.

At least I've got the house to myself for once.

As she sat at the kitchen table dividing her time from writing the occasional paragraph and tucking into her cold plate, Anna chuckled to herself thinking about the mayhem Vinny might well be causing at that very moment as he practiced for the Christmas carol concert at the church.

I wonder how Mum and Dad are coping with thirty excited children, all wanting to hear their own voice above all the others?

Walking the few yards to pour herself a tumbler of water from the sink tap, she gazed out of the window to take in Lipton's streetscape as the daylight faded, then up in awe of an angry sky, its billowing black clouds now rapidly filling the few remaining wisps of the deep blue atmosphere.

With luck, there shouldn't be any bombing tonight if the cloud cover builds.

Suddenly her attention fell on the tall, lean figure of Tom Bradshaw, who, she observed, appeared oblivious to her presence as he strolled past on his way to the kitchen door.

Beating him to it, she opened the half-glazed door. A surprised looking Tom stood motionless for a second. 'Oh, hello. Any chance of a cuppa?' he said, having recovered his faculties.

'I suppose so, you just sit there and make yourself comfortable, I don't mind doing all the work,' replied Anna with a wry smile.

Tom winked and did as instructed.

Anna smiled as she busied herself preparing the tea, all the time waiting for Tom to say something.

'Well?' she said, having realised the expected report was not forth-coming. 'Your date? Is it a state secret, or are you about to spill the beans?'

Tom scratched his head as if confused with the world. 'Don't ask.'

'I am.' Anna put a hand on each hip to reinforce her determination to hear his news. 'It was that bad, was it?'

'If you must know, we didn't even get as far as the cafe... and Fanny isn't happy.' Tom gratefully accepted his tea and took a sip after blowing over the rim of his cup to cool the soothing refreshment. 'The cottage hospital rang with the initial results of the crash victim's autopsy.' He hesitated.

'Go on,' urged Anna.

'A broken neck. Most probably an impact injury from his head snapping forwards when he hit the hedge.'

'Do you agree?' asked Anna.

Tom took a second sip from his cup before placing it back on to the table. 'To be honest, I don't know what to think, and that's my problem. Inspector Spillers says he thinks I should close the case pending identification of the victim.'

'But?' replied Anna, sensing Tom was holding back.

'I can't put my finger on anything, but he's acting out of character.' said Tom.

'Who is?'

'The Inspector. It's not like him to want to get rid of a case this quickly, at least not with so many unanswered questions. It makes me think—'

'And then there's the Scarlet Pimpernel.'

'What?' exclaimed Tom, losing his train of thought because of Anna interrupting him.

'Eddie, you know, "They seek him here, they seek him there," etc, etc.'

He's looking at me, but he isn't seeing, thought Anna.

'So what do you think is happening?' He blew on his tea.. Anna waited.

Tom looked at the window. 'It's... Oh, I see. I got lost for a moment.' He blew across his tea again, this time taking a longer sip.

'You don't go with all this tragic accident, guff, do you? Tell me you don't, please.'

Anna's question did the trick. 'No, not for one moment. I don't know how, or why that man died, but I'm certain it's not down to an innocent set of arbitrary circumstances.'

'That's more like it. Do you want a tea cake?'

Tom smiled, 'Is that a bribe?'

'Absolutely.'

'Then I'll have two. Seriously though, Inspector Spillers has given me an order, and I can't ignore it.'

His host vanished into the larder before quickly returning, bearing a battered round tin, the top of which took Anna several attempts to dislodge. 'Who said anything about ignoring him? I know you can't do that.'

Tom peered into the tin before frowning at Anna.

'Vinny O'Conner, I'll swing for you one day,' said Anna as she glimpsed Tom's disappointment and investigated the tin herself. 'There were two left this morning. I'm all for feeding a growing lad, but I ask you. Oh well, it'll have to be a crust and a dab of dripping. Is that OK?'

Tom smiled ruefully and accepted Anna's offer. 'I suppose the findings from the autopsy will take a day or two yet. Then there's all that paperwork. And, of course, I still must identify the dead man. That could take ages.'

'You're catching onto this game, Tom Bradshaw. See, it's not about deceiving your boss, or even telling fibs. You're simply being a diligent police officer who wishes to leave no stone unturned in giving the dead man the dignified send-off he deserves.'

'I think that makes up an overabundance of cliches Anna, don't you?'

Anna handed Tom a thick-cut slice of bread, one side covered with a thin film of beef dripping.

I don't like seeing Tom like this. He's torn between his boss and where I'm pushing him. I've no choice. We must move on.

'How do you fancy a couple of hours at a college for trainee vicars?'

Chapter Seven: A Strange Question

A disturbed night's sleep did little for Anna's mood as she woke to an overcast Wednesday morning with an accompanying wind that rattled the loose pane of glass in her bedroom window.

I wonder how Tom's feeling about yesterday. Did I do the right thing?

Convincing herself she was correct to push her friend not to act too hastily to close the case, Anna knew the responsibility fell to her in keeping him out of trouble with Inspector Spillers and helping to find out what caused a man's death in the most dreadful of circumstances.

She kept her conversation as light-hearted as possible for the ninety-minute journey to their destination, Appleby Theological College in Cambridge.

Having waited patiently by the garden gate for Tom to collect her, she gave a friendly smile and ignored the biting breeze as she slipped into the passenger seat of the old Wolseley police car.

I hope this turns up something useful.

Her plan for a distracting chat about nothing in particular to pass the time worked to perfection as Tom pulled the car into the grand driveway of Appleby College with five minutes to spare before their eleven o'clock appointment.

This must have been someone's country pile at one time. I bet they left it to the church to buy their way into Heaven.

Before them, a perfectly symmetrical Georgian mansion spread its grandeur across the landscape, the access driveway leading to a point on the centre line of the statuesque building. Students on their way to lectures walked across the parkland before vanishing into the college's vast interior.

'It reminds me of police college,' said Tom as he slowed the car to a crawl. On one side of the great front entrance doors of the college his brakes snatched, causing a slew of gravel to fly forward as the Wolseley suddenly stopped. 'Sorry about that.'

Anna recovered her composure, having braced herself by reaching out to the dashboard. 'There's never a dull moment in this jalopy, I'll give you that.'

Once out of the car, the pair encountered a steady stream of polite, smartly dressed and clean-shaven young men eager to wish their visitors a good day.

If they're curious about seeing a uniformed policeman and a young woman, fair play to them for hiding it so well.

'Good morning to you,' said a portly man in a black three-piece suit and old-fashioned winged starched collar, narrow black tie, and mirror-clean shoes. 'Miss Grix; Sergeant Bradshaw, welcome, the principal is waiting for you in his office. Please, come this way.'

He can get a move on for an old fella, thought Anna as she hurried to keep up as the trio crossed a beautifully proportioned hallway and down a long, wide oak-panelled corridor with its herringbone patterned beechwood floor stretching before them.

'Did you have a pleasant journey?' asked the soberly dressed man as he pressed on.

'Yes, mostly,' replied Anna. 'But we came across a great deal of military traffic. I suppose they must be on manoeuvres or something of the sort.'

'Or something,' said the man without turning. 'But we mustn't speculate, must we? Who knows, someone might be listening.'

'You're quite correct,' muttered Anna, chastened by the suited man's polite rebuke.

I bet he's ex-military, thought Anna.

On and on the corridor went until, at last, the man slowed his pace, faced an elegantly white-painted panelled door, and tapped twice with a clenched knuckle. He opened the door wide before standing to one side and announcing his charges. 'Your visitors, principal.'

Behind a large, oblong desk sat the Reverend Peter Wilks. His smile filled the spacious room, its walls and ceiling painted in delicate pastel shades of pale blue and white.

'Thank you for seeing us at such brief notice, reverend, it's so kind of you.'

Wilks stood before extending an arm to show where his visitors should sit. 'Please, Miss Grix, call me Peter.'

She smiled, 'And I'm Anna.'

The reverend turned to Tom, 'sergeant, so nice to meet you. Please, sit and tell me how I might help?'

He *seems a happy chappie*, thought Anna as her host settled back into his leather swivel chair.

'It's a wonderful place you have. The students must love it,' said Anna.

'I'm not sure they'd agree with you when exam time comes around, but yes, we're so lucky to have this place. Mind you, it can feel a little isolated. Devoting your life to God is no simple task for a young man. Many struggle on their journey before seeing the true light... and of course, a good many cannot stay the course.'

Before Anna could delve deeper into the principal's statement, the door opened.

'You asked to see me, Principal?'

'Ah, Mr Teesdale, your timing is impeccable, as always. May we have some tea? And I wonder if there might be any of that wonderful jam sponge cake left? Perhaps you might ask cook?' Wilks looked at Anna. 'We are so blessed to have several local ladies who bake and donate the most scrumptious of cakes to us. We are indeed fortunate.'

Teesdale withdrew without further comment, closing the wide door in silence.

Anna got down to business. 'I hoped you might provide us with a little background on Sidney Langham?'

Her direct approach had the desired effect. Wilks' smile faded as he reached for a paper folder that sat front and centre on his desk. 'Ah, yes. I suppose we should deal with the matter at hand. A most curious case which, even now, I pray has a happy ending.'

Anna exchanged glances with Tom.

I think it's going to take more than prayer, she thought.

'Sidney's background is a sad one. His father, like so many, died in the Great War. It seems life was hard for his mother as she struggled to make enough money for them to survive on, yet it seems her faith was strong, and this was something she seems to have instilled in the boy. Tragedy remained tethered to the family and a few years later, Sidney's mother also died.' The principal flicked through the pages of his file. 'The circumstances of her death are vague and it's not something we've been able to get Sidney to talk about—he's a strange mix of steely determination when the moment takes him, and extreme vulnerability. I take him to be a man who exhibits an intense dislike to any change in his routine.'

Anna gazed at the open file, attempting unsuccessfully to read its contents upside down. 'I guess that's no surprise given the two biggest changes in his life involved losing a parent.'

The principal nodded. 'As you say, Miss Grix, yet it gets worse for poor Sidney. Having no living relatives left in the country, he was sent to his aunt in Belgium. From what his file tells me, this was a happy time for him. Indeed, the only time I've ever seen any flicker of emotion from him has been at the mention of his guardian.'

Tom leant forward in his chair, 'Do I sense a "but" coming?'

Principal Wilks raised an eyebrow. 'I see that your police instincts are fully charged. Correct, sergeant. As I mentioned, tragedy is a terrible demon that takes full advantage, given half a chance. His aunt ran a school in Brussels and—'

'You use the past tense,' interrupted Anna.

Wilks closed the foolscap file and rested back in his chair. 'Forgive me, Miss... sorry, Anna. In May 1940, Sidney returned to England. It seems he got out with hours to spare before the Nazis overran the country. What little we know is that Sidney maintained regular contact with his aunt, who he clearly adored.' The principal glanced at Tom. 'Before you ask, yes, I'm about to add a further, "but". Although it seems his aunt was allowed to continue running her school, recently it was closed down and his guardian taken into custody.'

'Custody?' asked Anna.

'I gather from my spiritual brothers in Belgium that although arrested by the police, she's being held by the Gestapo.'

The principal's guests let out a collective gasp.

'But,' spluttered Anna before losing her thread.

'I know how hard it must be for you to take this information in, but there we are. Word has it that the Germans are convinced private institutions such as Sidney's aunt ran are a vital part of an escape chain used by our brave service personnel, particularly downed aircrew, to make their way back to our sceptred isle. Whether his aunt is involved or not, it seems she's a victim of the recent crackdown by the SS… and if she's found guilty, I'm afraid—'

'Yes, we understand,' said Anna, keen to save the principal from spelling out the awful consequences. 'How much does Sidney know?'

Principal Wilks leant forward and placed his elbows on the desktop. 'It's hard to say. As I mentioned, the man, though I'm convinced he is dedicated to God, remains an enigma. Certainly, I've told him nothing of what my Belgium brethren have told me. However, he's clearly aware something isn't right. It maybe that the sudden absence of correspondence from his aunt has alerted him to a problem–the thing is, his recent mood tells me he may indeed know more, or at least a version of what's going on.'

Wilks' explanation triggered a thought in Anna's mind. 'Did Sidney speak with an accent?'

Wilks studied her for several seconds before responding. 'My pupil seems to have immersed himself in his life in Belgium and has a gift for languages, so if you mean did his foreign accent attract unwarranted attention among those who cannot spot the difference between Flemish and German, yes. However, he seemed to take things in his stride. I advised he should see such unpleasantness as a test from God, and the result of a country in fear for its survival.'

Anna watched as Wilks turned to look at a crucifix high on the wall to his left, then back to her with an intensity she found uncomfortable.'Does he have any close friends you know of?' asked Tom.

'Do men form close friendships in the way women do?' replied their host, his eyes not moving from Anna.

91

Have I got two heads? thought Anna as she attempted to remain calm under Wilks' intrusive stare.

'I'm not sure,' continued the principal. 'However, he seemed close to one student.'

At that moment, the office door opened.

'Ah, talk of the Devil, so to speak.' Wilks' shoulders rose and fell as he giggled.

What a creepy thing to say. Why does he make me feel so uncomfortable? thought Anna.

'Allow me to introduce you to Walter Teesdale.'

Teesdale stepped forward carrying a tray of tea and sponge cake and set it on his superior's desk without comment or engaging anyone in eye contact.

'We've been discussing Sidney. Is there anything you'd like to share? Anything? It may just help.'

The man remained silent, his only acknowledgement a quick glance at the principal and an almost imperceptible shake of his head.

Poor man, he must be beside himself wondering what's happened to his friend, thought Anna.

The principal shrugged his shoulders. 'Very well, Walter, you may go, but please remember what I said. Keeping too much to yourself can be harmful. The path you've chosen to follow will be difficult. You cannot serve your parishioners if you can't look after your own wellbeing. This isn't about being selfless—in fact the selfless path is to share with others, which may involve food, money, love… or information.'

Walter turned without making a comment and strolled back to the open door. His progress slowed as another man entered.

He's got to be a lecturer, but why give the lad such an icy stare? thought Anna.

'Ah, there you are. I asked Dr Janson to join us. He's Stanley's spiritual supervisor. His mentor, so to speak.'

Tom stood to greet Dr Janson as Anna swivelled around in her chair and smiled.

He's a cold fish, she thought.

Janson gave Tom's outstretched hand a cursory shake and nodded to Anna, before taking his seat to one side of the principal's desk.

'Tea, Dr Janson?' asked Wilks.

Janson shook his head. 'Thank you, but no.'

'You speak beautiful English, Dr Janson. Were you taught in school?' asked Anna.

Dr Jenson smirked. 'I received a private education on our estates in Poland.'

A well-heeled family then, thought Anna.

'That sounds like an idyllic childhood, Doctor?'

What have I said? thought Anna as she observed the man stiffen.

'My home country was corrupt. The church has allowed me to spread the word to a new generation of young men who will change the world.'

'As God has been doing for almost two-thousand years,' added Wilks, his voice sounding resolute.

'Only men?' responded Anna with a polite smile.

Neither cleric answered Anna's challenge.

Things will change, thought Anna, working hard to keep her anger in check.

'Now, what can you tell us about Sidney?' she asked, determined not to show her contempt for the two men.

'Mr Langham was a troubled man. I had many difficult conversations with him, of course none of which I can share with you.'

There's that collective nodding again, thought Anna.

'His childhood,' continued Janson. 'He told me he saw some dreadful things which he seemed unable to let go of. I don't think I'm breaking any confidences by telling you he attempted to end his life on two occasions during his time at this institution.'

What? thought Anna.

She noted the intensity with which the principal fiddled with his fountain pen while staring unblinkingly at his desk.

'Suicide?' said Anna.

The doctor frowned. 'I'm certain Mr Langham saw it more as a release. Although we thwarted both attempts and maintained a close watch on him, his demise is of little surprise to me.'

'What are you talking about, Dr Janson?' Tom's tone gave away his irritation at the doctor's presumptive statement.

'Please, sergeant, let us not play games with one another. Mr Langham is missing, and you're here. The principal requested I join you. Perhaps the two matters are linked?'

Don't bite, Tom, thought Anna.

'I understand Mr Langham was late for his train?'

Well done, Tom.

'It seems one of our suppliers; the local butcher, stepped in to save the day and conveyed Sidney to the train station.'

He's holding something back, thought Anna. 'Have you any idea what made him late?'

The doctor sniffed, as if clearing his nostrils. 'I'm sure I don't know... Oh, wait a minute. Yes, he came to see me. I was rushing to give a lecture to my students on transubstantiation. It slipped my mind. Please forgive me.'

Oh, yes? she thought.

'What did he want?'

Janson hesitated for a few seconds before patting one of his trouser pockets. 'Money. Sidney said he needed two shillings for the bus journey from the train station to St Paul's.'

Before Anna could press further, a loud bell rang.

'Ah, the call to lunch in silent contemplation to give thanks for our blessings. If there's nothing further, Miss Grix; sergeant?' The principal rose from his chair and gestured toward the door.

I can take a hint, she thought.

As Tom twisted a heavy brass doorknob, he turned. 'One more thing, Dr Janson, could Sidney Langham drive?'

Janson frowned. 'What an odd question to ask, sergeant. I've no idea.'

'I've also a last question,' said Anna. 'Principal, did Sidney specifically request he be sent to St Paul's, or did you make that decision?'

The college head looked at Janson for confirmation, who nodded. 'As a matter of fact, it was he who asked I allow him to follow his path in that part of Norfolk. As I said, he is a deep fellow, and I assumed he had friends there, which I considered might be of benefit to such a lonely soul as Mr Langham.'

'What do you make of those two?'

'One plays the "Hail fellow well met" and the other a cold fish,' replied Tom. 'Who knows, perhaps they showed their true colours. It's hard to say. All the same, I feel there's more going on in this place than we're being allowed to see.'

Unlike at their arrival, the campus now appeared deserted as the lunch bell did its work, except for a lone figure Anna noticed closing on them as she opened the passenger door of the police car. 'It's Walter Teesdale. This should be interesting.'

By the time Tom had looked up from unlocking the car, Walter had reached Anna.

He looks as though he's seen a ghost, she thought.

'Are you OK? It looks as though you're going to—'

'Miss Grix… er, I wonder if I might have a word?'

'Don't throw up over me, Walter.'

Walter's shoulders slumped as he gazed at the gravel driveway. 'He's such a good man, and that's his trouble.'

Anna looked across the top of the car at Tom, then at Walter. 'I'm not sure I understand. What do you mean, "trouble"?' You can tell us, Walter, you're quite safe.'

Her remark caused Walter to look behind.

'What's up? Do you think someone is watching us?'

Still, Walter hesitated.

'If you're worried about your safety, we can get you away from here. In fact, you can come with us now?' Tom's reassuring tone settled the nervous young man.

'No, it's fine. I'm being stupid.'

'You wanted to talk to us, Walter. Come on, remember what the principal said, don't risk hurting yourself. Not like Sidney.'

Walter suddenly came to life. 'That's the point, Miss… I mean, Anna. Sidney was fine until about six months ago. Then, for no reason, he changed. His moods swung widely. One moment he'd be fine, then… and the anger. That's when he… he tried to…' The young man's voice tailed off.

Tom strolled around from his side of the car to stand next to Anna and Walter. 'Do you think he worried about his placement at St Paul's? Perhaps it was all getting too much for him and he didn't know how to express himself?'

Walter began shaking his head before Tom had finished. 'No, no. He was looking forward to it. I know he was.'

He's mad about something, thought Anna.

'If it wasn't St Paul's, did anything else happen that might explain his mood swings?' said Anna.

Walter shook his head again. 'I know he wanted to go. He said he'd important work to do to save people. But now? What's happened to my friend?'

'Save people?' asked Tom.

Walter frowned at the sergeant. 'That what we're trained to do... to save souls.'

'No, I get that, Walter, but according to you, Stanley specifically said people, not souls?'

'Are they not the same thing?' replied a confused Walter.

Tom looked at Anna. 'In my world, not necessarily.'

Anna placed an arm around the young man's shoulder.

Good, he isn't pulling away.

'It's curious, don't you think?' said Anna.

'What is?' replied Tom.

'Sidney saying continuing his training at St Paul's was a release. Don't you think that implies he wanted to get away? Almost as if he were running from something.'

'Or someone,' added Tom.

She felt Walter tense before he lifted her arm from his shoulders and take a step back.

'It's hard here. No one knows what we go through, but what do you mean about him running from someone? Sidney said something odd the other day, though,' said Walter.

'Odd,' repeated Anna.

'He asked me if I thought God would forgive someone who committed a sin to save one of his children.'

I've seen my father wrestling with the same dilemma, thought Anna.

'You mean he intended to travel to Norfolk to commit a crime, thinking he was serving a higher cause?' said Tom.

Walter shook his head. 'I don't… I mean… I just told him God always forgives those who truly repent. I thought it might help. Now I'm not so sure.'

Tom lightly touched Walter's elbow with an open palm. 'It's OK, Walter. I didn't mean to upset you. It's the way the police think, it's what we're trained to do.'

'And the police have a very clumsy way of saying things. Right, Tom?'

Anna's attempt to lighten the atmosphere worked as Walter showed the first signs of a smile. 'That's better. You have a lovely smile, you know. That'll come in handy when telling your flock off for something or other. Believe me, I'm a vicar's daughter.'

Walter's smile broadened as he looked at his watch. 'It's the silent time. I must go… but thank you both. I wanted you to know… well, you know.'

'We do,' said Anna. 'And remember, if you need to talk, give either of us a ring. The numbers are in the telephone directory.'

Walter offered a smile before heading back to the Georgian edifice.

Within two minutes, Tom had pulled the car back onto the main road and gathered speed.

'You know what, Tom? The more we dig, the more complicated this gets. You'll have to pick your moment to tell Inspector Spillers what you're up to. Don't make the mistake of getting too far out on a limb. If there's foul play afoot, you'll need his full support, and protection.'

Tom smiled. 'And on that subject, I want to call in on a motor dealer I know on the way back. We've still to identify that car and if anyone can it'll be him.'

Forty-five minutes later, Tom parked the police car, this time avoiding jamming the brakes. A sign above two huge open timber doors read:

Thetford Motorcar Sales and Service

'You must joke?' said Anna as she scanned the thinning thatch and peeled paintwork from the sign. 'Would you buy a car from this place?'

'Don't be such a snob, Anna Grix. Looks can deceive,' said Tom as he stepped from the car and strolled to the open barn doors.

'I know a cowboy outfit when I see one,' replied Anna. 'The fact you know him must mean you've come across the man in, how shall I put it, a professional capacity?' By now she'd caught Tom and tamely prodded his back with a finger to reinforce her point.

'Oi, that hurt, but you're sort of right, and wrong,' replied Tom as he caught hold of Anna's hand. The physical contact made them both stop in their tracks. After a fleeting meeting of eyes, Tom let go.

'That's what I call hedging your bets. I'm right or wrong, but not both.'

Whew, that was… strange.

'Alright, confession time. Yes, I nicked him once for selling stolen goods—'

'I knew it.'

'But he turned out to be the innocent party. He thought the car was legit and was only doing a favour for an old chap who'd recently lost his only son with the British Expeditionary Force, who needed a car urgently. In fact, the chap you're about to meet helped us track down the rogue who sold him the car, and we got a conviction. You might say we have been professional colleagues ever since. What he doesn't know about cars isn't worth knowing.'

I've heard everything now.

'What, you mean like if a car's stolen or not?'

'Ah, I thought it was you.' A gruff sound came from the depths of the barn. Seconds later, the crouched frame of an elderly man shuffled from its interior, complete with an oily smudge covering his forehead and nose.

'You're joking?' whispered Anna.

'There you go again with your assumptions. Don't judge a book by its cover and all that. Believe it or not, that bloke is an incredible engineer. I'm telling you, he's our man.'

Several seconds passed before the old gentleman stood within handshaking distance of his visitors. 'Herbert Trethel at your service.' He gave a small bow from the neck.

Quite the charmer, aren't you?

'Mr Trethel, your reputation goes before you.' Anna extended a hand, which the man eagerly shook while giving Tom a curious side glance.

'I see, I hope nothing too damaging?' He offered a toothless smile as he turned his full attention on Anna.

Priceless.

'I'm oily from adjusting some tappets on that miracle of science and engineering, so forgive me if I've got your hand mucky, miss.' Herbert turned to the barn and pointed to a car standing in the corner of the cavernous space.

'I'm thinking you're not here to pass the time of day with me, young fella?' said Herbert as he pointed a grubby finger at Tom's stripes. 'A sergeant now, whatever next?'

Tom made as if to polish his stripes with the opposite cuff of his jacket. 'A lot of hard work went into getting them, talking about which, I have some work for you if you're interested?'

'Where is it?'

Goodness, they've done this before.

Tom spent two minutes briefing Herbert on the car accident without

100

giving too much away by way of evidence, or anything that might inadvertently influence his report.

'We got a local farmer to lift it onto a trailer and take it back to his place. It's about forty-minutes from here. Don't worry, I'll arrange some extra petrol for you.'

'In that case, leave it with me. I'll look at her for you.' Herbert winked at Anna.

If you were twenty years younger, I'd wallop you.

Tom covered the onward journey from Thetford to Lipton St Faith in an hour.

'I need to call in at the thrift shop,' commented Anna as they entered the village. 'What are you up to for the rest of the day?'

Tom applied the handbrake to the Wolseley before scratching his head. 'I've got today's little outing to put into my report, but before that, there's the minor matter of making things up with Fanny to sort out... even if I'm not sure this date thing is a good idea.'

'You'd better make your mind up double-quick, Tom, because if you're not struck, you'd better be honest with the girl or she'll be getting the wrong idea–and that never ends well. So, a piece of advice; if you intend to go through with things, less is more. Don't go spinning all sorts of tales. Tell her what happened and offer to take her out. If you've any sense, it'll be tonight. Fanny will probably say no because she's washing her hair, but that's all part of the game.'

'What game?'

Anna looked at Tom as if he were a little boy in need of a plaster for a grazed knee. 'Poor Tom, you don't have a clue, have you? Never mind, you'll get better with practice. Now, I'm off. Think on, short and sweet... and smile at her.'

Anna left Tom with a puzzled look on his face as she slammed the passenger door shut before walking the few yards to the thrift store entrance. By the time she strolled in, Tom had taken off in a cloud of grey-blue smoke as his car coughed its way down the high street. Stepping inside the thrift store, Anna smiled at shop volunteers, Alice Stanmore and Flo Bassett, as they chatted to one another, interspersed with brief bouts of conspiratorial laughter.

'What are you two up to?' asked Anna.

Flo scrunched her nose and giggled again. 'A woman who shall remain nameless came in before, "looking for something special".'

'That's nice,' replied Anna. 'Perhaps she's going to a dance or the like.'

Alice laughed. 'At her age as well. Mutton dressed as lamb, I say.'

Anna joined in with the general hilarity. 'Why do I think I know who you're talking about?'

'Because it can only be one person who, as you say, shall remain nameless.'

The three women huddled around a selection of dresses the shopper had considered before making her eventual choice.

'She said she was looking for a present for her best friend,' said Flo.

'Oh, yes. One that wears trousers and sports a moustache,' added Alice. 'I ask you, what woman on the wrong side of forty wears a neckline this low?' She traced a daringly low line across her chest and began laughing again.

'Forty is hardly old, girls.'

Alice and Flo looked at each other and burst out laughing.

'You speak for yourself, Anna Grix. I can't even imagine being that old, but I suppose you're older than us two.'

Anna pointed a finger at the two volunteers. 'I'm twenty-six, which makes me just over two years older than you pair.' She intuitively investigated a long dress mirror to check her appearance.

Alice looked at Flo. 'Twenty-six, can you imagine being that old?'

Flo shook her head in disbelief. 'Not for one minute, I'm not looking forward to being twenty-five, never mind the same age as Anna.'

'Ah-hem, I'm still here, you know. Did she find anything nice?'

Flo put a hand to her mouth in mock horror. 'You should have seen the thing she picked. There's more fabric on my little sister's favourite dolly. I hope she's wearing her thermal underwear when she meets her friend, or she'll catch her death.'

'Too much information, Flo. Time for a cup of tea to calm our nerves, I think.'

'Good idea,' laughed Flo.

'Two sugars for me,' chipped in Alice.

'You know mum's rules, girls, one sugar each and that's your lot. I'll be back in two shakes of a lamb's tail.'

Busying herself filling and putting the kettle on and getting everything ready, Anna smiled to herself as she reflected on her conversation with the volunteers and imagined the woman they all knew in the daring dress. That was, if the girls were to be believed.

Are they ever going to stop giggling?

As the kettle came to the boil, Anna thought she heard the old brass bell that hung above the front door herald a new customer. Distracted by the high-pitched whistling of the kettle and steam quickly filling the tiny kitchen, Anna couldn't quite catch the conversation between Alice, Flo and whoever had entered the premises.

'Here we are,' announced Anna as she finished making the tea and carrying three cups and saucers on a cardboard shoe box lid. Her entrance met with silence.

What's up with them?

'Is everything OK, you two?'

Both girls hesitated; neither looked at Anna.

'For goodness' sake, is it bad news? Who's hurt? Or is it one of our fighting men?'

Mention of such serious matters prompted Flo to speak. 'Er… no, no, nothing like that.'

'Thank heavens for that,' replied Anna as she set the shoe box lid on the countertop. 'What is it?'

Flo reached over for the drink and handed it to Alice before retrieving her own. 'It was a man.'

Anna waited for more. 'And?'

Alice broke in. 'He wanted to know if there was a Liverpool lad living in the village.'

Both girls looked pensive as they took a sip of their tea.

'And what did you say?'

'We didn't let on. You don't think we'd—'

'No, sorry, girls. A bit of a shock, that's all. Did he say who he was?'

The girls exchanged a brief glance.

'That's the odd thing, or at least I think it's odd. He said he was a welfare officer come to check on a rumour about a runaway evacuee.'

'And,' added Alice, 'he said if we knew something but didn't tell, we'd be in serious trouble with a judge and could go to jail.'

Anna took a sip of her tea while giving the appearance of playing down the seriousness of the stranger's visitor. 'Oh well, I'll check with the office to see what it's all about. Do me a favour, will you? Say nothing to anyone about this. If he comes back, tell him you don't know what he's on about, will you?'

Flo lifted two fingers to her lips as if sealing them.

Chapter Eight: The Wanderer Returns

It's rare I get a personal invitation from a pub landlady to drop in for a chat.

Anna raised the thick collar of her coat to cover her ears as she closed the garden gate to the vicarage, crossed the narrow road and set a brisk pace for her meeting with Betty Simpson, widowed owner of the King's Head pub.

The village looks desolate in the blackout. I suppose it looked this way for most of its existence before the electricity came.

In the near distance, Anna heard an exchange of angry words as two youths harried Lipton's platoon of Home Guard as they practiced repelling a Nazi invasion, while doing their best to keep out of the icy December wind.

It's about time they all had the same uniform, never mind real rifles.

Smiling to herself as the platoon sergeant sent the two boys away with a flea in their ear, she grabbed for a brass door-pull and opened the entrance door to the pub. Inside, she noticed the regulars each sat in their favourite chairs. Clarence Woodman, a pig farmer whose bark Anna knew to be worse than his bite, sat chewing his pipe while playing dominos with two others. On the far side of the small bar,

Anna noticed Jo Blackburn, the ARP warden ensconced on a high-backed pine settle facing away from the prevailing draft.

At the bar, Betty occupied herself serving a young serviceman home on leave and eager to celebrate his temporary freedom with his two brothers.

There was a time when a woman coming in here alone would've stopped the clock. Now we're a piece of the furniture.

'Eight o'clock on the dot. You're always on time. How do you do it?' Betty gave Anna a broad smile as she finished pouring a pint of beer from a large, white enamelled jug and nodded at a roaring fire. 'Get yourself warm. I'll be with you when I've finished with these three great lumps.'

The three lads cheered and slapped each other on the back.

Keep safe, boys. That's all we ask.

As Anna sauntered towards the fire, Betty's raised voice pierced the air. 'Don't you dare.'

Everyone froze, each checking for any misdemeanour unwittingly committed.

'You, I mean you, can't you read?' All eyes fell on a wizened old man as Betty pointed to a hand-painted sign above the mantle. 'It says no spitting in the grate without permission. You don't have my permission.'

The old man rested inelegantly between a seated position and standing at an angle

'Your missus might let you do that at home, but not here, so either get rid of whatever's in your gob outside or have it for supper. Which is it to be?'

The bar erupted into laughter as the old man dashed for the door as best he could before he vanished into the icy night air.

'It gets my goat, does that,' said Betty as she beckoned Anna over to the bar. 'You'd have thought everyone learned their lesson from the last outbreak of tuberculosis, horrible thing that is.'

Anna leant on the bar after first checking her patch was clear of beer spills. 'I just about remember it. I can still hear the coughs and going with Dad to visit patients at the cottage hospital, all lined up in their beds on the veranda, whatever the weather.'

Betty nodded as she turned to check if the three brothers needed anything. Instead, they pored over the front page of a newspaper.

"HITLER SENDS IN C.-IN-C. TO STOP ROUT."[i]

'It's not them Germans we should worry about,' commented Betty. 'They're getting what they deserve.' She pointed to a much smaller heading. 'That's the one to watch. Can you read what it says?'

Anna tilted her head to one side so she might get an unobstructed view.

"F.D. R REVEALS JAPANESE ARMY MOVE"[ii]

'Do you reckon the American President knows more than he's letting on?' said Betty, 'I've got family out in Singapore. I hope they'll be OK.'

Anna frowned. 'It's a world war in every sense, now, isn't it? I have no idea what President Roosevelt does or doesn't know. I hope he can keep us all safe.'

'He can't keep us safe from the other side of the ocean, can he?' said the ARP warden.

Betty shook her head. 'Get on with your dominos or I'll confiscate them for the duration.'

'That's you told,' said one.

'Best keep quiet,' offered another.

In the genial atmosphere, Betty leaned across the bar and whispered to Anna. 'But I know someone who might have an idea.'

'Sorry?' replied her confused guest.

The landlady half-turned to her left and pointed to a narrow door at the end of the bar. 'In there. There's someone who wants to speak to you.'

What on earth's got into the woman?

She followed Betty's low-key prompt to follow her. As they passed through a familiar door which led to the landlady's private sitting room, Anna grew increasingly anxious.

Betty slowly opened the door until Anna glimpsed its sole occupant. 'Eddie?'

Anna hadn't noticed Betty withdrawing, so fixed was she in trying to make sense of the untidy shape slumped in a chair by the small fire.

What on earth has happened to him? He looks awful.

Eddie had his eyes closed, his unshaven chin resting on his chest. Legs outstretched and arms flopped over the sides of the winged-back chair.

Anna took in a room she'd been in many times over the years. Although small, Betty had crowded the space with mementos of a happy married life and artefacts Anna knew reminded her host of happier times.

She neared the sunken figure.

He looks as though he's been dragged through a hedge backward.

In his bedraggled civilian clothes, Eddie might have passed for a man fallen on hard times looking for a free meal at the village hostelry.

I've not seen him like this before. I hope he's OK.

Anna wasn't sure why she felt so protective about the lieutenant.

'Eddie, wake up, Eddie, it's Anna.' Seeing no movement, she touched his knee with the back of her hand. This time the American stared.

In an instant, Eddie went from an exhausted slumber to a flame-eyed predator alert against every danger.

'It's OK, Eddie. I'm here. You're safe now.' Anna took hold of his hand and caressed it between hers. The physical contact did its magic, causing the lieutenant to relax a little. As the seconds elapsed, Eddie's posture became less threatening, his look calmer now.

'What on earth happened to you? You look as though you got yourself into a right pickle. Where have you been? I…'

What am I babbling on about?

He continued to stare blankly at a point somewhere over Anna's shoulder.

Is he even listening?

'I apologise for all the questions. It's… well, I'm worried about you, that's all.'

Slowly, Eddie redirected his look from the wall to his companion. He lifted his right hand and placed it over Anna's, who continued to caress his other hand. 'I have some explaining to do, don't I?'

He's done in. So vulnerable.

'First things first. Have you eaten?'

Eddie moved his hand to pat his stomach. 'Two helpings of Betty's hotpot… full now,' he whispered in a croaky voice.

The door interrupted the intimacy of their conversation.

'I thought he might wake up when he heard your voice. Now, get these down you—both of you.' Betty stepped into the cosy room holding a small tin tray on which sat two cut-crystal glasses, each containing a generous measure of whisky. 'It's too cold for your usual lemonade and his beer, so get those down you. I won't tell anyone.'

Alone again, Eddie reached for the glass, which shone against the open fire as its many cut surfaces refracted the soft light in a thousand directions.

Heck, down in one, he must have needed that.

'Goodness me, do you want mine, too? Here, but take it easy this time or you'll be singing Roll Out the Barrel to all and sundry.'

'You don't know how much I enjoyed that,' he whispered. This time he sipped slowly and gave a sigh of satisfaction each time the golden liquid hit the back of his throat.

A comfortable quiet fell over the room, the only sound a gentle crackling from the open fire. Flames danced in the grate, which projected mysterious shapes onto the cluttered walls of Betty's living room.

Eddie took another sip of his whisky before leaning forward with a groan and placing the glass on the hearth.

He's falling asleep again.

Anna watched as Eddie's eyes became heavy. For several seconds, she could tell he fought his impulse to sleep by suddenly opening his eyes wide before exhaustion once again took over.

He's checking I'm still here. It's best I let him sleep.

Moving towards the door and turning the doorknob, its creaking hinges roused the American.

'No, please stay. We need... I need to talk.'

He won't give in to it, stubborn man, thought Anna.

She closed the door and turned to face a barely awake lieutenant, retracing her steps.

Eddie reached down for his whisky, took a longer sip this time, before replacing the glass on the hearth.

'Suppose there was someone who wasn't anyone?' Eddie fell silent for a few seconds. 'Suppose this someone isn't who he thinks he is. Instead, he possesses phenomenal, almost primeval, courage, which he cannot see in himself. He is afraid, but not for himself; someone he can't help. What do you think this person might look like?'

What is he talking about?

Anna concentrated hard on what she thought Eddie meant but failed to comprehend his meaning. 'I don't quite understand what you're driving at,' she replied, her voice showing the hesitancy Anna spoke with when feeling unsettled.

Why is he looking at me like that?

'You do, Anna. Trust me, you do. Think about my words in your mind's eye. It isn't a riddle. Tell me what you see. How might they present themselves to the world?'

'Are we talking about a man or a woman?'

'It doesn't matter.'

'Only a man would say that. Now, man or woman?'

'Man.'

This sounds like a parlour game.

'He's courageous, but doesn't know it, and he cares more about the welfare of others than himself?'

'Good,' replied Eddie, Anna's response seeming to fortify him. 'Tell me more about this person. How does he behave in public?'

This is hard,

'Oh, I don't know. Perhaps he's restrained in his outward appearance and preferring to stay well out of the limelight, yet he'll come across as friendly, more interested in what others have to say than his own opinions. Perhaps he's learned to do this from experience. You know, keep his opinions to himself?'

Eddie nodded as he emptied the last of his whisky. 'And what might such a man do for a living?'

Anna laughed. 'Eddie, that's impossible to say. I'd simply be guessing for the sake of the riddle you've set me.'

Eddie suddenly came alive. 'No, you wouldn't, Anna. Does this man remind you of anyone?'

He's gone mad.

'Eddie, for goodness' sake, this has gone too far. How do you expect me to…' her voice tailed off as a thought began to crystalise.

No, he can't mean…?

'My father? You mean this person who isn't a person is a man of the church?'

'First prize goes to Miss Anna Grix. He is, or was, very much a person. A gentle soul at first deceived by evil people, then disposed of with no more ceremony or care than the flick of a cigarette lighter.'

The effort seemed to drain Eddie of his last reserves of energy as he slumped back into his chair, his heavy eyes unable to defy gravity any longer.

He's done, thought Anna.

'The rest can wait, Eddie Elsner, and there's no way in the world you're driving back to Three-Mile-Bottom in that state. You're staying at the vicarage tonight.'

'Welcome to Thursday. I thought you were going to sleep all day. Mind you, after the effort it took to get you back here from the pub last night, it should be me who's wiped out.'

Eddie scratched his head as he wandered into the vicarage kitchen, while examining his ill-fitting pyjamas. 'I don't remember a thing, including putting these on.' He pointed to a pair of trouser bottoms that were four inches too short for him.

'It was my father's spare set, or nothing… and it was cold last night. Now, sit yourself down while I get you some breakfast. We have the place to ourselves, so make the most of the peace and quiet. It won't last.'

As Anna whisked up a scrambled egg, she kept an eye out for how Eddie handled himself.

He's still not totally with it.

Minutes later, she joined Eddie at the table as he tucked into his breakfast.

'I've taken your egg ration.'

'It's fine. I got a couple extra from one of my host mothers, quite sweet.'

The room fell silent as Eddie concentrated on his food, while Anna fixed her gaze on her guest.

You'll have to tell me eventually, Eddie Elsner.

At last, he set his knife and fork on the empty plate, took a long swig of tea, and sighed. 'OK, I guess I owe you an explanation?'

'That's an understatement and yes, you do. I've been worried to death. Disappearing like that isn't like you and make sure you never do that again to me.'

Who am I kidding? They might post him somewhere at any time.

The American dropped his gaze to the table. 'I knew you'd hate me for what I did, but believe me, I didn't have a choice.'

'Choice? What's that supposed to mean, and please, look at me.'

He played with his empty mug of tea until Anna moved it out of reach.

'Eddie, I'm here. Now speak.'

After a few seconds of quiet, the lieutenant responded. 'I knew you'd noticed me looking at the dead man's ear. I suppose I over-reacted. You weren't to know it triggered a memory; something I had to check out immediately, if only for my peace of mind.'

Anna shook her head. 'Eddie, you're back to talking in riddles. For goodness's sake, what's going on? You say you had to check something out. Check with whom? Where did you go?'

Eddie's hesitation only made things worse. 'Look, if you don't want to say, that's fine, but think about this. If you have information that might help us put a name to that poor chap, you need to tell Tom, even if you won't confide in me.'

Eddie gathered his plate and ambled over to the kitchen's stone sink.

'Don't walk away from me.'

'I'm not. It's… Look, I'm trying to protect you.'

Anna exploded. 'Stop it, Eddie. I'm not a hairbrained little girl. Either you tell me what's going on, or—'

'Or what, Anna?'

His abrupt challenge stunned Anna into silence.

'I can't tell you. At least not yet. It's far too dangerous and what you don't know can't hurt you; nor can you tell anyone else, so stop acting like a child. War does horrible things to people. Trust me, that's all there is to say on the matter for now.'

Fierce glares exchanged, the pair held each other's stare, neither wanting to be the first to back down.

There are times when you're patronising, thought Anna.

Anna tried a fresh approach. 'Don't play with me. You spoke in riddles for most of last night and encouraged me to play your little game, and now this nonsense of "I can't tell you." Well, it won't wash, Eddie, which is more than can be said for you, so I suggest you tidy yourself up and think about what you say next. Dad has left a clean shirt and his spare shaving kit. I suggest we leave it there for now. But understand, you will tell me what happened. A man is dead, Inspector Spillers thinks it an accident, and I've turned up the missing curate's only close friend. You're not the only one who's been busy. So, think on.'

Anna busied herself with the dishes as Eddie made himself presentable for the day. Outside the kitchen window, she noted how bright it was.

Pleasant change from all that gloomy weather.

Ten minutes later, a quiet voice interrupted Anna's thought.

'I guess I've been a jerk.'

She turned to see Eddie wearing one of her father's old suits and watched as he abandoned his efforts to close the double-breasted charcoal jacket.

'You don't have to apologise. I know you well enough to sense something awful happened. What if I told you there's a chance the man we saw at the cottage hospital and our missing curate are one and the same? Then again, from that little parlour game of yours last night, I suspect you already know.' Eddie put a hand to his forehead. 'Don't you look at me like that, you're not my father,' continued Anna.

'Now who's acting like a child?' replied Eddie in a quiet, fatigued tone.

Poor man, he looks all in. I just want to hug... Oh, bother, it's not as if I'm his... thought Anna.

'Please sit down, Eddie, I've something I want to say.' The American glanced to his side to check where the chair was before slumping into its deep cushions.

Taking the seat next to him, she reached for his hand. 'You said it yourself. War does things to people. Look at us two. Six months ago, we hadn't heard of each other. In any other circumstance we'd never have met, yet that first crazy meeting led to experiences I suspect neither of us thought possible.'

Come on, Eddie, look at me.

'Mum says I need to be careful about getting too close to people.'

'People?' responded Eddie, eyes now fixed on Anna.

Wow, I didn't expect that, thought Anna.

'Vinny, you... whoever, you know.'

'Is he OK?' replied Eddie in a voice tinged with anxiousness.

'I think so... but never mind Vinny, I'm talking about you and me.'

'Us?'

'Yes, Eddie, us. Look, all I'm saying is anything might happen. A bomb, a stray bullet from a dogfight a thousand feet above our heads, even being sent to the other side of the world to fight the Japanese.'

'Japanese?' spluttered Eddie.

'Will you stop repeating what I say and listen?' shouted Anna. 'What I mean is, what's the point of hiding things from one another? We're supposed to be looking into Sidney's death together, but all you keep saying "I can't tell" or "I'm protecting you". The thing is, Eddie, that's not your gift to give. Do you understand, I'll decide—'

'A spy murdered him.'

Eddie's sudden outburst stunned Anna into silence.

'A Nazi spy murdered Sidney Langham. I don't know who this person is yet, but I know why it happened. The dead man? It's Langham, though that's not the name I knew him by.'

Chapter Nine: Missing

Anna's head was still spinning from Eddie's earlier revelation as she took a mid-morning stroll with the lieutenant through the tranquil countryside on the edge of Lipton St Faith. A brisk easterly wind scoured their reddened cheeks as the sun fought in vain to take an edge off the early winter chill.

Here's me feeling guilty about not getting last month's evacuee report into the office, while Eddie's convinced we have a spy on the loose—more than that, a murderer. Whatever's happened over the last couple of days, it's shook him up.

She turned to take a last look down High Street before passing the last and oldest cottage for miles around and scoured its ancient brick gable for a date she hadn't forgotten from history lessons at school.

There it is, 1661. Not a good year for Great Yarmouth's Member of Parliament.

She remembered that was the year Miles Corbet, one of those who signed Charles I death warrant, was hung at Tyburn in London by his son, Charles II, as a regicide.

I suppose revenge is best served cold, thought Anna.

'What are you looking at?' said Eddie as he pulled his leather gloves tight against the raw breeze.

'Oh, nothing,' replied Anna. 'Just something that reminds me that actions have consequences.'

'Is that meant as a dig?' replied Eddie.

He's touchy.

Anna paused, turned to Eddie, and frowned. 'I had someone closer to home in mind. Me, in fact.' She studied his facial features. *He looks older, somehow.* 'I know I can be stubborn. Perhaps it shows my…'

Eddie stopped a few yards ahead; suddenly aware Anna had gone quiet. He looked back to see her gazing over a low hedge to the flat countryside beyond, now in hibernation for winter. 'What are you trying to say?'

She shrugged her shoulders beneath her heavy coat, its collar turned up against the weather. 'I care a lot about you, Eddie. There, I've said it. Now let's change the subject.'

What have I done? Thought Anna, afraid she'd let her emotional guard down.

Eddie walked slowly back to her. 'I'm not sure I understand?' He stood less than three feet from his companion, yet she hadn't turned to face him. 'Look at me,' he said in a quiet tone.

Now what do I do? thought Anna. 'What I mean is… I…' she began, while drifting her position so she could see Eddie. 'Well, don't you think this is strange?'

'Strange, what do you mean?'

Anna gasped in frustration, 'Eddie, last night you looked as though you'd gone ten rounds with Joe Louis… and lost. Then earlier today you say a spy murdered the man we saw at the mortuary. And now, nothing. It's like the last few days didn't happen.' Anna's eyes moistened as her anger surfaced. 'Well, it did, Eddie. You've changed, and it's no use pretending otherwise. So what's it to be? Perhaps we just continue to pretend nothing happened. Perhaps there isn't a war on after all? Sorry, Eddie, that's not going to happen. I want you to tell me—'

The unmistakable sound of two Spitfire fighters drowned her out. A split second elapsed between the first sound of the deep, pulsating Merlin engines and a deafening, all-encompassing roar as both aircraft flew overhead, before quickly disappearing over the coast before executing a tight right-hand turn to the south-east.

Both friends instinctively dropped to their haunches, as if in danger of being clipped by the speeding aircraft.

Come back safe from your patrol, boys, thought Anna, suddenly reminded about the reality of war, and how her problems subsided into the shadows compared to the two young pilots she'd glimpsed as they raced overhead.

Eddie stood up and gently helped Anna to her feet. 'You were saying... you know, the bit about you caring for me... "a lot", I think you said.'

Anna blushed. *Where's this going?* she thought.

'I'm sorry, I didn't mean to tease and if you don't know by now that I also care for you, we may as well give it up as a bad job.'

Eddie brushed several strands of withered grass from Anna's coat, an act of intimacy that took Anna by complete surprise.

'Give what up?' responded a startled Anna.

Eddie smiled, 'You know, all this private detective stuff.'

Anna studied her friend's body language as she attempted to inter-pret any difference between what he said and how he behaved. *Either he likes me, or he doesn't, as if I care.*

The lieutenant's smile subsided as he rested a hand on Anna's right arm. 'I don't mean to be evasive, and I'll tell you everything

I know... once I've made sense of it all myself. I promise.'

Anna wasn't sure if she felt relieved or not.

As they continued their mid-morning stroll, Anna told Eddie about her visit to Appleby college and the chat she and Tom had with Walter Teesdale.

'In that case, we need to visit the butcher who gave Sidney Langham a lift to the train station,' said Eddie as a villager overtook them and wished both a good morning.

Reciprocating the friendly greeting, Anna smiled and wished the man a fruitful day's fishing as she dodged a sizeable wicker basket slung over the man's shoulder.

'It shouldn't be too difficult to trace him. Walter reckoned the man traded from a village less than a mile from the college.'

Eddie nodded. 'I agree, so it's agreed. We spend a couple of hours in Cambridge. No? Why the puzzled look? I thought that's what you wanted to do?'

'It's not that, Eddie. I'm still confused why you maintain there's a link between the man we saw at the mortuary and your spy?'

'What, any more than you think the missing curate is the man we saw on the slab? Anyway, I didn't say he was a spy,' responded Eddie.

'That's different. Two men in the same profession, one vanishes while the other turns up dead.'

'Anna, you don't know for sure they were in the same job. There weren't enough fragments of clothing on that body to tell what he wore; let alone that he was a curate.'

'You're forgetting the stud.'

'And you're forgetting Charles said they were common. In fact, I've probably got a couple of studs like the one you found knocking about somewhere. It's hardly firm evidence, is it?'

I hate it when he points out the obvious.

Eddie unlatched a field gate as Anna pondered what to do next. She realised what her companion had done. 'Er, I wouldn't do that if I were you.'

'Do what?' replied Eddie in a tone which reflected his confusion.

Anna pointed to an old hand-painted sign, which the hazel hedge had almost completely enveloped over the years.

'What?'

'Bull,' replied Anna, pointing at the barely legible sign.

Eddie moved several thin branches from in front of the notice with the back of his hand. 'This is so old I expect the animal is long past chasing folks. In fact, I imagine he's chasing a herd of heifers on a cloud somewhere as we speak.'

All was silent, except for the faint sound of someone who sounded as if they had a mild chest infection.

'I wouldn't be so sure about that, lieutenant.' Anna pointed to a black behemoth fifty yards to their front. 'That's Patrick.'

'Patrick?'

'Patrick. He has quite a reputation.'

Eddie studied the enormous animal as it kicked clumps of grass up with its front right hoof. 'What, you mean with the ladies… cows, I mean?'

Anna laughed. 'Er, well, see those notches on the gate post?'

Eddie turned to where Anna pointed. 'And?'

'He's a champion for the number of heifers he keeps happy each year—they reckon he courted 157 last year and sired 149 offspring. Word is the farmer's hoping for 200 plus this time around.'

Eddie surveyed the gnarled post again, 'Either that bull can't count, or he ran out of space. I only count eleven.'

Anna smiled mischievously. 'Don't be daft, Patrick hasn't learned to write yet—and there's twelve, not eleven. See that faded scratch?'

The lieutenant narrowed his eyes and leant forward. 'That's not a scratch.'

Anna laughed. 'Oh, yes, it is. In fact, the farmer maintains it's from one of Patrick's horns as he lifted the farmer clear over the gate a few years ago. Ever since, he's kept a tally of those daft enough to cross Patrick and he's had to rescue. Some even made it out without the need of an ambulance! And they're the ones the farmer saved. Heaven knows how many have actually got on the wrong side of that bull... literally... so you might wish to close the gate.'

Before Eddie could move, the bull charged.

'He won't stop, so I reckon you have ten seconds at most before he gets you.'

Eddie shot forward, keeping one eye on the beast as he grabbed the open gate.

'You mean us?'

'No, Eddie, Patrick is a lady's man. He thinks he's protecting me from a competitor. As far as he's concerned, I'm part of his, well, harem, I suppose.'

'Don't be so ridiculous. My grandpa brought me up on his farm. That bull won't... oh no,'

Eddie grabbed at the gate, which had become wedged on a large stone sticking out of the half-frozen clay.

'He doesn't sound happy, Eddie. I reckon another five seconds and—'

'Yes, yes, I get it.' Eddie frantically pulled at the gate.

'Might I suggest you lift instead of pulling?'

After one last pull, which almost resulted in Eddie losing his footing, the gate came free.

'Your lucky day,' said Anna as Eddie slammed the gate shut and secured the latch. Patrick, meanwhile, thundered to a halt so that he now stood less than six feet from his visitors.

'He's a handsome chap, isn't he?' said Anna.

'Not quite the word I would use,' replied Eddie as the bull got agitated again.

'Move away from me and whatever you do, don't look at Patrick in the eye. He thinks you want to rut with him.'

Eddie laughed but took Anna's advice. 'Rut? Don't be so ridiculous. I told you, I grew up on a farm.'

Anna shook her head. 'Remind me, Eddie, this farm of your grandpa's, was it a beef farm, or did he grow cereals?'

Eddie sniffed the air as he turned his back on Patrick, while maintaining a respectful distance between himself and the immense beast.

Meanwhile, Anna approached the gate and encouraged Patrick to approach her. By the time Eddie looked around, the bull was enjoying having the flesh between his ears softly massaged.

'Remember, don't look at him,' said Anna in a quiet voice as Patrick got agitated.

'I've had enough of this. Catch me up when you've finished your date.'

Anna gave Patrick an extra hard scratch. 'It's alright, the stupid man has gone now, but I'd better get after him before he gets into more trouble.'

Patrick blinked as Anna let go and pointed to the notches in the gatepost. 'Not today, Patrick. Not today.'

In the thirty-seconds it took to catch up with Eddie, Anna's mind turned back to their investigation.

That was a pleasant diversion, but we need to get on with things.

'Recovered?'

'I don't know what you mean. Are we going after that butcher or not? Come to think about it, I've got the perfect job for him.' Eddie looked back at the field gate to see Patrick's head poking out as he kept a close eye on developments.

'Shame on you, Eddie Elsner.'

'What?'

'You know precisely what I mean.'

'Hmm,' muttered Eddie as he resumed walking. 'Back to business. You reckon the curate is the same man as we saw at the cottage hospital.'

Good, he's back.

'All I'm saying is a curate leaves Cambridge for a country church in Norfolk and doesn't arrive. At the same time, a man dies in a car accident, except no one knows who he is and all identification seems to have disappeared from his car. Yes, I agree there may be a connection, but to say they're the same man is a leap of logic.'

'Oh, so only men can apply logic, can they?'

They both stopped walking to face each other.

'Now what have I said?' replied Eddie, shaking his head.

'Is that what this is all about?' said Anna, nostrils flaring.

'You've lost me.'

'You and me, Eddie. Perhaps you don't like it that Tom and I have been making progress while you were swanning around… well, I don't know where because you won't tell me, and don't pull that "I'm only trying to protect you" line or I'll knock your block off.'

Eddie reached out to hold Anna's hand. 'Listen… I…' Shaking his head again, he slowly released his gentle grip.

'What are you trying to say, Eddie?'

The American broke off eye contact and began walking again.

'Oh… nothing. It can wait. Now, are we going to Cambridge or not?'

What was all that about?

* * *

Having hurriedly made four cheese and pickle sandwich and grabbed two apples from the larder, Anna hurried down the vicarage path and slid into Eddie's sports car. 'Right, let's get going. We can have these on the way,' she said.

One topic that Anna hoped they might avoid was their awkward exchange while walking.

Perhaps it's best we put that one back in its box, thought Anna.

To begin with, she thought Eddie felt the same way, since the first half of their ninety-minute journey took place largely in silence, apart from the occasional general remark about how cold it was for the time of year, and their hopes the fine weather wouldn't bring with it a spate of new mass bombing raids on the various industrial parts of the country.

'A penny for them?' said Eddie.

At that point Anna knew their unspoken agreement was about to end. 'They'll cost you more than that.'

Eddie changed down a gear as he overtook a tractor on one of the few passing places the road allowed and pressed hard on the accelerator. His car reacted immediately, its exhaust giving a throaty roar as the vehicle sped up. 'How much?'

Anna wanted to look at her companion, but something held her back.

I don't feel comfortable talking about this.

'To be honest, Eddie, I don't know what I think. I—'

'Do you regret we ever met?'

Anna felt numb at Eddie's brutal comment.

Do I? Does he?

'You know, everything that it's led to?' added Eddie.

'Led to?'

'You know, the murder investigations and stuff. Perhaps you simply want to look after your evacuees?'

How dare he?

125

'Don't patronise me, Eddie.' Anna avoided looking at the lieutenant and instead gazed out of the passenger window.

'Stop it, Anna. What on earth's got into you? I simply meant, no, sorry, not simply... you're doing important work to help little folks who are having a tough time of it. I respect that. But is our stuff getting to you?'

What if he's right? What do I do?

'If I'm being honest, yes, it does.'

Should I have said that?

She sensed him looking at her.

'It's just, well... looking after the evacuees is the actual world for me. It makes me feel useful, you know, doing my bit and all that. This other stuff? I'm not a policeman and neither are you. Look at us now, dashing to Cambridge to talk to a butcher about a lift he gave to some man. I mean, Eddie, who are we kidding? Why not leave Tom Bradshaw to get on with it? What business is it of ours?'

Eddie slowed the car before bringing it to a halt on a small patch of grass off the narrow road. 'Because you care, Anna Grix. I've seen that look in your eyes when we solve, or at least help the police solve, a murder case. It tells me you know you've done the right thing. What if everyone looked the other way? Then where would we be?'

Anna felt herself blushing 'Having a much quieter life.'

Eddie started the engine. 'OK, do you want me to turn the car around and head back to Lipton St Faith, or are we going to spend a pleasant hour looking out on all these quaint little English fields?'

Anna smiled. 'Quaint fields? You see that tree ahead on our right? Well, that thing is older than your country.'

'And your point?'

'It's known as Kett's Oak. These "little fields" well, most were once open common land. That's a little over fifty years after Christopher

126

Columbus stumbled upon your country, and that oak was already standing tall. The landowners enclosed the fields, hence all this hedging you see now.'

'You've lost me,' replied Eddie.

Anna pointed to the ancient oak. 'You spoke about the consequences of people standing by and doing nothing. But there's also a price to pay when you get involved with something without thinking it through. That tree's named after Robert Kett. He owned land around here, but still backed the landless. He didn't need to get involved, yet he led a rebellion by marching to Norwich to demand the fields left open.'

'I guess it didn't go too well since the hedging is still here. In fact, it's everywhere you look.'

'And that's my point.'

'So how come all the hedges are still here? The king had him hung for treason at Norwich castle. Not satisfied with that, his brother got the same treatment, only at the Abbey in Wymondham up the road from here.'

Eddie shook his head again. 'Does that mean we're going to Cambridge?'

Anna shuffled in her seat. 'We may as well, the car's pointing in the right direction.'

Knapwall displayed all the signs of being a wealthy Cambridgeshire village. An abundance of large, well-maintained houses, a variety of shops to cater for those with the money and coupons at their disposal and two banks, which Anna thought curious for such a small place.

Perhaps there's too much cash for one bank to handle, thought Anna.

'I don't know about you, but I fancy a spot of tea and cake. That place looks nice.'

Anna pointed to a small, smart looking building that sat snuggly between a saddler and quaint bookshop. The sign above the cafe read:

Ye Olde Tea Shoppe

'What about those cheese and pickle sandwiches you made?'

'Don't worry, I'll save them for later. We can't waste them,' replied Anna as she gave her companion a knowing glance.

'It must be old, look at the spelling.' Eddie pointed to the sign above their destination as he got out of the car and walked the few paces to catch up with Anna.

'Don't be daft. No one uses spelling like that. It's done for the tourists. If the cake's fresh and the tea hot, they can spell the name of the place however they want. You're paying.'

The sound of a bell ringing as she opened the cafe door reminded Anna of her mother's thrift shop. With the added benefit, there were things to eat. Inside the empty, brightly painted space, a small selection of cake stands formed a neat display on a white linen-covered table.

'Don't they look gorgeous?' said Anna?

'Good afternoon, sir, madam. Perhaps you might like a window table?' A young woman dressed in a black uniform complimented with a sparkling white apron and waitress hat pointed to a small, square table complete with two place settings.

The waitress patiently waited for her customers to take off their heavy coats and settle into their chairs before giving a little cough as she held a small pencil over her order pad.

Anna glanced at the cake stands. 'May I have a slice of Victoria Sponge, please, and tea for one.'

The waitress nodded, noted the order down, and turned her attention to Eddie.

'I'll have the same, please, except I'll have coffee instead of the tea.'

Anna smiled as she watched the waitress scribble the order, as Eddie's instruction sank in.

'We only have Camp coffee, sir; will that be alright?'

'As long as it's coffee, I don't mind what it's called, young lady.' Eddie winked at the waitress, who blushed before making a hasty retreat.

'Have you any idea what that stuff is?'

'Coffee is coffee,' replied Eddie.

That's what you think.

'Do you know why she asked us to take a window table?' said Anna.

'She thought we could do with some extra vitamin D?'

Anna laughed. 'That's not bad for you. In fact, we are bait.'

'Bait?'

'Yes. What do people do when they see a crowd? They join it. What do people do when they see a group looking up into the sky? They, too, look up. Sitting us here gives the impression the place is busy. You know, customers beget customers.'

'You come out with some rubbish, Anna Grix.'

'It's true. I bet this place will be half-full by the time we leave.'

As if on cue, the doorbell rang, heralding more business for the waitress.

'Told you,' said Anna, as she watched a well-dressed man and woman enter and make their way to a small table against the far corner of the bijou establishment.

On cue, the waitress appeared from the kitchen, pushing a dainty stainless-steel serving trolly with one hand and held her order pad and pencil in the other. 'I shall be with you in one moment,' she said to the new arrivals, before delivering a small teapot, strainer and delicate cup and saucer to Anna, before depositing a mug of brown liquid in front of Eddie.

'I'll get the rest of your order.' Pushing the trolley back so that it rested across the kitchen door, the waitress walked smartly over to the cake stands, used a silver-plated knife to lift two portions of Victoria sponge onto their respective plates and returned to the table.

Meanwhile, Eddie continued to favour his mug of liquid with a curious glance.

'Wonderful,' said Anna as the waitress completed her task and wandered over to her other customers.

'Is everything OK?'

Eddie pulled a face prone to be observed when a child first encounters a lemon. 'To be truthful, I don't know. What is it?'

Anna's eyes sparkled. 'I warned you. That's cost you sixpence, so you'd better drink up.'

As Eddie took a first, tentative sip of his coffee, the shop bell rang again. 'Told you,' said Anna.

Eddie took a sharp intake of breath as the brown liquid hit his taste buds, causing him to cough. Regaining his composure after assuring the fellow diners that all was well, he pushed the mug to the centre of the small table and, instead, concentrated on his cake.

Fifteen minutes later saw the pair rising from their table after settling the bill. As Eddie opened the shop door for Anna, a familiar face appeared.

'Miss Grix, twice in as many days, we must have impressed you.'

Anna worked hard to disguise her surprise by concentrating on the woman standing next to the Reverend Wilks.

'Ah, forgive me, Miss Grix. May I introduce my wife, Estelle?'

'And this is Lieutenant Edward Elsner. As you can see, he's an American.'

'And what is an American doing in our tiny village, nay, country?'

Eddie offered a homely smile as he adjusted his ill-fitting jacket. 'Just passin' through, sir. Ma'am, it's great to meet you, too.'

Estelle smiled nervously, 'Great… I mean, nice to meet you, too, lieutenant.'

I'd better move this conversation along, thought Anna. 'Spires, The dreaming Spires of Cambridge. The lieutenant is keen to take in our history.'

The reverend ushered his wife forward while he closed the shop door. 'Oxford, Miss Grix.'

'I beg your pardon?'

'You mean Oxford, for that's the description given by Matthew Arnold's inspiring poem, *Oxford*… "And that sweet city with her dreaming spires". Wonderful, is it not?'

I hate academics.

'Of course, Reverend.'

'And what of you, lieutenant? I see you're not in uniform, you're not a spy, are you?' Wilks resorted to type by laughing at his own joke. 'And where do you hail from? Originally, I mean.'

'Southwest Colorado, sir. A long way away.'

'Goodness me,' replied Wilks. 'That certainly is a distance. What brought you among us? Business of some sort? Perhaps the opportunity to gain orders from the War Department?'

I don't like the way this conversation is going, thought Anna.

Eddie offered the reverend a disarming smile. 'Sir, I'm just passin' through.'

Anna watched Wilks' reaction closely.

He's a sharp one.

'I see, lieutenant, well, that's most interesting. And now I must join my wife, or I shall be in trouble. It's so easy to get into trouble these days, is it not?'

Handshakes exchanged, Anna and Eddie were outside the cafe and about to close the door when the reverend shouted after them.

'Have you any news about young Langham? Such an odd matter, don't you think?'

'Who is this Langham? Have I met him, Anna?' said Eddie.

You wily old dog, thought Anna.

'No, no, Bud,' replied Anna. 'Just one of the reverend's students up at the college.'

'You're a teacher?' asked Eddie.

Don't push your luck, fella.

The Reverend Wilks smiled but said nothing as Anna closed the tearoom door.

'Bud? you could have picked something more... well, imaginative?'

'Oh, you sort of suit the name. Did you see the way he looked at you?'

'He's suspicious alright, but why?'

Anna strolled down the path before checking if Eddie followed. 'It beats me, but one thing is for sure, there's more to that college than the instruction of would be vicars.'

It didn't take long for the object of their visit to come into focus, or at least the shop premises the butcher operated from.

'There it is. Come on, there's nothing coming. Let's cross the street.'

I doubt this place sees more than half-a-dozen cars an hour, thought Anna as she obediently checked for traffic, before stepping into the road.

'That's odd,' said Eddie, 'it's closed? I thought Wednesdays were half-day closing around these parts?'

Anna looked through the crisscross tape stuck to the front window in case of explosion. 'It is, but perhaps they have their own way of doing things in Cambridgeshire, who knows. The place looks deserted.'

'It's not like him to miss out on business. He'd skin a caterpillar and sell it for tuppence, given half a chance.'

The pair half-turned to see a woman pushing an old bicycle with a wicker basket to its front pass without looking at either of them or making further comment.

'Perhaps she missed out on her rations,' said Anna.

'I guess you don't get between a housewife and her family's rations in wartime, eh?'

Anna pointed a finger at her companion. 'Sexist, that, but I'll forgive you this once, mind.'

Eddie chose not to respond and instead explored a passageway that ran between the butchers and the neighbouring building. 'It's wide enough to get a horse and cart down here, I reckon,' said Eddie.

'What are you doing?' asked Anna as she held back as Eddie strolled to the far end of the passageway.

'Look at this. It opens into a yard. I suppose this is where he does the business with them that end up on his shop hooks.'

Walking tentatively down the covered passageway, Anna now stood in a space big enough for several carts. 'Melodramatic, Eddie, but I get what you mean.'

As Anna explored the space she saw from the corner of her eye Eddie moving towards the back door of the shop.

'Well, what do you know? It's open. Let's go in.'

'Hang on, Eddie, are you sure? The place looked empty from the front.'

Before she could make further comment, Eddie disappeared into the building.

Stupid man. He's asking for trouble.

With little other option, Anna followed her companion. Now both stood is a small preparation room, a dark space despite it having a white lime-washed ceiling and light green tiled walls. A heavily built beech table dominated the space, its concave knife-marked surface laying its purpose out for all to see.

'Where's my Daddy?'

The shrill voice of a frightened-sounding woman pierced the tiny space, making Anna and Eddie jump in alarm.

Turning towards the scream, Anna saw a bedraggled woman not much older than herself, though she found it difficult to tell given the tortured expression the woman wore combined with long, straggly hair which didn't look as though it had seen a comb for ages.

'Watch out.' Eddie's shout transfixed Anna's eyes onto a meat cleaver that the woman held aloft.

Why didn't I see that until now?

Before she had time to react, Eddie pulled Anna away from the woman and took up position between the would be attacker and his friend.

The crazed woman sprang forward.

Oh, no. No.

Chapter Ten: Who's Who?

'What's all this fuss about?'

The crazed woman stopped in her tracks as her intended victims readied themselves for seemingly inevitable violence. Eddie turned his head to see who the calming voice belonged to, making sure he kept the meat cleaver in his peripheral vision.

A short, stout man dressed in a traditional butcher's garb of white shirt, calf-length blue and white striped apron and straw boater stood in the open doorway. 'Your Pa's back, Flower. What are you going to do with that there thing? I've been looking everywhere for it. Best I take it and put it away for safekeeping.'

Anna looked on from behind the safety of Eddie's tall frame as the man slowly walked forward, his eyes never deviating from the woman's vacant stare.

This isn't fazing him at all.

Flower lowered her arm.

'That's it. Let Pa take that from you, so nobody gets hurt, eh?'

The room fell into a deathly silence, save for the sound of the butcher's leather clogs making a scratching sound on the sawdust-covered stone floor as he neared the woman, who stood as if in a catatonic state, staring at Anna. Both arms now hung limply by the would be attacker's side.

Anna felt Eddie's body relax as the butcher reached out with his right hand and carefully took the meat cleaver from his daughter. 'Isn't that better, Flower? No need to be frightened.'

The woman allowed the butcher to relieve her of the fearsome object as she continued to focus on Anna's concerned features.

'April, is that you? Where have you been all this time?'

Who on earth is April?

Anna looked over to the butcher, who'd put the cleaver out of reach.

'No, it's not April, Flower. These friendly people are our special friends who have come a long way to see us. Now, why don't I get you settled in your room and bring a nice cup of tea. Perhaps I'll find a biscuit for you. Now, come along, that's it.'

Flower allowed her father to take her hand and begin leading her back to the doorway through which she'd entered less than ten minutes previously.

'Will there be chocolate?' said Flower in a quiet, child-like tone.

The butcher lightly swung his daughter's hand as if they were taking a family walk in the woods. 'No chocolate today, Flower. Perhaps another time.'

Anna realised Eddie was feeling for something in the jacket pocket of his borrowed suit. She felt safe enough now to come out of the lieutenant's shadow in time to see him hold a half-bar of Hershey's chocolate up.

Either my father has a secret stash, or Eddie raided Vinny's supply this morning. Either way, there'll be trouble.

Flower's eyes lit up as she glimpsed the chocolate.

'There, what did I tell you, our friends have come all this way and what do they bring you but some lovely chocolate. Who's a lucky girl?'

Anna noted the thankful glance the butcher gave Eddie as he took the treat from the lieutenant's outstretched hand.

'Come along, Flower, let's get you back to your bedroom and I'll bring you tea and some of this lovely chocolate.'

Seconds later, Anna and Eddie were once again the room's sole occupants as the butcher chatted away to his unresponsive daughter in the hallway.

'What do you make of that?' said Eddie.

Anna sighed as she attempted to relax by standing at the open rear door and taking several deep breaths of fresh air. 'Do you know, I think I've just witnessed one of the saddest sights I've ever seen.'

'Sad? She tried to kill us?' replied Eddie.

'No, she didn't. Whatever she saw, it wasn't us. She's terrified, although what of, I don't know.'

The room once more fell silent as they listened to the muffled sound of the butcher's voice as he led his daughter upstairs and into her room. A minute later, the distinctive sound of the man's heavy clogs gave a running commentary on the butcher's position as first they traced their way back down the stairs, then clattered noisily on the hard floor surface of the hallway.

'She'll settle now,' the butcher said quietly as he re-entered the preparation room. 'Thank you for the chocolate, it made all the difference and... well, I'm sorry you had to see my daughter like that, I—'

'No! We startled your daughter and owe you an apology for entering your home without permission.' Anna exchanged awkward glances with Eddie.

The butcher fell silent.

Poor, poor man, thought Anna.

'It was a bombing raid on London. We'd only gone for one night to visit a sick relative, then...'

'You don't have to say anything if it's too painful.' said Anna in a quiet, respectful tone.

The butcher retrieved the meat cleaver he'd put out of harm's way and hung it on its allotted hook on the green tiled wall. 'Everything in its place, that's what my wife always said.'

'Will your daughter be alright?' asked Anna.

She watched as the butcher scanned the wall to check the tools of his trade were all accounted for before he turned and attempted a smile. 'Yes, she'll sleep now and will probably have forgotten all about it by teatime. I should explain, I—'

'Please, as my friend said, there's no need to,' said Eddie.

Ignoring the lieutenant's offer, the butcher continued. 'Flower lost her identical twin sister, April, on that visit. She also lost her mother and uncle, whose house got hit. I was the only one to get out. I still don't know how. Now it's the two of us trying as best we can to cope. I'm lucky, I have the business and people have been exceedingly kind, but Flower, well, as you can see. I don't like to leave her, but I've no choice. She doesn't normally come out of her room. I'm sorry you had to go through that. All the same, I'm sure things will be simply fine, isn't that what you Americans like to say?'

Eddie didn't respond.

'Always look on the bright side. That's what my Mary… my wife, used to say, so that's what I try to do. It's just, wel… Anyway, forgive me, my name's Jimmy Falkirk.'

There's such sadness and pain in those eyes and he looks old well beyond his years. How do you carry on having lost so much?

'We should explain why we're—'

'I know why,' replied Jimmy. 'You want to know what happened to young Sidney?'

'But how—' replied Eddie.

138

'Because you're not on my books, so you can't get meat from me, and I saw you talking to the Reverend Wilks. Only I lost sight of you because I got collared by a long-standing customer. I didn't think for a minute the back door was open, let alone Flower was downstairs.'

'Not to worry, but you're right, we are here about Sidney. I should explain, my father is a vicar and knows the church Mr Langham should have arrived at, except—'

'He didn't, did he? It's the talk of the village, I'm afraid. Nothing escapes their attention.'

Anna offered a rueful smile. 'I know what you mean.'

'So you know I took him to the train station, but as I told the lady, he seemed fine. Quiet, but fine.'

'A lady?' said Anna.

The butcher hesitated for a few seconds. 'Yes, a most striking woman. Well to do I should say judging by how she dressed and spoke, posh-like. She seemed genuinely concerned about his welfare. Sidney is her nephew, that's what she told me.'

'I didn't expect that,' said Anna as Eddie sped up out of Knapwall and headed due east.

'And I hoped we might get away before nightfall. I hate driving in the blackout. But you're right, that was an interesting experience.'

Anna burst into laughter. 'Interesting? is that what you call almost being chopped up with a meat cleaver?'

Eddie reciprocated. 'You're exaggerating, as usual.'

'And you've certainly got the hang of British understatement, lieutenant!'

Eddie looked up at the night sky and pointed at his windscreen. 'That's no understatement, though.'

Anna knew what her companion meant as she, too, looked to the Heavens. 'How can all that death and misery come from such a breath-taking place? It's a bomber's sky alright. I wonder if it'll be Manchester that gets it again? They've had a terrible time of it lately.'

The sudden change of topic from light banter to the realities of war cast a shadow over their journey as the sports car wended its way along the meandering lane of rural Cambridgeshire and over an invisible border into Norfolk.

As time passed, with each of the little car's occupants lost in their own thoughts, Anna knew Eddie had become preoccupied with checking the rear-view mirror. 'And I thought it was us women who were the vain ones.'

Eddie seemed not to understand her meaning.

'That.' She pointed to the mirror.

'There's a car. A long way back, but I keep catching its reflection in the moonlight. It's been with us for ages.'

Anna turned in her seat to see if she could catch sight of the car. 'Don't you think you're being a little paranoid? If I were you, I'd be more concerned about what might drop from the sky, not some car that's on the same stretch of road.'

Anna felt a sudden jolt as the car slowed.

'What the…' exclaimed Eddie as he manoeuvred the vehicle around a blind bend, only to be confronted with a stationary car that completely blocked the narrow lane. A man stood hunched over the rear wheel as if checking for a mechanical problem.

'What a place to break down. So dangerous,' said Eddie as he brought his own vehicle to a shuddering halt.

'Perhaps it's a flat tyre,' offered Anna.

Why isn't that chap looking at us? Surely it's the first thing someone would do in his position.

140

Seconds later, the car that Eddie had been so concerned about pulled up fifty feet to his rear.

'I don't like the look of this. You stay inside. I'll see what's going on. One thing, Anna. Whatever happens next, you're my girlfriend, right?'

'Girlfriend, have you gone mad?' she giggled.

'This isn't a joke, Anna,' responded Eddie, his unsmiling features leaving his companion in no doubt he meant it. 'There's no time to explain but prepare to play a convincing role. This might be nothing, but—'

'You've made you point. I get it… I think,' replied Anna as the lieutenant swung open his door, pulled up the collar of his overcoat and stepped out into the chill air of the early evening.

'Having a spot of bother?' said Eddie in a cheery tone as he approached the man looking forlornly at his rear tyre.

He plays a good part. I'll give Eddie that, thought Anna as she listened to her friend's upbeat tone.

The stranger looked at Eddie from beneath his wide-brimmed hat. 'Ah, an American. My wife is one of those.'

Eddie strolled casually forward. 'It proves we get everywhere; don't you think? You got a flat tyre?' Eddie pointed to the wheel.

'Not quite, Lieutenant Elsner, you might say more of a slow puncture.'

Oh no, how does he know his name?

Eddie ignored the bait as he casually glanced behind him towards the other car.

Who does Eddie know who talks with a plum in his mouth? I bet the bloke went to Eton, or Harrow.

The stranger looked past Eddie. 'Ah, Miss Grix, please join us. My two colleagues so want to meet you,' he said, doffing his hat before holding it aloft.

This proved to be the signal for the occupants of the second car to get out of their vehicle. In seconds, two men approached the lieutenant's car, one standing behind the other, feet away from the passenger-side door.

Extending a gloved hand, the man nearest Anna's door opened it and gestured in no uncertain terms that she should get out and follow them.

'You have me at a disadvantage, sir,' said Anna, standing opposite Eddie while studiously ignoring the other two.

'Yes, I do, don't I? I'll tell you what, why don't we dash back to my place and have a nice cup of tea? It's near to here.'

'But your car?' replied Anna.

The well-spoken gentleman kicked his tyre with an immaculately clean shoe and smiled. 'Isn't it marvellous what magic moonlight and patience does for the soul. My tyre is restored to full health.' What do you think about that? Now, will you join me for tea?

'Do we have a choice?' said Eddie.

The man smiled again. 'Of course, I have both Sian and green tea. You may have either, or perhaps try a cup of each?'

By the time they arrived at the stranger's house, having driven the sports car in convoy, sandwiched between their host's vehicles, the night had closed in. Above, the star-filled sky looked as if a million diamonds shone, varying in brightness as a full moon caught their multifaceted surfaces.

This place looks like something out of a horror film. Thought Anna.

'This'll be interesting,' said Eddie as their escorts approached his stationary sports car.

'There you go again with that understatement; you're becoming quite an expert.' said Anna.

'Remember what I said about being my girlfriend, yes?'

His sudden change in tone bothered Anna.

What have we got ourselves into?

Entering the faded grandeur of a once opulent tall, square hallway, Eddie and Anna crossed the vast space and followed their host into a large saloon that had originally showcased its owner's portrait collection.

'Ah, thank you, Davis,' said the posh man as the soberly dressed attendant silently entered the large room, set down a silver tray on a rich Brazilian mahogany sideboard, and left without comment.

'And what do you think of our little country?'

'What do you mean?' replied Eddie, maintaining his guard.

The posh man made a sweeping hand gesture to highlight the faded opulence of the grand room. 'Some might say dear old Blighty is past its best, just like this room, whereas your country continues to grow in power and influence… such a pity our current sovereign's ancestor, George III, gave it away, don't you think?'

Anna studied Eddie closely to see how he'd react to the stranger's provocation. *Don't let him goad you*, she thought.

To her relief, the lieutenant's facial features relaxed into a smile. 'Oh, you mean the Boston Tea Party and all that… well, I guess that's why us ex-colonial folks drink so much coffee. You know, perhaps tea still leaves a bitter taste in our mouths.'

Ouch, thought Anna.

Now the posh man smiled, 'You may have a point. That said, fresh-ground coffee can of itself taste rather bitter, especially if it's left to stew. Of course, without the French navy coming to your rescue at Chesapeake Bay, I imagine you'd all still be talking with an English accent and taking afternoon tea, don't you think?'

Eddie sensed victory, 'a favour we might someday soon repay to the French and throw in a free hand to the old country, too.'

Anna sensed the exchange might soon get out of hand. 'Enough, you two.' Turning to the stranger she continued, 'Let's stop this silly game and get on with whatever it is you want from us and—'

'And let me remind you,' interrupted Eddie, 'That I'm an American citizen under the protection of the United States.'

The posh man grinned, his lips parting enough to reveal a gold tooth in his upper jaw.

'Protection? Ah, yes, how is General Murphy? Do give him my regards when next you see him.'

Eddie disguised his surprise. 'Who?'

'General Bob Murphy, can you have forgotten your superior so soon? You spoke to him only the other day.'

Anna grew increasingly frustrated and launched herself into the exchange. 'What exactly is going on? And who exactly are you?'

Her interruption caused the two men to break eye contact.

'Please allow me to apologise, Miss Grix,' said the posh man. I'm forgetting my manners, especially to the daughter of a man who served his country with such distinction during the Great War.

What on earth is going on? Who is this joker? thought Anna.

'Enough!' barked the lieutenant. 'Why are we here and what do you want?'

Their host remained unruffled by Eddie's angry outburst as he sipped his tea while leaning against an Adams Fireplace. 'Tell me, lieutenant, how are things in Southwest Colorado at this time of year? Getting a little cool, I expect?'

Eddie got to his feet and closed on his host, who raised a hand to gesture Eddie should advance no further.

'Forgive me once again, lieutenant, that was rude of me.'

'You seem to do a great deal of apologising,' said Anna. 'Perhaps you might behave like a grownup instead of a poor imitation of Dick Tracy and get on with whatever it is you kidnapped us for?'

144

'Excellent, Miss Grix, quite remarkable, if a little harsh. My briefing file highlighted you possessed a fighting spirit, which appears to be the case. Yes, you're correct, it's time to get on with the matter in hand.'

The man gestured for Eddie to resume his seat while he settled into a deep red Chesterfield leather armchair.

'Lieutenant, you recently visited a certain establishment. We want to know why you went there?'

'What's he on about, Eddie?' asked Anna in a confused tone.

Their host clapped his hands quietly. 'Wonderful, Miss Grix, such impeccable acting.'

'She knows nothing about this!' barked Eddie.

This is getting surreal, thought Anna.

'About what?' she said. *He looks worried. I've not seen him like this before.* 'And who are you? You keep apologising for your poor manners, yet you haven't even introduced yourself?'

The man stood and walked back to the hearth. After retrieving a cigar from a silver case on the white marble mantle, he clipped one end and lit the cigar using a match he struck on the wall.

He clearly doesn't own the place, thought Anna.

'You're quite right, Miss Grix. Unforgivable on my part. You may call me... let me see; yes, Grey, I shall be Mr Grey.'

He's playing with us, she thought.

'Bletchley is a wonderful place, is it not, lieutenant, though I suspect not given the weather we've been having lately.'

So that's where Eddie disappeared to, thought Anna.

She once again turned to Eddie. 'Bletchley, there's only a train station and a few factories there. What's so interesting about Bletchley?'

The lieutenant gazed at the oak parquet flooring.

'Ah, we are so alike, you and I, Miss Grix. You anticipated my next question to your companion.'

Eddie stood rigid; his self-control tested to the limit. 'Keep her out of this.'

Grey curled his lips into more of a sneer than a smile. 'It's far too late for that, I'm afraid. In fact, we have a minor job for you both. The outcome will determine whether you become heroes, which no one will ever hear about, or arrested for treason and… well, things may not go so well for either of you.'

Chapter Eleven: Brandy, Anyone?

Shocked at the brutality of Grey's words, Anna felt the colour drain from her cheeks.

What have we got ourselves into?

A glance at Eddie confirmed her worst fears.

'Now, enough of business. Perhaps it's time for something a little stronger than tea. You'll both join me, I hope?'

This is beyond surreal, thought Anna.

With little other choice than to await the mysterious Mr Grey's pleasure, both his unwilling guests stood without saying a word and followed their host into the library, shorn of any books and instead its shelves home to a forest of spider's webs, save for a large radio placed at one end of the snug space. A large octagonal table, out of scale with its surroundings, sat in the middle of the room. At its centre rested a round silver tray with finely worked edges, upon which rested a crystal decanter with a heavy-looking silver topper. Three intricately hand cut lead-crystal brandy glasses traced a triangular shape around the fine container, three-quarters filled with a dark golden liquid that caused the flames from an open fire to appear as if the decanter was flaming.

'Please take a seat.' Grey gestured for Anna to sit, guiding her chair as if adopting the role of maître d'hôtel at the Ritz in London.

'And lieutenant, please.' Grey pointed to a chair opposite side. Taking his own seat, their host looked to the open doorway and gestured for someone to enter. Anna turned to see the sombrely dressed man walk smartly over to the table and pour three generous glasses of brandy.

I wonder where Grey got the brandy from, *has nobody told him there's a war on*?

'Wonderful, simply splendid,' said Grey as he gently swirled the brandy around in its glass, then lifted the container to his nostrils. He closed his eyes and took in the refined aroma of the vintage alcohol.

Grey opened his eyes to observe the sober-suited man staring at Anna, who looked sternly back at him.

'He's waiting for you to gesture if the brandy is to your taste. He doesn't speak... or at least I've never heard him do so, so I find it easier to point or shake my head.'

Words fail me, she thought.

Glancing up again at the man, Anna smiled and leaned back as a signal of satisfaction.

Eddie adopted a similar posture.

The suited man gave the smallest nod before formally acknowledging Mr Grey and leaving the room.

Their host glanced around the once exquisitely decorated library, then at the sparkling decanter. 'Perks of the job, one might say.'

'One might say many things, Mr Grey,' replied Anna. 'The question is, perks of *what* job?'

She waited while Grey once again savoured the contents of his glass before taking a delicate sip and allowing the liquid to linger on his palate. 'Wonderful, simply exquisite, don't you think.' He pointed to Anna's own glass. 'You must drink, it will keep the chill out.'

Anna complied.

I hate to admit he's spot on, thought Anna.

'And the "little" job?' asked Eddie, his irritation clear.

Making his guests wait until he'd finished his brandy, Grey raised his eyes as if searching for inspiration. 'I am but a humble clerk, a collator of information, a sifter of fact from fiction that ends up being stored in nothing more important than a dusty filing cabinet somewhere in my superior's office. I'm permitted, on rare occasions, such riches as we see before us this evening.'

As Grey finished speaking, a man appeared at the open doorway to the dining room, still wearing his heavy coat and hat from having left the cold evening outside.

Anna turned in time to notice the man give a single nod to Grey.

As if one strange man isn't enough for one night, thought Anna.

She turned back to face her host, who occupied himself by pouring himself a further quarter-glass of brandy.

'Good news?' enquired Anna.

Grey held up his glass. 'Delicious, is it not?'

'Enough,' shouted Eddie. 'What do you want of us?'

Grey delicately returned his lead-crystal glass to the finely veneered surface of the table.

'Perhaps you have a point, lieutenant, not least since all now seems in place.'

'What's "in place"?' demanded Anna.

'The required authorisations.' Grey turned his attention back to his glass and turned it between finger and thumb, causing refracted light from the fire to dance across the old table.

'Authorisations?' said Eddie.

Not for the first time, Grey's guests exchanged anxious glances.

'Oh, you know how bureaucracies work. All that making sure

the paperwork has the correct ink stamps and so forth; though on this occasion the fact you're an American complicates matters.' Grey ran his tongue around the inside of his mouth as if attempting to dislodge a rogue scrap of food. 'You see, my superiors have no wish to cause a diplomatic incident with our nearest and dearest friends.'

'By which you mean?' responded Eddie.

'Which means I'm pleased to tell you that Mr Churchill and your president have given their blessing to our little endeavour.'

Eddie sat ramrod straight.

'Oh, please don't look so shocked, lieutenant. Your reputation goes before you, and all agreed you're the man for the job. I have to say we are most thankful to General Murphy for putting your name forward.'

Anna frowned at Eddie. 'Do you know what this is about?'

'Not a clue,' replied the lieutenant, his demeanour changing from its usually relaxed state into one getting ready for fight or flight.

'I've no idea what you're talking about except I know for sure that my superior officer would not do such a thing without briefing me first.'

Grey gave Eddie a long, hard stare, his closed mouth giving an exaggerated downturn at each edge. 'I thought you might say that.'

He reached into an inside pocket of his jacket and withdrew a single piece of crisply folded paper. 'You might wish to have a glance at this.'

Eddie collected the note from Grey's outstretched hand and studied its contents before sharing it with Anna.

He's been done up like a kipper, thought Anna.

The lieutenant took one last look at the signatures at the foot of the document before handing it back to Grey.

Several seconds passed as Anna and Eddie watched Grey fumbling in his trouser pocket, while still holding the piece of paper with his free hand. Eventually their host produced an elegant silver Dupont lighter and held it to the bottom right corner of the paper.

'What on earth are you doing?' exclaimed Eddie, seated too far from Grey to influence events.

They watched in bewilderment as Grey lit the document, maintaining a fingertip hold on the flaming object until the heat compelled him to drop the last remnants onto the table as it crumpled to ash.

'Why did you do that?' said Eddie in a quiet, determined tone.

Grey smiled. 'I told you, if you succeed in your task, you'll join the legion of unsung heroes who helped defeat our joint enemies. If you fail and suffer the consequence, let's say it's better no evidence exists of any link to, er… officialdom.'

'And me?' asked Anna in a sharp tone.

'You offer the perfect foil, not to say cover, for the lieutenant.'

I'm glad I come in useful for something, thought Anna.

'But enough of this gloomy stuff. I have a surprise for you both, please, follow me.' Grey downed the last of his brandy and rose from his chair.

Why are we following this man like sheep? thought Anna.

They enetered a chilled narrow room furnished with a slide projector at its centre, next to which stood a man. Three chairs faced a white sheet hung on the far wall.

'I'd like to show you a few snaps, and I promise they're not endless images of my last holiday in the Alps prior to 1938, interesting though it was.'

Grey's words served as a signal for the projectionist to turn the single naked lightbulb off and bring the projector to life.

The first slide illuminated a familiar-looking figure. 'Here we have Mr Langham on campus at his college… and in Appleby. Ah, yes, with his best, nay, some might say, only friend, Walter.'

The projectionist changed slides at a relentless pace. 'And here,' continued Grey, 'here we see Sidney with his spiritual supervisor, one Dr Janson, I believe. They don't look at all happy, do they? My mother taught me never to point at anyone, yet here we have Sidney's mentor do precisely that. I wonder what he was so angry about?'

And I remember the look they exchanged when Walter left the principal's room, thought Anna.

'Oh look,' said Grey. 'Here we have a shot of where Mr Langham spent much of his older childhood growing up. It's his aunt's house in Belgium. And here we have a picture of the two of them together.'

They look devoted to one another, thought Anna as she mulled Sidney's age in the over-exposed image. *Six, possibly seven?*

'Now,' continued Grey, 'here's something a little different. An extra brandy for whoever correctly identifies the location.'

Projected onto the stretched cloth, which rippled in response to a chill breeze that entered the room from its ill-fitting window, stood the statuesque figure of a gentleman dressed in a top hat and morning suit.

'That's Ascot races,' said Anna.

'You win the brandy, well done, Miss Grix… though I suppose things were a little loaded against the good lieutenant given the nature of that most august of British racing traditions.'

'Wait a minute,' exclaimed Anna. 'He's in the Royal Enclosure. Why are you showing us such a picture next to images of Sidney's everyday life?'

Grey offered a brief burst of applause. 'Oh, Miss Grix. You are so perceptive. Yes indeed, show you the image of an English gentleman at leisure juxtaposed to a little boy in foreign climes? Three more slides and I shall explain.'

The remaining slides followed a theme. They all featured aerial views of a rural landscape.

'Forgive the obvious, but why are you showing us these?' asked Anna.

Grey gestured to Eddie, his hand piercing the light from the projector so that an exaggerated shadow flashed across the cloth screen.

'Perhaps you might direct that question at the lieutenant,' replied Grey.

Anna glanced at Eddie through the darkness. *He looks as though he's seen a ghost. What's the matter with him?* she thought.

At that precise moment, the room lights came on, causing Eddie and Anna to shield their eyes against the sudden change in conditions.

'Well?' asked Anna.

Eddie fidgeted with his shirt cuff.

'I'm waiting, Eddie. Why have those pictures shocked you so much?'

The lieutenant continued to preen his ill-fitting jacket without looking at his companion.

Anna stood to confront Eddie. 'I've had enough of this, Eddie. Whenever I ask what you do, you're evasive, or else you palm me off with some stupid answer that treats me like a child. Well, this has gone far enough. Look where your secrets have got us. Talk to me.'

Eddie shot to his feet. 'The same mission I had well before I met you. I didn't ask to play Watson to your Sherlock Holmes.'

'And I didn't expect to be saddled with an American version of Jekyll and Hyde.'

'That's enough, Anna.'

'Enough? It's not half enough.'

They stood square on to one another, faces inches apart as the shouting match continued.

'Never speak to me like that again, or—'

'Or what, Anna?'

The challenge silenced both antagonists. Instead, they continued to glare at each other, faces contorted with anger.

'Have we quite finished?' said Grey in a controlled, quiet tone, 'because I know lover's tiffs can be quite intense and go on for some time. However, perhaps we might continue?'

Lovers? I wouldn't marry that stupid American if he was the last man on earth.

'Please, might we continue?' repeated Grey.

'You can start by telling us what all this crazy stuff is about?' said Anna.

Eddie disengaged from Anna, who similarly appeared to welcome the release.

'Do you mean your lover's tiff? Only you two can answer that. If you're referring to my slide show, I suggest we retire to the morning room. I'm in the mood for a fine cigar and more brandy... and there'll be a fire.'

Once again, his guests followed his prompt without comment, while resisting any temptation to exchanges glances. Within the minute, Anna sat at one end of a long leather sofa, Eddie choosing the opposite end as if his companion didn't exist.

Grey offered refreshments, which they both refused without uttering a word. Retrieving a long, thick Havana cigar from a mahogany case on a nearby table, Grey clipped the tip of one end off and lit the pungent tobacco with his lighter.

Decanting a large measure of brandy into a lead-crystal glass, Grey seated himself on a deeply buttoned leather chair at an angle to his guests. 'Sidney Langham is, or rather, was, a deeply religious young man who committed his life to the Almighty at a young age. His early childhood was traumatic, having lost both parents, which prompted his move to Belgium. His aunt, the lady in the slides, took the boy in and raised him as her own. It appears from everything we know they were devoted to one another... although I suspect you already know much of this.'

Neither Anna nor Eddie changed their downcast expression 'And this is important because...?'

'A relevant question, Miss Grix. You see, several months ago, the enemy picked his aunt up. She suffered a dreadful interrogation.'

'Why pick an old lady up?' commented Eddie.

'Also, a relevant question and one that puzzled us at first. However, it seems she was nothing more than an unfortunate victim of gossip. Details are sketchy, but it seems someone with a grudge, or ulterior motive, told the Gestapo that she formed a resistance cell helping British Airmen get back to England after being shot down. That was enough to get her arrested by the local police at the behest of the Gestapo. Who knows, perhaps the person who told tales wanted the old woman's apartment or saw the chance to earn some extra rations from the occupying forces. Who are we to judge when people simply wish to survive from one day to the next under the most desperate of circumstances whose cruel invaders control every move?'

I hope I'd have made a different decision, thought Anna.

'But if she wasn't involved in getting airmen back to Britain, what use was she to the Gestapo?' asked Eddie.

Grey tapped the arm of his chair with his brandy glass, almost causing its contents to spill. 'Of course, they wouldn't have known that at first, though I suspect given the techniques used to elicit information, the poor woman soon convinced them of her innocence... on that matter. However, it seems she told them about her English nephew and his location studying to be a pastor. Who knows, perhaps she thought it showed how harmless she was to them.'

'And just how do you know all this?' asked Anna.

Grey gave her a long, lingering look as he puffed on his cigar. 'We take a keen interest in who the Gestapo pick up. If the prisoner is one of the lucky few to be released, it's for one of two reasons; either they've agreed to work for the Nazis, or their captors want to see what the person does once "free". The natural thing to do is run for safety. That might be to friends or family... or, perhaps, to alert your fellow resistance colleagues of imminent danger if that's what the person is involved with.'

'And so, lead the Gestapo to—'

'You understand everything, Miss Grix. And it's for that reason that our own operatives are most careful only to make contact when it's safe to do so.'

Anna looked confused. 'What, even if the person isn't up to anything dodgy?'

Grey nodded. 'Our enemies do not welcome our visits to the continent as a rule. However, we need to gather as much information as possible. Many lives can turn on a misplaced comment or gesture when a prisoner of the Nazis is under the threat of torture, or worse. Now, does that answer your original question, Miss Grix? Oh, and by the way, all that you have seen and heard this evening is to remain confidential. You must tell no one. You should know you're subject to the Official Secrets Act. If you divulge anything to anyone about these matters, you'll get arrested for treason. There, that's another bit of bureaucracy dealt with.'

For the first time in twenty-minutes, Anna and Eddie exchanged glances.

'Please, don't be so shocked, I'm sure it won't come to that,' said Grey. 'After all, Miss Grix, you're a vicar's daughter and the lieutenant is, I'm certain, above reproach.'

'The man in the top hat,' said Eddie.

Grey looked puzzled. 'Top hat? Ah yes, The Royal Enclosure at Ascot. I'm glad you reminded me about that gentleman because it brings me to the crux of the matter. He's one Lindsay Fox-Marsden, or to give him his noble title, Sir Lindsay Fox-Marsden, Second Baronet of Sidborne in the County of Norfolk.'

'Never heard of him or his title,' said Anna.

Grey downed the last of his brandy. 'That's because it doesn't exist, at least not now. King Henry VI recalled the title when its last incumbent died without a male heir in 1422. Our chancer maintains he discovered a direct link via his family tree, which is nonsense, but it serves some people of influence to encourage his delusions.'

'Like whom?' asked Anna.

Grey took another long puff on his cigar. 'So, we arrive at our destination, so to speak. Fox-Marsden inveigled himself with Oswald Mosley and his thugs—probably because he thought he might get his title if the Germans win the war. Although we've interned Mosely, we know he has a network of loyal followers working to further his fascist aims. We suspect that through them, Fox-Marsden is acting as a spotter for an enemy agent who is, in turn, feeding Mosley's delusions to help the Nazis defeat our country.' Grey turned to Eddie, 'And mark my words, lieutenant, once the Axis forces have finished with us, they'll come for America, ably assisted by forces from where the sun first rises.'

'And we connect all this to Sidney Langham's death?' said Anna as Eddie sat in silence digesting his host's words.

Grey nodded. 'You must contact Fox-Marsden. As things stand, he's the only hope we have of identifying who the enemy agent is. Our concern is it may be someone at the heart of the British establishment who can do this country much harm. As a further complication, you only have until nine o'clock on Sunday evening when certain most important persons will speak by telephone. I must have my answers in time for that telephone call.'

As the pair stood and made ready to leave, Grey offered a parting shot to Eddie.

'Unusual fit of clothes you're wearing, lieutenant. Perhaps you might change into something that hangs on you a little better when you get home. Keeping up standards and all that, you know.'

Chapter Twelve: Red Wine

As Eddie reversed his car to execute a rapid three-point-turn in front of the once grand house that had, until a few minutes earlier, acted as a detention centre, Anna felt a wave of relief wash over her.

Thank Heavens we're out of there. She checked her watch. *Ten-thirty. Did that really take two-and-a-half hours?*

Her joy at being free soon turned to anger as she considered where several strands of their ordeal came together. 'Stop the car.'

'Are you mad?' replied Eddie. 'We need to get away from Grey and his sidekicks pronto, and you want me to stop?'

'I said stop the car.' Anna glared at her companion, making it clear she expected him to comply.

'This is plain crazy,' replied Eddie as he pulled up instead of turning onto the main Norwich to Cambridge Road. 'OK, what's going on?'

'A good question. In fact, that's what I want to know?'

'Anna, I don't know what you're talking about. You heard every word Grey said. I know as much as you do. Why the third-degree? Now, can we get going?'

Anna put her hand over the gearstick knob before Eddie could engage first gear. 'Not until you tell me what's going on… and don't give me that "I don't have a clue" rubbish. When Grey showed us the aerial photo-slides, you looked as if the world had ended. Then I asked you directly what you're doing in Norfolk. I'm still waiting for an answer.'

Eddie reached for the ignition key and twisted it to the off position. An uneasy silence fell as the low roar of the car's engine ceased, to be replaced by a gentle rustling of what few leaves remained on the surrounding trees in the night breeze.

'You might well look uncomfortable,' commented Anna as she watched his eyes close and shoulders drop. 'This has gone on long enough. What started as helping Tom Bradshaw solve a traffic accident has turned into a nightmare of murder and, it seems, espionage. On top of which a man neither of us has ever met, or at least that's true in my case, all but kidnaps us and pulls a letter from his jacket pocket like a rabbit from a hat giving him permission to direct you, and me, to do his bidding… and to cap it all gives us until Sunday night to accomplish whatever it is we're supposed to do. Doesn't that strike you as odd?'

Eddie tapped the leather covered steering wheel with two fingers of his right hand, while running the remaining hand through his blond locks. 'What do you want me to say?'

'I'm talking about what I *expect*, not want,' retorted Anna. 'Like it or not, whoever Grey works for has latched onto what you're up to. That connection has put us both at risk of either being killed or arrested for treason. I'd call that Hobson's choice, wouldn't you?'

Eddie placed both hands back on the steering wheel and gazed out of his side window.

'If you're looking for inspiration, Eddie, you won't find it out there. I—'

'My job is to scout locations for possible US military airfields in East Norfolk, and all I've ever tried to do is protect you. Since it seems

159

you're determined to put yourself in danger, what's the point?' said Eddie in a voice devoid of emotion.

So that's why I've seen him talking to local farmers, thought Anna.

Anna hesitated for a few seconds before gathering her wits. 'I'm not a china doll, Eddie. The whole "we must protect the women" stuff gets my goat. Judge me by what I can do, not what you think I *should* do, and I'm not criticising you for that, but times are changing. When the war is over, it won't be like the last one when the women were all sacked and sent back to their kitchens. This time we'll keep tight hold of the skills we've learned and things we've done. There's no going back... we won't let go.'

The companions slowly met each other's gaze.

I wonder what he's thinking.

'I... I don't want you...' Eddie's voice tailed off as each suddenly disengaged after briefly moving nearer to each other.

'So, we're going to see a lot more of you lot over here?'

Anna's question allowed both to regain their composure without the need to explain.

'That's above my pay grade and we haven't declared war on anyone as far as I know. All I know is if the balloon goes up, Norfolk will feel like one huge aircraft carrier with all the guns pointed at Europe. The Nazis have already sunk some of our ships and who knows what the Japanese are up to.'

I wonder what Mr Churchill and his president are really up to? thought Anna.

After a few seconds of quiet, Anna's need for further explanations took over from her urge to return to the vicarage. 'And Bletchley Park?' She immediately sensed Eddie stiffen.

'As you said in the house a while back, there's a train station and some factories, that's all.'

'A visit to which caused you to end up looking like a down and out. I don't think so, Eddie.'

He banged an open palm on the steering wheel. 'No more, Anna. I can't tell you even if I wanted to. Grey talked about treason before. Believe me, some things are way bigger than you or me. More important even than ships at sea that could've been saved from Nazi submarines, but which are now lying at the bottom of the North Sea; bombing raids that do terrible things to your cities that might have been much worse. In the scheme of things, we don't count. Your Mr Churchill had it right in October when he said of war, "Never give in, never give in, never, never, never, never—in nothing, great or small, large or petty—never give in except to convictions of honour and good sense."'

Blimey, I didn't expect that, thought Anna.

'Don't look at me like that,' said Eddie. 'As it happens, I'm a great fan of your prime minister. Perhaps he might teach my country a thing or two.'

Anna smiled as she glanced at her companion. 'Well, he is half-American on his mother's side after all, so I suppose that almost makes him one of you lot.'

Eddie returned her smile. For the second time in as many minutes, their eyes locked together. This time, Eddie shied away first.

'OK, I'll tell you what I can. The mortuary—'

'The mortuary?' said Anna, cutting Eddie off in his tracks.

'Do you want to know or not? The lieutenant's voice revealed a sharp edge born of frustration with his companion. 'To tell you the truth, I thought the man at the cottage hospital looked familiar and noticed your reaction to me checking his earlobe. I told the truth about calling my boss, but it was to ask permission to visit Bletchley, not submit a routine report.'

Well, knock me down with a feather. He's finally letting me in. I wonder what changed his mind? thought Anna.

'We now know his name is Sidney Langham,' continued Eddie. 'I knew him by another name—only for a short time; less than a week in fact, but that old cut in his ear stuck with me.'

'You met him at Bletchley Park, didn't you?'

Eddie nodded. 'Don't expect me to tell you the how's and why's, but what I will say is they found him wandering in the grounds and held him for interrogation. I was involved in that interrogation. The man was terrified and told us a story about getting off his train at the wrong station and looking for someone who could tell him which train he should catch to Cambridge.'

'Cambridge?' said Anna.

'You got it; we didn't believe him for a second given he could have asked anyone at Bletchley station. Anyway, he persisted with his story. I have to say the slight accent he spoke with didn't help— an odd mixture of French and Dutch as far as I could make out. Anyway, we concluded he didn't pose a threat and let him go under surveillance, and that was the end of my involvement with him. Nothing more was mentioned of the man, so I assumed they had assessed him as not posing a threat—otherwise he'd have been locked up, or worse.'

What else don't I know about Eddie?

Anna shook her head. 'And you've kept this to yourself all this time?'

'Sometimes we don't have a choice. Anyway, it happened before we met. In fact, I travelled here straight from… well, the place we're talking about. That's when—'

'You almost killed me by knocking me off my bike.'

'I was going to say that's when I came to Three-Mile-Bottom to begin my new job. The two were completely unrelated.'

'Until now,' replied Anna as she glanced in the rear-view mirror of Eddie's sports car.

'As you say. But I wasn't to know. We put him through the mill, I can tell you, but he stuck to his story. In hindsight, it was a mistake to release him, because if we'd kept him in custody, he'd still be alive.'

Anna glanced at the rear-view mirror again. 'But that still doesn't explain the state you got yourself in the other day, even you must tire of wearing my father's clothes by now?'

Anna's question prompted her companion to inspect his ill-fitting suit. 'You can say that again,' he muttered as, for the hundredth time, Eddie pulled on the end of his jacket sleeves to cover his exposed flesh.

'I went back to Bletchley Park to check the files, to see if there was anything in Langham's interrogation notes that might give me a clue, but discovered nothing other than confirmation of the crescent-shaped injury to the man's ear. I wasn't the only one interested in him. Someone broke into my room while I slept. I imagine they'd been watching me, thinking I'd have something of use to them, a file, or notes. Either way, I woke and realised someone was in the bedroom. That's when he, or they, hit me. I remember little after that. To be honest, I wandered around Bletchley for the next day or so in a bit of a daze. Concussion, I expect, but finally I recalled where I'd come from, except I remembered the pub, not my billet. The rest you know.'

This gets crazier by the minute. But at least it's making sense. Poor Eddie, thought Anna.

Anna checked the rear mirror for a third time.

'What are you looking at?'

'See for yourself.'

Eddie spent a few seconds with his head turned towards the old house. 'Nope, I don't get it, there's nothing there.'

Anna frowned. 'That's my point. It's as if we were never inside. Look, the cars have gone. In fact, thinking back, I'm not even sure they were there when we came out. I dunno, there must be a back way out. Look, the place is in darkness... way beyond shutting the curtains for the blackout. See, not a single chink of light because there aren't any lights on; the place looks deserted. It's as if we never went inside.'

Eddie took a second, longer look at the run-down property. 'Perhaps our Mr Grey is telling us something. Time to go, not least as Grey made clear, the clock's running.'

Eight-thirty on a Friday morning followed the pattern of every other school day as Helen coaxed young Vinny to get a move on, ready for the three-minutes' walk to school. This time Anna remained clear of the fray as she thought through the events of the previous day and what might lie ahead.

How do we get Fox-Marsden to talk to us? And what do we say if he agrees? And there's proving a link to Sidney. Plus...

Vinny shocked Anna out of her internal musing as he crashed into her bedroom, ran to the dressing table, and gave her a hug as she attempted to finish combing her hair.

'Let me breathe, young man, you're getting so strong.'

The youngster let go of his surrogate sister and folded his arms at ninety-degrees as if mimicking Mr Universe. 'Look at them muscles. I'm stronger than anyone at school.'

'Perhaps you are, my lad. Make sure you use your muscles to beneficial effect, and not to show off. Now, get yourself downstairs or you'll have you-know-who after you.'

Mention of her mother sent the lad scampering down the stairs, despite Anna's plea for him to be careful.

I'll miss that little chap so much when he goes back to Liverpool, thought Anna.

Five minutes later, calm had returned to the vicarage. Relishing breakfast alone, Anna took a last glance at her reflection in the dressing table mirror before sauntering downstairs and into the kitchen. No sooner had she done so than the back door opened and two familiar figures entered.

There goes my peace and quiet, she thought.

'If you think I'm making breakfast for you two, you're mistaken. A mug of tea and that's your lot — and you're only getting that because I'm making one for myself. Now, sit and don't make a noise, I'm still waking up.'

'That's us told off good and proper,' said Tom Bradshaw as he winked at Eddie, who now wore his full military uniform.

The two men sat opposite one another at the pine kitchen table and chatted quietly among themselves as Anna fried two slices of bread in the smallest amount of butter and fat. The egg she'd expected to have with her bread failed to materialise as she looked forlornly into the larder.

That'll be Mum being soft with Vinny again, thought Anna.

Settling for bread only, Anna brewed the tea, popped the fried bread on a plate and transported the lot to the table in two short journeys. 'And you can both keep your eyes off my bread. Come anywhere near it and you'll get the sharp end of my fork.'

'I'd forgotten you're not what we call a morning person,' said Tom.

Their host studiously ignored them as she tucked into her bread and glanced at her father's newspaper.

Not like Dad to leave it in here, she thought.

'Look at this.'

The men broke off their own conversation to glance at the paper.

"NAZI RUSH TO TOBRUK"[iii], read the headline.

'Do you think we'll lose it?' said Anna.

Eddie studied the paper's short analysis. 'Rommel is a top-notch commander; I'd say he's the best the enemy has, and it doesn't look good from what I'm reading here.'

A deflated atmosphere descended on the kitchen as Anna crunched her fried bread as quietly as possible, while her guests each sipped their tea without making further comment.

Just then, the vicar strolled into the kitchen, hands in pockets as if he hadn't a care in the world. 'Judging by the general air of despair, I assume you've seen the news about North Africa? A canny man, Rommel is. If we give an inch, he'll take more than a mile, you wait and see.'

With that, the vicar turned on his heels and left the way he'd arrived.

Charles' sudden appearance and vanishing act caused the other three to break into laughter.

'I'll say this for your father,' said Tom. 'He certainly knows how to leave an impression.'

Anna picked up on the levity. 'Right, that's enough of the doom and gloom. I'm awake now. Who is doing what today?'

Anna's sudden burst of energy caught the men by surprise as they concentrated on their refreshment.

'Blimey, that's a quick change of gear,' said Tom. 'Er, well, I intend on catching up with Herbert Trethel to see if he's come up with anything that can help us identify the car's owner.'

'And we have a certain top-hatted gentleman to talk to,' said Eddie.

'A top—'

'Don't ask, Tom. The truth is a strange thing. We'll tell you if anything comes of it.'

Anna gathered up her plate and empty mug and placed them

into the deep stone sink, returning for the other two mugs before reuniting them all in the soapy water that Helen had left from earlier in the morning to save wasting it.

As she cleared a thin film of butter and fat from her plate with a scouring pad, she noticed a man stood on the other side of the street.

Is he watching the house?

Distracted by Eddie asking where Ascot was, Anna momentarily took her eyes off the man. When she looked again, he'd gone.

Strange?

Thinking no more on the matter, Anna finished the dishes and left them to dry on the beechwood drainer.

'Well, I'd best be off,' said Tom as he made his way to the back door. 'Catch up later?'

'See you,' said Anna. 'Oh, and by the way, have you sorted a new date with Fanny yet?'

'Don't ask,' he responded after poking his head back around the open door, before finally disappearing, giving Anna a cheery wave as he passed the kitchen window.

Both the kitchen's remaining occupants seemed content to allow quiet to descend as Anna completed her final bits of tidying up, while Eddie thumbed his way through the Daily Express.

After several minutes, Anna moved towards the hallway. 'Time to make that call. You or me?'

Eddie looked up from the sports pages. 'You, I think. Men are suckers for a woman's charm.'

'Why did I know you were going to say that? I'll give you charm, lieutenant. Now, get yourself sat on those stairs while I see if I can trace his number — not that there's any guarantee he'll even be in.'

'Just remember what we agreed. He's desperate to get some evidence that proves he's an aristocrat, so all you need to do is say you've some important information... I reckon he'll bite your hand off for it,' said the lieutenant.

Anna nodded, 'yep, I agree, I'll... oh, it's connected,' she replied, her heart racing at the thought of knowingly telling an untruth.

'Yes, that's right, operator, Fox-Marsden, although you might have him down as the baronet of Sidborne... yes, that's it... you're so kind, yes, I'll wait.'

The two friends exchanged frustrated glances as the operator took what felt like an age to come back with the results of her endeavours.

'Crikey, she's putting me through. now. I didn't expect that. Come here so you can catch what he says.'

Eddie sprang to his feet and hunched over so that he was at the same height as Anna, listening through the Bakelite telephone handset.

'Second Baronet Sidborne. To whom do I have the pleasure of speaking?'

She heard a voice on the crackling line.

'Hello, to whom am I speaking?' repeated the man.

Here goes, thought Anna.

'Yes, I hear you. My name is...' she hesitated as panic set in. Searching for inspiration, she looked around the hallway until her gaze settled on the hat stand. 'My name is Hat... ter. Patricia Hatter.'

'And what may I do for you, Miss Hatter. I presume it is miss?'

'Oh, yes, indeed.' Anna could feel herself cringe at the crassness of her words. 'I... I have something to your advantage. A tree, you might say.'

After a momentary pause, the man answered. 'A tree? I'm not in need of such a thing, good day to you.'

'No... no, please wait.' Anna listened to check if he'd ended the call.

'I'm waiting, young lady.'

'Oh, thank you and I apologise for not making myself clearer. It's come to my attention, family you know, that certain elements within the nobility doubt your claim to the baronetcy.' She paused, expecting the man to respond. The line again fell silent. 'I think such people are being beastly to you and should act as befits their rank in society.'

'I see,' said the man. 'And…'

Anna didn't hesitate this time. 'I have your family tree and can prove your lineage. I can show without doubt that you're entitled to the title Second Baronet Sidborne, but I must see you to hand over the document.'

'Let us do precisely that, my dear. Where are you?'

Anna panicked again. Eddie prompted a response she might try.

'I'm in Cambridge now, but only for today. It's hush-hush after that, if you understand my meaning?'

'Oh, yes, we must keep things hush-hush.' Anna mouthed to Eddie that she thought the man misunderstood her meaning. Eddie leaned back from the telephone to avoid the sound of his chuckling being heard at the other end.

'Are you still there, young lady?'

If he calls me young lady once more, I'll pull his tongue through the telephone cable, thought Anna.

'Yes, I'm here. Can you meet today?'

'That will be perfect. I'm in Newmarket later this morning. It's not that far from Cambridge. Do you think you might pop across and show me what you have?'

Anna looked at Eddie, who'd recovered and now heard every word.

'Absolutely,' he whispered.

'I beg your pardon. Do you have a cold?'

That was enough to set Eddie off again. This time Anna pushed the American away to put distance between her telephone call and his giggles.

'You're so perceptive. In fact, I'm recovering, but thank you for your concern and yes, I can be in Newmarket at, shall we say, one o'clock.'

'Splendid,' replied the man. 'Meet me in the Jockey's Boot tea shop on High Street. You can't miss it. Until then, goodbye young lady.'

Anna almost threw the handset back onto its cradle on once again hearing the refrain she hated so much.

'That was the simple bit. Now you *must* turn on the charm if we are to get anything out of that oaf.'

Chapter Thirteen: To Newmarket

Newmarket, King Charles II's favourite racecourse and for other royal pursuits of an amorous nature, nestled in its soft Suffolk landscape surrounded by racing gallops and stud farms which merged seamlessly into the town itself.

As Eddie's car navigated a crossroad on the edge of Newmarket that gave them access to the high street, the town's iconic Victorian clock announced to the world it was twelve-forty-five. 'We'll have to split up once we find the Jockey's Boot in case our erstwhile baronet catches on that I've brought company,' said Anna.

Eddie pointed to an advertising sign hung above a cafe fifty feet ahead. 'I agree, I'll stay in the car but park so that I can see who comes and goes from the place. Are you OK with that?'

Anna gave her companion a sideways glance. 'I can look after myself... most of the time, so yes, that's fine. I'll come back to the car as soon as I'm done.'

'Hang on a minute, I've an idea.' Eddie scanned the roadside for a suitable place to park while remaining unobtrusive among the Jockey's Boot patrons. 'Why don't you walk to the train station when you've finished? That way if anyone follows you, your cover story of having travelled from Cambridge will look genuine.'

'Why should anyone follow me?'

Eddie gave his companion a wry smile. 'Anna, you are naive. You don't think someone like our would-be baronet travels alone, do you? Not if he's hitched up with Oswald Mosley's lot. Unless he's one of their top men, they'll watch him.'

'So how do we know who the good guys and baddies are?'

'We don't, Anna. And that includes our new friend, Mr Grey.'

The lieutenant pulled up a good fifty feet from the cafe and tucked his vehicle behind a large saloon car, but with an unobstructed view of Anna's destination. 'This should do. Remember, play your cards close to your chest. Get him to talk. My guess is he's used to babbling on to anyone who'll take this baronet stuff seriously, but remember, he'll be wary of you. Think about how you'd feel if the reverse had happened. You'd think it a trap. He knows the authorities are watching him. We have to hope his obsession to prove his title will overcome the doubts about you he will have.'

'Got you,' replied Anna as she opened the tiny door of the sports car. 'I'll put my poshest voice on and tell him I heard about his plight from a distant cousin who went through something similar years ago.'

Eddie looked flabbergasted. 'Is that true?'

'Sort of. He's a distant cousin who now lives in Argentina. I'll tell Fox-Marsden that we remained close, and I get the occasional letter from him, post permitting. I've never met the man. Dad told me about him years ago.' Anna became aware Eddie was giving her a perplexed look. 'What?'

'Are you telling me you're related to the king?' replied Eddie.

Anna burst out laughing. 'The king? What are you talking about? Members of the British aristocracy aren't all related to the royal family you know. Granted, some are, often the result of trysts out of wedlock, but the vast majority aren't. A baronet comes bottom of the pile, in fact, below a baron, but above a knight of the realm.'

'I'm confused,' replied Eddie.

'What's confusing about being the lowest rank of the British aristocracy?'

The lieutenant shrugged his shoulders 'Outranking a knight sounds OK, I suppose.'

'Don't confuse money or influence with a title', said Anna, 'Most of them are broke now—inheritance tax laws after WWI saw to that. The secret to their success is their title makes them cocky… snobbish. It opens doors to power and influence for them and is the sort of thing that allows them to get away with murder, literally sometimes.'

'If that's the case, it's more reason to watch yourself with Lord Snooty over tea and caviar, or whatever it is the British upper class have for lunch.'

As Anna went to close the car door, she gave Eddie one last glance. 'I suspect it will be tea and currant cake without the currants, but yes, I'll take care. By the way, I presume you'll follow me to the train station. I don't fancy sharing a train back to Norwich with a carriage load of leave-happy soldiers. So, none of that American sense of humour, OK?'

'Me?' replied Eddie as he winked at his companion.

He watched as Anna sauntered down the busy high street as if she didn't have a care in the world, stopping occasionally to take in the latest fashions on display in shops that all referred to their French lineage.

Eddie peered through the small windscreen of his sports car as Anna looked up at the unmissable image of a jockey boot above the doorway, before disappearing inside the cafe. The lieutenant looked to the side and rear of the car to check if anyone had followed his companion into the establishment.

Satisfied she wasn't followed, Eddie settled in for what he expected to be a long wait.

The tall town clock, which looked for all the world like a miniature version of London's Big Ben, continued its relentless progress. As the clock struck two o'clock, Eddie sprang to life as he spotted Anna leaving the cafe. Despite what they'd agreed, she fleetingly looked in his direction, before realising what she'd done and distracted herself by checking her hair remained tidy in the reflection of a men's footwear shop next to the cafe. After a few seconds, Anna moved off, strolling in the station's direction. As before, she occasionally stopped to look in a shop window as if an item had gained her attention.

Eddie turned the car ignition, making sure not to rev its engine and attract unwanted attention. As he moved forward, a man came out of the Jockey's Boot Cafe, looked to his left, then right, before taking off at speed. Only when Anna momentarily looked back did the man stop and turn his back to the prevailing breeze to light a cigarette.

The walk to the station took Anna less than five minutes, during which she avoided further backward glances. As she entered the station, the man came to a halt, waited for two minutes, turned around and began walking back to the town centre.

'Did he follow me?' said Anna in a breathless tone as she climbed into the sports car and gave Eddie an anxious glance.

'He did, although I have to say he was hardly the world's best mob goon, or whatever he does for a living. You'd have thought getting a good quality thug to do that sort of stuff should be easy in wartime. Perhaps they don't pay enough.'

Anna frowned at her companion. 'That's not funny, Eddie. I wondered about him in the cafe, sat on his own in the corner nursing a half-empty cup of tea. The waitress looked as though she was fed up with him. People were waiting for a table and there he sat, like a sleeping Buddha. I honestly thought at one point that—'

'The baronet, Anna? What about your lunch partner?'

The lieutenant's abrupt interruption stopped Anna in her tracks. 'Alright, Mr Bossy Pants, there's no need to be rude… and don't you shake your head at me, or I'll biff you one.'

Did that sound as ridiculous as I think it did?

A spontaneous bout of laughter filled the tiny car as both its occupants gave in to the absurdity of the situation.

'Come on, turn this car of yours around and get us back home, and I'll tell you all about the deluded one.'

As they left the train station, drove down the high street and passed Newmarket's miniature Big Ben, Eddie put his foot down as they sped along a ramrod straight road that skirted one of many stable gallops and made for Lipton St Faith.

'… We ordered our tea and cake. He went for the apple pie and I chose—'

'You're doing this on purpose, aren't you?' said Eddie as he made rapid progress towards the A14 main road.

'On purpose?'

'You know precisely what you're doing, so stop playing about and let's get serious, shall we?'

'Spoilsport,' replied Anna, wearing a mischievous smile. 'If you must know, Lindsay was charm itself.'

'Lindsay, is it? You remember why we contacted the man?'

'Of course I do, but to be convincing, I had to make friends with him. He now thinks Patricia Hatter is the best thing since sliced bread.'

'Patricia? Old-fashioned, don't you think?' replied Eddie.

'Old money is old fashioned, so I thought it fitted the bill. He seemed convinced about my erstwhile Argentinian relative. After that, he treated me as an equal, though I have to say keeping that posh accent up was a bit of a trial. I dropped a bit of cake onto my napkin and allowed my Norfolk accent to creep through. I'm not so sure he noticed, though. He seemed nervous, you know, always looking out of the window to see if anyone was watching.'

The lieutenant turned right onto the main Cambridge to Ipswich trunk road and kept his eye out for a split in the road that led onto the A11 Norwich Road. 'I suspect he was looking anywhere but at the goon in the corner. Of course, what we don't know is whether he employed the, what did you call him? Yes, the sitting Buddha directly and made a ham-fisted attempt to distance himself from his minder, or if Oswald Mosley's organisation had "gifted" the thug to Fox-Marsden. Either way, something isn't right.'

Anna thought about what her companion had said. 'Do you know, I think you have a point. After spending an hour with Lind... I mean, Fox-Marsden, it's clear he isn't the sharpest chisel in the toolbox. In fact, I found him dim, except on the one subject he obsesses about, his title. Mention that and he comes alive with a mixture of anger, indignation and entitlement.'

'That's fine,' said Eddie as he veered off the A14 and onto the Norwich Road. 'But our Mr Grey must have his reasons for, err, "suggesting" we contact the man. Did he say anything at all that might satisfy Grey?'

'Eddie, after an hour of him grandstanding about the great wrong he'd suffered, and how my additional evidence would change everything, I felt exhausted. It was hard to shut him up, it was all about...'

'Yes?' replied Eddie after a few moments of silence.

'There was one thing. He prattled on about Greece. I thought it odd, but he tied it back into his claim for the baronetcy. Now, what did he say? It was something like, "O lykos erchetai". It made little sense to me, still doesn't.'

Eddie shook his head. 'Nor me, but it might mean something to the mysterious Mr Grey. Anyway, once I've told him that will be that and we'll be shot of him.'

'Are you sure about that?' said Anna.

The lieutenant looked at his passenger without commenting.

Within a short time, the familiar sight of Lipton St Faith's squat Norman bell tower came into view.

'Look, Tom's waiting for us. I wonder if he's got any news for us?' said Anna as she pointed to a police car parked outside the vicarage.

Once stationary, Eddie and Anna left the sports car behind to greet their mutual friend. As they approached, the driver's door swung open.

'Fanny,' said Anna. 'I was expecting Tom, but it's nice to see you all the same. Is he in the vicarage?'

Why is she looking so serious? thought Anna.

'I've been assigned to drive you to… well, that doesn't matter for now. Could you get into the car, please?'

'What?' said Anna as she checked with Eddie to make sense of Fanny's request. 'Can't it wait? It's almost five and I'm starving… and it's dark.'

The driver moved to the rear kerb-side passenger door and held it wide open. 'I'm afraid not. I have my orders. Not even Tom knows I'm here and to tell you the truth, I don't feel comfortable about this, but—'

'It's OK, Fanny, and I apologise if I sounded short with you. It's a shock, that's all.'

Fanny gestured toward the passenger door. 'What I can tell you is where we're going is less than fifteen minutes away and a familiar face will be there to meet you.'

Bless, she's doing her best to reassure us. I wish it did.

The brief journey took place in silence as Anna made a mental note of each location she recognised in the early evening darkness. As they neared their destination, she realised where they were being taken.

It's St Benet's Abbey. There's nothing else down here.

As the police car wended its way down ever narrower lanes, bordered by high hedges, Anna knew that after a final precarious blind bend, the scant remains of the Abbey and mill would come into view in its desolate landscape.

'We may only be a short distance by car from the village but it might as well be in the middle of nowhere.'

Fanny brought the car to a halt with its headlamps pointing towards the red brick conical shaped building, which had long ago lost its sails and canopy. A single opening, large enough to hoist grain between floors, pierced the upper floor. At ground level, its flared base merged with the derelict remains of a now unidentifiable Abbey building.

'Best see what's going on,' said Anna as she opened the car door and stepped into an overgrown patch of grass. 'Charming, I don't think,' she mused.

Eddie suffered the same fate as he alighted, while Fanny remained steadfast in her seat. No sooner had the pair walked forward a few paces to stand side-by-side than a figure appeared in a doorless opening in the shattered brickwork.

'So glad you both could make it. How was Newmarket?'

Grey, how did he get here? thought Anna.

'You seem to know a great deal about our movements. Why does that not surprise me, Mr Grey?' said Eddie.

The man held out an open palm while holding a lit hurricane lamp at head height with his other hand. 'As you can see, I've nothing to hide. I asked that you contact Fox-Marsden, which you did, and now I wish to know how lunch went at the Jockey's Boot, Miss Grix.'

We came straight back, so there's no way he could know where I met the baronet without having tapped the vicarage telephone line?

'Why don't you tell me since you seem to know everything else the lieutenant and I get up to?'

A second figure emerged to stand behind Grey. He, too, held a hurricane lamp, which gave both men the ghoulish appearance of the undead.

'Inspector Spillers. What are you doing here?' Anna's surprise was complete.

What on earth is going on?

Spillers maintained a stoic silence as his eyes bore into the back of Grey's head.

'I shall reveal all in a few minutes,' said Grey. 'We await our last visitor... Ah, I see him now.'

The sound of a car's engine filled the chill evening air.

Another police car... It can't be?

Anna's intuition proved correct as Sergeant Tom Bradshaw emerged from the gloom.

'Let's get out of this breeze, shall we,' said Grey as he turned, forcing Inspector Spillers to stand aside, and vanished into the decrepit building's roofless interior.

Tom Bradshaw gave Fanny a brief glance as he approached his two friends.

He seems cool towards her, thought Anna.

'What's this all about, Tom?' said Eddie.

'Beats me. I took a call at home telling me to get here pronto. So we'd better get on, they're waiting for us.'

Tom pointed at the ethereal glow from the hurricane lamps as they cast an eerie, soft glow around the abandoned building's interior. 'Come on.'

They could have given us a light. I can't see where I'm treading, Thought Anna.

Once inside the brick cone of the abandoned mill, Grey took centre stage. Setting his hurricane lamp on the floor, the up-lighting effect cast a giant's shadow on the convex shape of the old brick walls. 'I apologise for all this clandestine malarky, but one can never be too careful about who's listening.'

'What, like tapping someone's telephone line, Mr Grey?' Anna's pointed question had the desired effect.

'Ah, that. Well yes, you're, of course, correct. Although most distasteful, I felt it necessary in the circumstances.'

'Circumstances?' spat Anna.

Grey clasped his hands together and held them out, as if pleading for forgiveness. 'I had to be certain you would put the call in. In other circumstances I would apologise, but as it is, well, it's my job.'

Anna looked at Inspector Spillers, who immediately lowered his gaze.

'Did you know about this?'

Grey answered for him. 'No, no. Please be aware that the civilian services have no power to do such things. Inspector Spillers was neither consulted nor told about the outcome of my actions. He is here because I have something to say to you, once you've briefed me on your meeting with Fox-Marsden, although his actual name is Jeremy Kipper.'

'Kipper,' exclaimed Eddie.

'I agree, lieutenant, not as regal as Lindsay Fox-Marsden, Second Baronet of Sidborne, is it? The fact of the matter is that we gave him that identity five years ago.'

'We?' commented Anna.

'Let us simply say he agreed to serve his country, just like you two have, except it went to his head. Although he failed miserably in his task, so fulsomely did he adopt his role that he now believes himself to be that person — quite mad of course. This makes him dangerous because of what he knows and who he now associates with. However, I was correct, wasn't I? Your offer to prove his case, which I thought brilliant, opened a metaphorical door?'

Eddie neared the hurricane lamp so he could get a clear look at Grey's features. 'And does that goon who followed Anna to the train station belong to you?'

Grey shook his head. 'lieutenant, we listened in on Miss Grix's telephone call. I didn't have anyone on the ground in Newmarket, nor do I know what you discussed, hence our little gathering this evening. I imagine he was, shall we say, "chaperoned" by his handler courtesy of Mosley's network.'

Anna joined the lieutenant. 'I thought you said last night that Mosley's interned?'

'He is,' replied Grey, 'And as I also said, he's kept many followers; too many for us to track, so, from time to time, something interesting pops up we wish to look at. Our hapless would-be baronet is one such interest. Now, Miss Grix, did the man say anything of interest to you?'

Anna spent the next five minutes briefing Grey on her meeting, which he listened to without interrupting.

'Is that it?'

'Mr Grey, do you want me to make something up? I can tell you he was furious. You said he was mad. Well, I don't know about that, but he certainly holds a grudge. Now I know it's aimed at you... or whoever you work for. Now, it's been a long day and after listening to an endless diatribe why Fox-Marsden... or Jeremy Kipper, or whoever, feels he's entitled to a baronetcy and droning on about Greece, well, I've had—'

'Greece, Miss Grix?'

Anna looked perplexed. 'That's what I said, didn't I? He spoke gibberish… well, actually, I think it was a bad attempt at Greek.'

Grey became animated as he picked the hurricane lamp up and held it up to Anna.

'That's close enough,' said Eddie, as he moved in front of her.

Isn't that sweet? thought Anna.

Grey took a step back. 'Forgive me, I didn't mean to alarm Miss Grix. Please accept my apology, but you said he spoke Greek. Can you remember what he said?'

Anna thought for a moment. 'If you make fun of my pronunciation. I'll stop and won't repeat myself. Do you understand, Mr Grey?'

Grey nodded. 'Please, Miss Grix, continue.'

Anna reflected for several seconds to recount the man's words as best she could. 'He said something like O lykos erchetus… no, he said erchetai.'

'The wolf comes,' said Inspector Spillers. 'He said "The wolf comes".' I studied ancient and modern Greek at University. Clearly some of it stayed with me. The question is, what does it mean?'

Grey lapsed into his own world.

As Anna watched, she noticed his eyes darting from left to right as if speed-reading the most important document in the world. 'Does it mean something to you?'

He nodded. 'We know of an enemy operative who uses the code name "Lykos" who, it seems, is an active Nazi agent. We suspect they work for British intelligence, which makes this person a serious threat to the war effort, and, therefore, the country's very existence. We must stop them whatever the cost.'

I don't like the real world, thought Anna.

Grey moved off, prompting Eddie into action. 'Two questions for you: You keep calling the person, "they" Don't you know who he is?'

The man shook his head. 'We've been aware of someone leaking low-level information for a while now, but they're astonishingly good at what they do and hiding their identity, so no, we don't know who this person is. Our hope is that Fox-Marsden does. You said two questions?'

'When we convened, you mentioned you wanted to say something to us. Perhaps you might now enlighten us?' said Eddie.

Grey walked to the mill entrance before turning to face his audience. 'I had intended tell you your mission was complete and apart from the usual stuff about the Official Secrets Act, leave it at that.'

'I feel a "but" coming, Mr Grey,' said Anna.

'Yes, Miss Grix, given what I now know, you're all at risk and safer working with my people. You won't know who they are. They will introduce themselves when required. They may act to protect you without either informing you beforehand or briefing you on the outcome of their actions. Please understand this, if I'm correct in my thinking, Lykos is in the area for a reason I don't yet understand. You must play your part in helping to identify and track this person. Once we know their whereabouts, we'll deal with them.'

'Deal with them, how?' asked Anna.

Grey gave her a steely look before disappearing into the night.

Chapter Fourteen: From the Shadows

An invitation by Inspection Spillers to gather back at Lipton St Faith police station to pool their intelligence proved an easy one for Anna and the lieutenant to accept.

By seven o'clock, Tom, Anna, and Eddie each occupied a seat in the Inspector's sparsely furnished office.

'Time to put our cards on the table,' began Spillers. 'I have no wish to see anyone put in harm's way. However, that's where we find ourselves. Bradshaw, are you content to continue leading the investigation into what I think we can say is now a murder enquiry?'

Tom's serious features mirrored those of his companions. 'I am, sir.'

'Good,' replied Spillers. 'Be assured that I won't leave you exposed. In normal circumstances, you know as well as I do that a junior officer, no matter how high they're held in esteem by their superior, would not be let loose on a murder enquiry. However, these are far from normal circumstances, so have your wits about you. Remember, always maintain contact with me and do nothing that puts either yourself, or these two, in danger.' Spillers pointed a finger at Anna, then Eddie.

'I understand, sir.'

Fanny brought in a tray of tea.

'What are you still doing on duty, Miss Coulson?'

Fanny smiled as she set the refreshments on the Inspector's desk. 'I thought you could all do with a nice cup of tea after being out in the cold before I set off for home, sir.' She gave Tom a sideways glance and smiled. Anna noticed Tom reciprocating the intimate gesture.

Turning to leave the room, Fanny got as far as the door when Spillers spoke. 'Wait a minute, Miss Coulson. Perhaps this affects you as much as the rest of us.'

'This?' replied Fanny as she let go of the tarnished brass doorknob.

'You'd better stay. If we were under surveillance out at the Abbey mill, you may also be at risk of harm. I can't go over all the details now, and much of what we shall speak about will sound odd. However, I'll leave it to Sergeant Bradshaw to fill you in on anything else he feels you need to know. For now, I need your absolute assurance that what you hear remains in the strictest of confidence. Lives, including yours, may depend on it.'

A confused looking Fanny slowly nodded as she moved to stand behind Tom's chair. 'You have my word, sir.'

She's picking fluff off Tom's shoulder. Hmm, thought Anna. He'll have to decide about her soon.

A momentary silence fell across the room as its occupants took in the Inspector's solemn words. All, except for Fanny, took a sip of their drink. Eddie half-turned in his chair and offered her a share of his, which she declined.

'Let's recap what we know, or at least *think* we know,' began Spillers. 'It's our joint belief that the body in the car was that of Sidney Langham, who was on his way from Appleby in Cambridge to further his ecclesiastical journey local to us at St Paul's.'

'We also know he couldn't drive, and that his train route took him to Aylsham, from where he would've taken a taxi to St Paul's,' added Tom.

185

'Good point,' responded Spillers. 'So how does a young man in full church garb come to die in a car accident on the outskirts of Lipton St Faith?'

The room fell silent again.

'And there's the fact that Sidney's mood changed suddenly about six months ago. At least that's what his best... well, his only friend at college, Walter Teesdale, told us. He also said Sidney's spiritual supervisor, Dr Janson, shouted at him before he left the college for the train station,' said Anna.

'Didn't Janson say he was Polish?' added Tom.

'What has that got to do with anything?' responded Spillers. 'Many Polish people came here before their country fell to German forces. In fact, some of our finest and bravest RAF pilots are Polish. Think back to their vital contribution to repelling Hermann Goring's onslaught in 1940.'

Tom hesitated before answering his superior's point. 'It... well, when he joined the meeting Anna and I had with the college principal, he, well, he was angry.'

'And don't forget the look he gave Walter. That stare was sharp,' added Anna.

Spillers sat back in his chair and took another sip of his tea. 'It seems to me it might be worth going back to that college to dig a little deeper into Dr Janson's background. Bradshaw, sort that out, will you?'

'Yes, sir.'

The office door opened to reveal the portly figure of Dick Ilford, the desk sergeant.

'Sergeant Ilford,' said Spillers, almost spilling his tea as he placed it back down onto his desk. 'I don't want to hear another word about Mrs Clifford's cat. It's not the Christian thing to say, but I don't care if the mangy moggie has got himself catnapped by the Nazis. I refuse to meet that woman again.'

The surprised look on the other members of the meeting mirrored the desk sergeant. 'Er, no, sir. I thought you'd like to know your wife's been on wanting to know when you'll be home. It seems your tea is spoiling and I'm to tell you if you're not back by eight-thirty, the dog's having it.'

All eyes fell on the Inspector who occupied himself looking at the ceiling and shaking his head. 'Yes, yes, never mind all that. Thank you, Ilford, that will be all.'

The sergeant made as if to speak again.

'I said that will be all,' repeated Spillers.

Anna did her best to stifle her giggles. Looking at the other three, she knew they were having the same issue.

'As you say, sir,' said Ilford as he withdrew, while quietly closing the office door.

'Now, where was I?' said Spillers, as if the previous two minutes had never happened. 'Oh, yes. Bradshaw, you see to Janson.'

'I will, sir,' responded Tom, while pinching his earlobe, hoping the pain might distract him from his superior's embarrassment.

Eddie, who had been silent until this point, roused. 'I suppose we should talk about the elephant in the room.'

'Grey, you mean?' replied Spillers.

'Yes. We know he had Anna and me under surveillance when we visited Appleby, presumably because he knew about my trip to... er.'

Spillers smiled. 'It's OK, lieutenant, you need not mention the location by name.'

Eddie visibly relaxed. 'Well, the man clearly knew I'd been there. Who knows, perhaps it was his goons that broke into my bedroom.'

Why didn't that come as a surprise to the Inspector, he didn't react at all?

187

'And when he "invited" Anna and me to spend the evening with him, all he seemed concerned about was us contacting the fake baronet who, as we now know, had previously worked for him, whatever he does.'

Tom looked shocked. 'This is all new to me.'

'There's more, Tom,' said Anna. 'Why do you think Grey reacted so strongly when he heard me say "Lykos"? My guess is there is a direct link between a rogue agent using the cover name Lykos, and Sidney Langham. I don't know what it is yet, but I'm sure there's something that connects them.'

The room once more fell into silence, allowing the occupants to absorb Anna's assessment.

'So,' began Eddie in a slow drawl. 'Perhaps Sidney was blackmailed into doing something he didn't want to do, got in deeper than he felt comfortable with, and tried to back out of the deal. What if Lykos murdered him?'

Spillers rose from his chair to walk a circuit of his small office. 'Which leads me to believe his task compromised this country's security and wellbeing of those who work to keep us safe.'

Anna turned to track Spillers' progress. 'Then why did Grey go so heavy on implying we were in danger? Surely if Lykos had dealt with Sidney, they'd scarper. After all, why risk hanging around and being picked up by our intelligence services?'

Spillers stopped pacing the room as he neared his desk and gave its mahogany top a loud slap, which made the others jump in unison. 'Because the mission, whatever it is, remains to be accomplished. Think about it, Langham refuses to do what he was told. Pays for it with his life, yet Lykos' handlers still demand the mission completed. That means—'

Eddie interrupted the Inspector. 'They're still in the area and on an active mission. The question is, what is that mission?'

* * *

'I need a pint after that,' said Eddie as he led Anna, Tom and Fanny into the packed bar of the King's Head. 'It's great to have a pub in every village. At home you have to travel for hours to get to one.'

Anna strolled through the main entrance, whose door Eddie held open. 'It serves you right for having such a big country,' she replied without looking at her companion.

'That's what you get for being chivalrous, eh, Tom?'

Bradshaw laughed as he took advantage of the lieutenant's polite act. 'What did you expect? It's Anna you're talking about?' At which point Fanny also breezed through.

'She is different, isn't she?' said Tom.

'Fanny?'

'No, I meant… oh, never mind,' replied Tom.

Both men laughed as they entered. The sight of a policeman brought the pub to a silenced standstill as a dozen pairs of eyes looked at Tom with suspicion.

'Settle down, lads. I've come off duty so you can relax, unless any of you have a crime you wish to admit carrying out?'

After a few seconds of continued silence, a roar of friendly derision filled the bar as the locals resumed their games of dominos and darts.

'I bet you love doing that,' said Betty Simpson, the pub owner, as the small group made it to the bar.

'I shouldn't, but I do,' replied Tom as he winked at Betty.

'You lot look as though you could do with a stiff drink, no cordial for you tonight, Anna. Am I right?'

You've no idea, Betty, thought Anna.

'I don't suppose we could use your lounge for a bit of peace, is there?'

'That bad, eh,' replied Betty. 'Of course, you can. You know the way. Two pints and two sherries, is it?'

'Thanks, Betty. Great job,' replied Anna as she led the way to their host's private quarters.

'Thank goodness for that,' said Fanny. 'And I can't wait for that sherry.'

The four companions settled into the comfortable space, each looking into the coal fire's calming glow.

'So, how is everyone feeling?' enquired Anna as she glanced at her three companions.

'I have to say, it's not how I expected my day to go,' said Fanny. 'I'm a part-time driver for the police, not a spy catcher... but it's sort of exciting, isn't it?'

Anna smiled while watching Eddie frown, while Tom gave Fanny a reflective glance.

He doesn't know if he feels anything for her, thought Anna.

A knock on the door signalled the arrival of their drinks. Tom sprang from his chair to help Betty by swinging the door wide open.

'Here we are, m'dears, get them down you. I can't stay; that lot want another round before I ring the bell for last orders.'

Anna glanced at her wristwatch.

Blimey, a quarter-to-ten already.

'That doesn't include you four. You're my private guests, isn't that so, Sergeant Bradshaw?'

'That will be in order, Mrs Simpson, although I shall have to make a note of it in my pocket-book.' Tom made as if to retrieve his official notepad from a breast pocket.

'Get away with you, you daft lump,' replied Betty with a broad smile as she withdrew and closed the door.

'A wonderful woman is Betty,' said Anna. 'Not everyone could have carried on after losing her hubby. I imagine running a pub is hard at the best of times, but to do it on your own, well...'

Tom nodded. 'Landlords... and landladies have a lot to put up with. If it's not rowdy drinkers, it's the likes of me checking up on them, and the excise duty people making sure the beer hasn't been watered down. I don't envy Betty one bit. That said, I admire her pluck.'

Fanny turned to Tom. 'Are you saying a woman can't do the job?'

I like your style, thought Anna.

Tom looked flummoxed. 'All I meant was—'

'I'm joking,' said Fanny, whisking her hand across Tom's knee.

Oh, yes.

'Oh… er, I see,' replied Tom.

He doesn't see at all.

As the group exchanged banter at Tom's expense, the door opened. This time, no knock heralded the interruption. Inspector Spillers stood back-lit by the dim lights of the bar, observing full blackout and smoke from a dozen pipes, causing a bluish haze to envelop the air.

'Has something happened, sir?' said Tom, getting to his feet.

'Trethel's been found dead. It looks like murder.'

Chapter Fifteen: The Missing Lecturer

The shock of Inspector Spillers' news still reverberated within Anna's head as the foursome followed him out of the pub without uttering a word, and down the darkened high street of Lipton St Faith.

'If you crush up, there'll be room for you all,' said the Inspector as he unlocked his car, which awaited its owner patiently outside the police station. With Tom Bradshaw in the front passenger seat, the other three crammed into the rear seat as Spillers brought the vehicle to life. Within seconds, the windows steamed up because of the breath of five anxious individuals filling the unheated interior of the car and condensing on its cold glass surfaces.

'I need you to keep the windscreen clear, Bradshaw, but make sure you don't knock the car out of gear leaning over to my side. It's temperamental.'

Tom complied, as Spillers sped from the village as rapidly as a blackened sky and shaded headlights against enemy bombers allowed.

'Where are we going, Inspector?' asked Tom.

Spillers leaned against the steering wheel, trying to get a better view out of the partially clear windscreen as he navigated around a blind bend. 'The garage where our recovery lorry took the car, Miss Coulson, you know to which garage I'm referring?'

'My uncle's place.'

Tom looked behind him, 'Are you OK, Fanny?'

That's the look of a policeman, not a suitor, thought Anna.

Within a few minutes, Spillers had successfully navigated the last of the meandering narrow lanes and eased the police car to a halt outside the garage. A dim light broke the otherwise unbroken darkness, and someone held a small oil lamp behind an almost closed door.

'We'd better get in, the clouds are breaking; we don't want to attract unwanted attention from forty-thousand feet above,' said Spillers.

Inside the sizeable garage workshop stood Fanny's uncle, his morose look testament to his sad discovery. 'The poor fella's over there, by the back of the wreck you brought the other day. I doubt he knew what hit him.' Fanny rushed over to her uncle and gave him a hug. 'Now, now, lass. Your old uncle is fine. Why don't you go to your Aunt May? She could do with the company?'

Fanny gave her uncle a lingering look, before landing a gentle peck on his cheek and making for the house which adjoined the garage complex.

Spillers and the others moved forward cautiously, being careful to avoid the risk of disturbing any evidence that might still be present at the crime scene.

'Have you moved or disturbed anything?' asked Spillers.

The garage owner shook his head. 'I thought we had a thief about the place - we get black marketeers trying their hand at nicking engine oil occasionally, but Boris always sees them off.'

'Boris?' said Spillers.

'Our dog. A great, scruffy lump of a thing who'd lick you to death given half the chance. But he hasn't half got a bark, so he scares folk off before he has a chance to show his soft side. He's loud enough to wake the dead, which in my case is a good thing because my wife says the only way she knows I'm still alive in bed is because I snore like a pig.'

In any other circumstance, that'd be funny, thought Anna.

'But you woke up this time?' said Spillers without reacting to the garage owner's surreal explanation concerning either his sleeping habits or his dog's habit of licking strangers.

'Well, to be fair, it was the wife who woke me. She's got sharp elbows when she wants. I came over and there he was.' The man nodded towards the corpse. 'I had a quick look around but found nothing. Boris had gone back to sleep, so I knew whoever had been here had run for it. Mind you, at first, I thought this chap was one of those black-market types I mentioned, but I saw that bruise on his neck. I can't see any way he did that to himself or fell on anything nearby that might have caused it.'

He's no fool for all his looks, thought Anna.

Spillers bent over the body, which lay prone on the oil-spattered concrete floor. 'He went down like a sack of potatoes. I doubt he knew what hit him.' The inspector closely examined a small, circular purplish-blue bruise to the base of the victim's skull. 'This is no argument among thieves or an accident. Whoever did this knew what they were doing. Look at the small puncture wound in the centre of the bruise; my guess is that severed his spinal cord. They had no intention of allowing the man to leave. The question is, why?'

Tom Bradshaw stepped forward, his police notebook open and ready to record events. 'I told you Herbert had agreed to look at the car for us, remember, sir? Perhaps the two connect? Him looking at the car and his death, I mean.'

'Yes, Sergeant Bradshaw, I'm quite aware what you meant. Are we to believe he found something to identify this car that led back to Sidney Langham's killer, or was this a pre-emptive strike by the murderer to remove the risk of anything coming to light?'

Fanny came back into the dimly lit space holding a tray of tea.

'Can you leave that over there, Miss Coulson, so we don't contaminate the crime scene?'

She did as Spillers asked and set the tray on top of a metal toolbox.

'How's your aunt?' asked her uncle.

'Grumpy. She's not happy at being woken up.'

'Good old Bess, she's feeling better,' replied Fanny's uncle. 'Best you get back to your aunt. It'll keep her mind off things, eh?'

Fanny smiled before giving Tom a sideways glance and exiting the workshop.

Leaving the tea where it rested, the garage's five live occupants stood in a semi-circle around the crumpled body of Herbert Trethel. Anna noticed Tom's restless demeanour. 'Are you OK, Tom?'

Whatever he says, I know he's not, thought Anna.

Tom didn't answer for a few seconds, instead he gazed unblinkingly at the body. Folding his arms, he turned to Anna. 'If I hadn't insisted we called in at his place on the way back from Cambridge the other day, he'd still be alive.'

Spillers cranked his head as if alerted to an unknown threat. 'We'll have none of that, Sergeant Bradshaw. You did your duty as you saw fit. Do not take responsibility for this dreadful event. If you wish, or expect, to progress in your career, you must set personal feeling aside. As an officer, you made a professional decision. There will be many other such decisions facing you in the years to come. It's for you to decide whether senior leadership is what you want. If it is, you must learn to protect yourself, otherwise you're of no use to me or those you'll command. Do you understand, Thomas?'

Goodness, I've never heard Spillers call him by his full name before, thought Anna.

Bradshaw snapped out of his melancholy. 'Yes, sir. I do.'

'Good man, now, what do we know of Herbert Trethel's working habits?'

'What do you mean?' asked Anna.

Spillers walked over to the tea tray and lifted a light blue mug with a small chip on its rim. 'Better get one before they go cold.'

The other three followed the Inspector's advice and joined Spillers around the toolbox.

'To answer your question, Miss Grix, Sergeant Bradshaw briefed me on, shall we say, Trethel's eccentric ways. Perhaps therein lies the possibility that our victim left something in that car to help us identify him. What do you think, sergeant?'

Tom frowned as he blew over the top of his tea mug and took a sip of the fiery liquid. Without warning, he put the mug back on the tray at such speed that some of its contents overspilled onto the tray. 'His arms.'

'What?' said Eddie, who'd remained in the background.

'His arms. Herbert never carried paper. He reckoned people might use it as evidence against him—he was a bit of a chancer, after all.' Tom briefly glanced over to the still shape of the motor engineer and offered a knowing smile. 'To avoid forgetting things, he was forever scribbling notes on his hands and arms. In fact, that's how he proved to me he was innocent over that car deal I told you about, Anna.'

Spillers and Eddie looked at Anna, expecting a measure of clarification.

'It's too long a story, but I know what Tom means.'

The other two exchanged glances and engaged in a mutual shaking of heads.

Tom made several brisk steps until he reached Herbert's body. 'Can you help me, Eddie? We need to get his jacket off so I can check his left arm.' The sergeant looked at his superior. A nod told him he had permission to continue.

Eddie joined his colleague and together they relieved the dead man of his jacket. Tom removed a gold cufflink from Herbert's left cuff and slowly rolled up the dead man's sleeve. 'You were right, Inspector. He left us something.'

Anna resisted the attempt to join Tom and Eddie. 'What have you found?

Tom looked at a brief series of letters and numbers. 'I think it reads: CE 1761.'

'That's a Cambridge registered car number plate,' said Eddie excitedly.

'How do you know?' said Anna, her voice tinged with scepticism.

Eddie smiled. 'It's one of those things that sticks in my head. I told you months ago the men in white coats said my brain works in funny ways, well number and letter sequences and what they mean is one of those things. Don't ask me how I do it, but I'm telling you. If our dead friend is correct, that car is registered in Cambridge.'

'Which only helps us if its original owner still owns the car.'

Tom shook his head. 'Not necessarily, Inspector. The car logbook would list all subsequent owners if it changed hands. We need to get a copy.'

'Wait a minute,' said Anna. 'Could there be a connection to Janson? He works and lives in Cambridge. Might he own a car? After all, he was seen arguing with Sidney Langham, wasn't he?'

All eyes fell on Inspector Spillers. 'It's doubly important you get yourself back to that college, Bradshaw. Get some sleep before driving back there with Miss Grix first thing tomorrow. I'll square it with the Chief Constable of Cambridge constabulary—providing his force gets the credit for any convictions, he'll be happy enough. Meanwhile,

I'll finish up here. I must find where on that vehicle Herbert Trethel discovered the index number. Without it, we have no firm evidence, and that poor man can't add to what he's already provided.'

Anna was still feeling the effects of the late night of the previous evening when she strolled languidly into the kitchen, only to be confronted with a young Liverpudlian devouring a large bowl of porridge, while talking twenty-to-the-dozen and shuffling a leather football between his feet under the kitchen table.

'He wants to go to the village green for a kick-about, but I've told him it's still too early,' said Helen as she prepared her daughter's breakfast. 'So, stranger, what were you up to yesterday? We hardly saw you, but I heard you come in. My bedside clock said it was half-past midnight. What on earth were you doing?'

She motioned towards Vinny, who remained busy with his porridge and football, while firing incessant questions at the vicar who did his best to concentrate on his newspaper while offering Vinny an occasional, *I see, Vinny,* and *is that so?*

'I get it,' whispered Anna's mother as she pointed for her daughter to take her seat at the table.

'You look knackered,' said Vinny, to the astonishment of the adults. The vicar allowed the top half of his paper to fold down to expose his surprised expression. 'Vincent O'Conner, where did you hear such distasteful language?'

I remember dad giving me that special look as a child!

The Scouser looked surprised at being admonished. 'It's where horses go when they can't pull their weight, everyone knows that.'

He's a sharp one.

'That may be, but Anna isn't a horse. At least last time I checked, she wasn't.'

'Hilarious, father.'

'No, but she looks like Mr Swanson's old nag before it went to the kna—'

'Yes, that will do, Vinny. I think we get the picture,' responded the vicar. '"She" is the cat's mother.'

Vinny stopped eating his porridge and frowned at the vicar. 'No, she isn't. If she isn't a horse like you said, she's your daughter. We don't have a cat?' Without saying another word, the Liverpudlian returned to his porridge and dribbling the football between his feet.

The three adults exchanged stupefied looks as they attempted to dissemble the boy's logic.

'I give up,' muttered the vicar as he flicked the top half of his paper up again.

Helen busied herself at the kitchen sink while Anna played with her breakfast.

I wonder what we'll find out at Cambridge today? she thought.

'You've a visitor,' said Helen.

Anna glanced at the wall clock. 'Heavens, I'm late. Don't let him in until I'm upstairs, he can't see me looking like—'

'A cat, or a horse, or whatever,' said Vinny, without lifting his gaze from the last of his porridge.

'You'd better get a move on,' said Helen, while turning to Vinny and running her wet hands through his thick locks. 'And you're a cheeky chap.'

Vinny shrugged his shoulders and carried on eating without breaking his stride.

In the few seconds between Helen saying Tom had arrived and him entering the kitchen, Anna had vanished, a thumping rhythm coming from the staircase the only evidence of her presence.

'I've caught her out?' said Tom as he pointed a finger at the ceiling.

Helen laughed, 'You have. Tea?'

Tom shook his head. 'Thanks, but no time. We've a lot to do today.'

The vicar folded his paper and laid it on the table so that Tom could read the headline. 'What do you think the Japanese are up to, eh? Oh, and by the way, good morning to you.'

Tom ambled over, taking his turn to ruffle young Vinny's hair. He read the bold type. 'All I know is I'm glad I'm nowhere near Indo-China. I don't like the look of that lot one bit.'

The vicar nodded solemnly as he retook possession of his paper.

'Right, what are we waiting for?' said Anna as she breezed into the kitchen, winter coat draped over her left arm and raring to go.

Tom and Helen exchanged glances.

'What?' exclaimed Anna.

'Oh nothing,' replied Tom. 'Come on, we'd best be going.'

As the pair reached the back door, Anna turned to Vinny. 'You watch yourself, young man, and don't talk to any strangers.'

Vinny and Helen gave Anna an identical look of bemusement.

'It's Lipton St Faith we're talking about, my dear,' replied Helen.

Anna smiled. 'Just saying, that's all.'

Once in the car, Tom asked Anna what she meant.

'I don't know, it's just a feeling. Someone came into the thrift shop the other day asking the girls if they knew the whereabouts of any Liverpudlians in the village. I was in the back making some tea, so didn't see him. But later I saw someone from the kitchen window standing opposite the vicarage. By the time I'd turned away for a few seconds and looked again, she'd gone.'

Tom glanced at his companion as they left the village for the open roads to Cambridge. 'She? I thought you said it was a man who called in at the shop?'

Anna frowned, 'Yes… well I did, but that doesn't mean… what I'm trying to say is… I don't know, perhaps they're working together?'

'Don't you think you're being a little paranoid?'

Anna paused while she thought about Tom's reaction. 'To be truthful, that's what I thought at first, but… you know, what with these two killings and talk of a foreign agent around the place? What if it's true? I'm so fond of the lad, I couldn't bear it if any harm came to him. Vinny's already been through enough back in Liverpool.'

Anna was glad that Tom didn't follow up on her explanation. The last thing she wanted was to dwell on what might or might not happen to her precious Scouser. Instead, they spent the ninety-minutes it took to reach Appleby college, mostly in a comfortable silence only possible between close friends.

'Here we are again,' said Tom. 'I wonder what awaits within?'

Minutes after passing through the ornate wrought iron gates of the former country house, Tom's police car came to rest next to the front entrance of the impressive Georgian building.

'It must have been a sight for sore eyes when it was a private estate,' said Anna as she admired the perfect proportions of the square-shaped reception hall.

'I suppose you're right, provided you lived upstairs. I wouldn't fancy trying to keep this place going, never mind the grounds. It must have been a nightmare,' replied Tom.

Anna laughed, 'As you say, not if you spent your life in the upstairs rooms.'

The light-hearted interval ended as a familiar figure entered the vast space.

'Walter, what a coincidence. How are you?'

Sidney Langham's only friend looked stunned at the visitor's presence. 'Miss Grix, and… sergeant?'

'Oh, I'm forgetting my manners,' said Anna. 'This is Sergeant Bradshaw.'

Tom smiled and extended his hand.

'Goodness,' replied Walter, shaking Tom's hand. 'It's rare we see a policeman here. It must be serious. Is it about Sidney?'

Anna took hold of Walter's hand after Tom had released his iron grip. 'Nice to see you again, Walter. I'm afraid there's nothing more we can tell you at the moment.'

'So why have you come?'

'It's Sidney's spiritual supervisor we're here to see. Do you know where he might be?'

That hit the spot, thought Anna.

'He's probably in his office. It's down there; third on the left,' Walter pointed to one of three corridors that led off the reception hall.

She offered Walter a reassuring smile. 'Don't worry, you're not in any trouble. We want to ask Dr Janson if he can tell us anything further about the day Sidney asked him for money for his train, that's all.'

'Oh, you mean the day he shouted at him?' replied Walter.

'Well, he was in a rush to get to a lecture, wasn't he? That's what you told us the other day,' said Tom.

The young man looked at the sergeant. 'Did I? Perhaps I did.'

There's something he's not telling us.

'Walter, is everything OK? You look, well, if you don't mind me saying, terrified. What is it?'

Walter looked at the ornate tiled floor before words tumbled out of his mouth in an incoherent stream.

'Hey… hey, calm down… breathe… that's it.' Anna's calming voice and cupping of his shaking hands with her gentle touch did the trick. 'Now what is it? Take your time.'

'Dr Janson didn't take that lecture. Some of the other students were laughing in the refractory yesterday. When I asked them what was so funny, they told me another Master took the lecture at brief notice and didn't have a clue what he was talking about. Do you think Dr Janson had anything to do with Sidney's death if he wasn't where he said he was? What if he comes for me next?'

Anna gave Walter a hug, which the man seemed in no hurry to disengage from. 'I tell you what, when this is all over, why don't you spend the weekend with us at Lipton St Faith. I know it will delight my father to show you the church. Perhaps he might even get you to St Paul's so you can meet the vicar Sidney was due to work with. What do you say to that?'

Walter's broad grin gave Anna all the answers she required. 'That's settled then, I'll be in touch.'

As Walter turned to the left, Anna walked straight ahead, following the young man's directions to Janson's office. One sharp tap on the door brought the response Anna had hoped for.

'Enter.'

Anna opened the solid oak door to see Dr Janson sat behind a massive desk piled high with papers, the walls covered with fully stocked bookshelves and against one large window, an armchair sat at an angle allowing its occupant to gaze over the extensive grounds of the college.

'Miss Grix, Seargeant, to what do I owe this honour?' Janson laid his fountain pen on the desk and sat back in his chair as he gestured for his guests to sit in a matching pair of wooden chairs on the far side of his extensive desk.

'Thank you for seeing us without an appointment, Dr Janson, you see, something's come up.'

Janson took a pencil from his breast pocket and twirled it between his fingers. 'It must be of a serious nature to bring you both all the way over here on a Saturday morning, Miss Grix?'

No point is mucking around. Here goes, thought Anna.

'Dr Janson, someone saw you arguing with Sidney Langham on the day he left for the train station. Why was that?'

The directness of Anna's question appeared to ruffle Janson as he twirled his pencil at ever greater speed.

'What are you saying, exactly, Miss Grix?'

'I'm stating a fact, Dr Janson, you shouted at a student, one whose temperament had suddenly changed, and who was at the end of his tether. Were you the cause of this change?'

'Now wait a minute, Miss Grix. Be careful what you accuse people of, I—'

'I'm not accusing you of anything. Either you shouted at Mr Langham, or you did not. If you did, it's not unreasonable to think there may be a link between his obvious unhappiness and your behaviour towards the man.'

Such was the force with which Janson now held his pencil that he snapped it in half. The act temporarily brought the heated conversation to a halt.

Janson gathered the fractured pieces of his pencil from his lap and placed them in a neat row on his desk, arranging them in order of length. 'Miss Grix, sometimes one's spiritual supervisor must intervene when his student is underperforming in his studies. What others witnessed on that day was only me reminding Langham of his responsibilities, both to himself and those he'd shortly preach to at St Paul's.'

'And as you say, Dr Janson,' said Tom, 'you were in a rush to get to a lecture, isn't that so?'

'Precisely, sergeant.'

'The problem is, Dr Janson, we now know you did not give that lecture, so where did you go, Aylsham, perhaps?'

Chapter Sixteen: Missing

'I think you'd both better leave now. I have nothing further to say,' said Dr Janson as he rose to his feet, crossed the few yards to his office door, and swung it open. 'You have no jurisdiction to involve your-selves in church matters, let alone the private discussions between a pastor and a member of his flock. If you please?' Janson extended a hand to show his visitors the door.

Tom Bradshaw wasn't yet ready to vacate his seat. He spoke without turning to face Janson. 'Understand that if you don't cooperate with the police, the matter will escalate?'

'Is that a threat, sergeant?' replied the academic, still holding the door wide open.

'The Cambridge constabulary is aware of my visit today, for which courtesy I'm honour-bound to submit a report of its outcome. Do you want the police crawling all over this place? What would the Reverend Wilks say? I doubt he'd thank you. And there is the matter of your background.'

Don't push too hard, Tom, thought Anna.

'My background? Don't you think that's a little racist, sergeant? I escaped exactly this sort of persecution when I left my home country at the beginning of the war. I did not expect to find such attitudes in your country.'

Tom sprang to his feet and spun around to confront his accuser.

He's baiting you, Tom, thought Anna.

Anna placed a hand on the sergeant's elbow. Her touch proved a suitable antidote to his uncharacteristic flash of anger.

'And nor will you find evidence of such in my actions. However, it's a fact that you're a guest in this country. As you know, the government has interned many, while you've been granted the privilege of continuing your work here at the college. I'm simply suggesting the continuance of that situation must be preferable to waiting out the end of the war in a camp on the Isle of Man?'

Good on you, Tom. I didn't know you had it in you.

'Whom is to spend time on a small island sandwiched between our sceptred isle and Ireland?' The college principal's deep-toned voice filled the corridor as Wilks strolled up to his subordinate.

'I can deal with this, principal. We are merely discussing the pros and cons of internment from a spiritual standpoint.'

'Is that so?' responded Wilks. 'Now, Miss Grix; sergeant, what is all this about? I'm surprised to see you both again so soon. Perhaps it may have been courteous of you to have informed me of your visit before approaching one of my senior staff?'

Oops, he's got us there, thought Anna.

'It's of no matter,' he continued, 'I understand standards have slipped because of the war. However, perhaps you might explain to me why you're here?'

That's an object lesson in having your head cut off without feeling the blade, thought Anna.

Tom Bradshaw crossed the room to offer Wilks a handshake, which the principal did not try to reciprocate. 'As Dr Janson has said, we—'

'Sergeant, please do me the courtesy of not treating me like a child. You have no more travelled all the way from the east coast to discuss abstract theology than Mr Hitler is a bastion of fair play and reasonableness.'

Anna, sensing the encounter might spiral out of control, stepped in. 'Dr Janson, will you tell your superior, or shall we?'

She looked for signs of panic on Janson's face. *Hmm, cool as a cucumber,* she thought.

The principal glanced at his subordinate, wearing an expectant look.

'Principal Wilks, the fact of the matter is that our guests have accused me of abusing my immigration status by simply doing my duty to one of my charges.'

Wilks retrieved a handkerchief from a pocket and dabbed the tip of his nose. 'Inflamed sinus… they are rather bothersome, and my doctor holds out little hope of a satisfactory resolution soon.'

Why has he changed the subject? thought Anna.

Several seconds passed by the time the principal had neatly folded his handkerchief into a square and pushed it back deep into his trouser pocket.

'I assume this is about Mr Langham?' said Wilks. 'What makes you think my colleague has anything to do with the unfortunate matter concerning Mr Langham?'

He's a cute one turning the tables on us like that, thought Anna.

'We believe Dr Janson drove to Aylsham the day Sidney left for the train station with the butcher,' said Anna.

Tom joined in the fray, 'We also have reason to believe this gentleman did harm to that young man and I shall prove it, despite any attempt by the church to protect him,'

Wilks smiled, 'Come, come, sergeant. Let us not be so dramatic. It is one thing to say, Dr Janson is in some way involved with a student's disappearance. It is, however, quite a leap to suggest the church has thrown a veil of conspiratorial silence over the matter. Should we not be concentrating on the welfare of that unfortunate young man, rather than machinations of dark doings in God's House? However, I look forward to you sharing with us any proof you have concerning what is, if I may say, a rather wild accusation.'

Brilliant, thought Anna.

'I take my instructions from the Lord. It is He who directs my every action, and it is to Him I shall answer. My conscience is clear.'

H*ow convenient,* thought Anna.

The principal's smile widened. 'Now, what say we call an end to our impromptu meeting. I promise to speak to Dr Janson about the matters you've raised. In return, all I ask is that you show me any evidence you have, to confirm your, er… position, sergeant.'

Tom replaced his police helmet. 'We follow the evidence, Revered Wilks, and nothing more.'

'Quite,' replied Wilks in a quiet, confident tone. 'Now, we mustn't detain you. I'm sure you are both busy people, as are we.'

The principal held out an arm toward the main entrance.

That's that, thought Anna as she and Tom left their hosts following the most cursory of parting nods and made for the car park. She looked over her shoulders one last time before leaving the impressive interior of the college to see Wilks in a heated discussion with Janson at the doorway to the latter's office. Although she couldn't hear what was being said, their body language made it clear all was not well between the two clerical academics.

'What do you think of that?' said Tom as he held the passenger door open for Anna, before walking to the driver's side and settling himself at the wheel.

'My father always warned me to be wary of people, especially the clergy who spouted nonsense like that. Dad's always been clear that we decide for ourselves... and bear the consequences of our actions. Janson is hiding something from us. I don't know what and I'm not sure if the Reverend Wilks is in on it, but there's something, that's for sure.'

Tom switched on the car ignition and headed for the ornate entrance gates to the college. 'I agree with you. Whether he's guilty of murder is a long shot, though. What conceivable motive does he have, still less going to all the trouble of following Sidney Langham to Aylsham when he could've got rid of the man here, or at least somewhere local to the college.'

Anna took in the soft Cambridgeshire landscape and allowed her mind to wander as the police car made steady progress towards Lipton St Faith. An idea suddenly sprang into her head. 'Why don't we call in on our friendly butcher to see if he's heard anything on the grapevine about Dr Janson? He's in and out of the college all the time delivering stuff. I bet there's no better source of gossip than the kitchens.'

'Good idea,' said Tom. 'But I don't fancy a run in with his daughter like Eddie and you had. Do you reckon he'll be in? It's half-day closing.'

'He's bound to be. Saturday morning will have been busy. What time is it now?' Anna looked at her wristwatch to answer her own question. 'A little before two o'clock. I bet he's still cleaning the shop down.'

No sooner had Anna made her point than the police car entered the high street. A minute later it sat motionless outside Jimmy Falkirk's butcher's shop.

'Look. I told you he'd be in.' Anna pointed to the shop window, where Mr Falkirk was busy wiping down several white enamelled trays. Noticing his visitors, Jimmy held a hand up in acknowledgement and hurried to unlock the shop's entrance door.

'Good afternoon to you two. I see you've brought a bobby this time, Miss Grix. What brings you back so soon?'

'Oh, nothing special, and by the way, this is my good friend, Sergeant Bradshaw. Ignore the uniform. He's a tame one. We called in at the college to tie a couple of things up,' said Anna as the pair walked the few paces from the police car to greet the butcher.

'I see,' replied Jimmy. 'Well, you're welcome here anytime, you know. Will you come in for a cup of tea? I've finished in the shop, so I'm having one.'

Tom nudged Anna, showing he was desperate for a drink. 'That's so kind,' she said, 'and how is Flower today?'

Jimmy smiled as he led the way into the back room that had hosted the pair during their last visit. 'She's fine. We had a good night for once. She slept through. One of her oldest friends is with her at the moment.'

'She doesn't sleep well?' asked Anna.

'Not since that night in... well, you know how it is... or I hope you don't, but—'

'It's fine, Mr Falkirk. No, I can't comprehend what you went through, but I'm glad she still has friends to keep her company. People rarely know how to react, do they? You know, it's the same with a physical disfigurement, or knowing someone who's terribly ill. People avoid the situation instead of confronting their fears, don't they?'

The butcher gave a knowing nod. 'You've hit the nail on the head, Miss Grix. But I can't blame people for reacting the way they do with Flower. She's so different to the bubbly girl everyone remembers - but there we are, we manage as best we can and are thankful for our blessings. Now, I'll make that tea, and by the way, it's Jimmy.'

Anna smiled as the butcher crossed into a tiny side room, filled the kettle from a single cold-water tap attached to a white-painted wall, then placed it on a paraffin powered heating ring. 'In that case, I'm Anna and this lump of a policeman is Tom.'

A few minutes later, Jimmy returned with their refreshments. 'Here you are, and good health to you both.'

The trio chatted away contentedly about the situation everyone found themselves in from the tediousness of rationing, which Anna and Jimmy agreed was likely to get worse the longer the war lasted, to how cold it had been recently and the likelihood of a white Christmas. Only at the end of their genial exchange did Anna bring up the subject of Sidney Langham's death.

'Is there anything else you can remember from you taking Sidney to the station?'

The butcher slowly shook his head, 'Not really,' he replied, 'as I told you last time, he was quiet, but apart from that, no, nothing sticks in my memory.'

Anna wore a resigned look. 'He said nothing about meeting anyone? You know, being collected from Aylsham. That sort of thing?'

'Oh, yes,' said Jimmy.

What?

His visitors exchanged excited glances.

'He did?' said Tom. 'Did he say who?'

The butcher thought for a moment and shook his head. 'No, at least I don't remember him saying... wait a minute, now as I think about it, he mentioned something about a chum, but I thought nothing of it, other than to remark how nice it was to meet old friends.'

Why didn't Sidney say anything about that to his best friend at college, or did Walter decide not to tell us?

'What did Sidney say to that?' asked Anna.

Jimmy investigated his almost empty mug and swilled the tea leaves around the base of the glazed clay container. 'Nothing, except I remember him pulling a face. I thought he was feeling sick because of my driving. I didn't half go at a lick to get him to the train station on time.'

We've got to speak to Walter.

Anna noticed Jimmy quickly glancing at a clock on the wall to his right.

That'll do.

'Listen, Jimmy. we've taken up too much of your time already and you've been a great help regarding Sidney, but we need to get a move on if I'm to help my mother prepare the family meal.'

He looks relieved.

'Well, yes, and I suppose I should drop in on Flower to see how the pair of them are doing. Out of interest, what are you having for tea?'

Anna looked surprised by the question, 'Er... fried tinned SPAM and potatoes.'

Jimmy disappeared into his cold store for a short period before reappearing, carrying a string of pork sausages. 'You take these from me. I won't take no for an answer. I never got to thank you properly for how you and the lieutenant handled my daughter the other day. She still talks about the chocolate he gave her.'

I can't take them; he can't have much to sell.

'Go on, I'm not putting them back into my cold store now, so they'll go to waste if you don't have them.'

Fibber, thought Anna as she saw a warm smile wash over Jimmy's face.

'That's so generous, Jimmy. How can I ever thank you?'

The butcher wrapped the sausages up in two pieces of grease-proof paper and handed the neat package to Anna. 'Understanding my daughter's illness is all the thanks I need, Anna. Now, you'd best be off. I know it's a long journey back to Norfolk and you'll be needing your passport if you leave it too late.'

What a lovely man.

Anna took a step forward to place a gentle kiss on Jimmy's forehead.

212

'Let's hope next time we meet it will be purely social. You never know, we might've won the war as well.'

Jimmy threw his hands up and laughed as he led his visitors back through the shop and opened the door for them. 'I'm afraid that might be awhile coming, Anna, but we all live in hope for a quick victory. Sergeant, it's been a pleasure to meet you and thank you for all you do in keeping us safe.'

Tom offered an embarrassed smile. 'It's my pleasure, Jimmy, and make sure you keep that daughter of yours safe—and you, too, mind.'

No sooner had the pair got back in the police car, said a last fare-well, and drove off than Anna returned to the more serious business of Sidney Langham. 'We have to speak with Walter, Tom.'

'Anna, there's no way we can go back to the college. They'll never let us in, and I have to be careful because I don't have any jurisdiction here. I imagine Dr Janson has already been on to Inspector Spillers, never mind the Chief Constable of Cambridgeshire.'

He has a point, I suppose.

'It'll have to be by telephone, look there's one a little way ahead.'

Ten minutes later, Anna, having made the call using one of the country's familiar red public telephone boxes, walked back to the parked police car with a spring in her step.

'He took some finding, and he didn't want to talk at first, and to be honest, I thought I was about to run out of coins, but—'

'Anna, stop.'

Tom's sharp words startled his companion.

'What?'

'Take a breath, will you? Ok. let's start again, shall we? We've established Walter seemed reluctant to say anything. Continue.'

Rude man, I don't know why I find him so attractive. Why am I even thinking that?

213

Anna gave Tom one of her well-practiced indignant looks. 'As I was saying, Walter was quiet at first, and then he told me.'

'And?' said Tom after what seemed like an age.

'Walter said that someone came to see him at the college a few months ago. He reckoned Sidney said it was a relative, but Walter didn't believe him.'

Tom slowed the police car as he reached the brow of a hump-back bridge so that he had a chance to spot anything coming before it was too late to avoid a collision. 'But why didn't he say anything the other day?'

Anna fixed her gaze on Tom. 'He said he was too scared to say anything.'

No sooner had Tom and Anna arrived back at Lipton St Faith police station than Inspector Spillers called to them from his office through the half-open door. 'In here, now, both of you.'

'What have we done now?' said Anna as she glanced at the smiling desk sergeant.

'He's been in a foul mood for over an hour and there's no calming him down. I even found an old chocolate biscuit in the back of the kitchen cupboard, but that didn't help one bit. You'd best get in and face the music,' said Dick Ilford.

'Sit and don't speak.'

It's a long time since I've seen him like this.

'I've had the Chief Inspector of the Cambridgeshire Police onto me before I could get to him. What on earth did you accuse that Janson bloke of?'

The pair looked at one another as if seeking inspiration.

'I didn't accuse him of anything, sir. I simply asked the man if he'd travelled to Aylsham to follow Sidney Langham,' said Tom.

'And the racist comment?'

'That's not fair, Inspector Spillers. I—'

'I'm not concerned about what was or wasn't fair, whatever that's supposed to mean in the context of a police investigation, Miss Grix. Neither am I concerned whether you consider what is and isn't racist. The fact of the matter is that Dr Janson considered the comment as such. Now what have you both got to say for yourselves?'

Before either could answer, the office door opened to the familiar figure of Sergeant Ilford.

'Not now, Ilford,' barked Spillers as he gestured for the policeman to withdraw and close the door.

'But Inspector, a—'

'I said, not now. Which bit of that did you—'

'A letter, Inspector. We've received a letter which you'll wish to read immediately, sir.'

That's certainly one brave man, thought Anna.

She watched as Spillers thought about the matter.

'Very well, bring it here, and it had better be important,' said Spillers in a grouchy tone.

A flushed Sergeant Ilford stepped forward, stretched to place an opened envelope on the inspector's desk, and left without further engagement with his superior, or the room's remaining occupants.

He's not happy, and I don't blame him.

Spillers looked at every inch of the envelope, paying particular attention to the post-mark. He removed a single piece of folded paper from its cover, placed it on his desk, and read its contents.

Come on, Inspector, how long can it take to read a few lines of writing?

Eventually, Spiller straightened up, before resting back in his chair with his hands together as if praying, the tips of which rested below his chin.

Why doesn't he look angry?

The inspector lifted his gaze from the letter to engage Anna and Tom. 'Forget what I said before. You now have my full authority, and for the benefit of doubt, I shall put it in writing, to pursue Dr Janson with all the powers at your disposal, sergeant.'

'Sir?' said Tom in a surprised tone.

'Perhaps you might like to read this aloud so that Miss Grix may understand why I issued that order to you. It's unsigned, as is often the case with such letters.'

Tom took the paper from Inspector Spillers, quickly digested its contents and gave his superior a concerned glance.

What on earth's going on?

Tom read the brief note out loud: "I saw Dr Filip Janson arguing with a young man dressed like a vicar on Sunday last, near Three-Mile-Bottom. He made the man get into a car and drove him off quickly."

'But that means—'

'Yes, Anna, it means Dr Janson is very much our prime suspect. I'll speak to my opposite number at Cambridge Headquarters. I'll let him decide if he wishes to brief his chief constable. My preference is that the contents of this letter remain known to the fewest possible people until we can prove whether Janson was near Three-Mile-Bottom. If he was, it—'

'Makes him our murderer,' interrupted Anna.

'Or at least heavily involved in the man's murder. Now, get to it sergeant, do you still feel you're up to it?'

Tom straightened in his chair. 'Absolutely, sir.'

As Tom opened the door to allow Anna to pass through, Spillers looked up from reading the letter again. 'Make sure you keep Miss Grix safe, Thomas.'

'Sir,' replied Tom, before closing the office door.

'Blimey, what did you do to him? He sounded almost human again.'

Anna winked at Sergeant Ilford. 'Nothing to do with us; everything to do with the letter you brought him.'

Leaving the police station, the pair turned right for the short walk to the vicarage.

'Wait until Mum sees these sausages; I'm going to be in her good books.' Anna held out the grease-proof package in triumph, having recovered it from her overcoat where it lay safe during their tense meeting with Spillers.

'And I can't wait to see Janson's face when we confront him about the contents of that letter,' said Tom.

As Anna opened the front door to the vicarage and led Tom down the vestibule and into the lounge, she expected to see the smiling faces of her parents. Instead, her mother sat hunched up with a handkerchief to her mouth.

Mum's been crying.

Her father stood over a large open map-book he'd placed on a coffee table.

'Mum, Dad, what's the matter?'

The vicar looked at her without smiling, his ghostly complexion adding to Anna's concern. 'Vincent has gone missing. No one has seen him for hours.'

Oh, no. No, this can't be happening.

'What do you mean he's gone missing?' said Anna.

Helen dabbed her eyes before standing. 'It's as your father says. We allowed him to use the village green to play football. Several villagers saw him playing at various times this morning. After that, nothing. He seems to have vanished.'

Tom placed his arm around Anna.

I feel safe with Tom around.

'We've come from the station,' said Tom. 'Sergeant Ilford didn't say a word, which is more than odd.'

'They don't know yet,' said Anna's father.

'You haven't reported Vinny as missing? Why? It'll be dark soon and he's been out since this morning. What were you thinking about?' said Tom, his voice breaking with incredulity.

Helen broke down, which no amount of comforting by her husband or daughter could quell.

'A couple of locals saw Lieutenant Elsner speeding out the village in his car and thought he might have a passenger. We assumed he'd taken Vincent for a run out. You know what boys are like with cars. Well, I've rung Hilda Cross, and she says they haven't seen him since breakfast. I thought you might know?'

Anna shook her head, the colour draining from her face. 'No, I've… I don't know where Eddie is or why he was in the village. Anyway, what is "thought" supposed to mean? Either he had someone with him, or he didn't?'

The vicar traced his hand along several deep furrows of on his forehead. 'That's what they said. Perhaps he didn't have anyone with him, but why rush from the village in such a manner? We must assume, no, pray, he *did* have Vinny. At least that way, we know the boy is safe.'

'I'll get back to the station and get things started,' said Tom. 'If your mum or dad think of anything else that might help, make sure you let me know, OK?'

Tom sped from the room without waiting for her to respond.

What have you done, Eddie?

Chapter Seventeen: Where's He Gone?

Anna did what she could to console her mother. However, she knew that the visible display of terror her mother exhibited manifested itself inwardly on her father.

I hope this doesn't push Dad over the edge.

She knew that her father occasionally joked about depressive episodes Mr Churchill called his "Black Dog". In her heart, Anna knew her father wasn't joking at all. It was more of an acceptance of what he suffered from after acute stress.

'Are you OK, Dad?'

'Oh, don't you worry about me. It's your mother we need to get right. Now, come along, I suggest we nip into the kitchen and at least try to eat the meal your mother's been preparing all afternoon.'

That's exactly why I worry about you, Dad, always showing concern for other people, especially family, instead of taking care of yourself.

'I'm not hungry,' said Helen as she dabbed the tears from her eyes again. 'What if something dreadful has happened to Vinny? I'll never forgive myself.'

'Mum, Vinny will be fine. You know what a little terror he can be, which also means he can look after himself.'

I must believe what I'm saying. Vinny, please be safe.

Helen shook her head while clinging to the arm of the sofa as if to stop herself from collapsing onto the floor.

'Perhaps a cup of tea?' said the vicar. He caught Anna's attention to show she should follow him into the kitchen.

'We'll be back in five minutes with a nice hot brew. You rest. I know Vinny will be back before you know it.'

In the kitchen, the atmosphere regarding Vinny's disappearance proved more realistic.

'It's not looking good. Your mother and I haven't discussed the matter, but I can't help wondering if the lad's been taken by someone.'

'You mean Eddie?'

'No, no, Anna. You know as well as I do the lieutenant would've taken care to tell us he'd taken the boy for a spin. No, I'm afraid the lieutenant's departure is a separate conundrum that has nothing to do with Vinny. I meant the man who called in at the thrift shop asking after Liverpudlians, then you seeing a stranger looking at the house from over the road.'

Anna filled the large kettle and placed it on one of the AGA's heating plates before turning back to her father, who busied himself cleaning down the already spotless beechwood draining board of the sink.

'I knew I should have taken that more seriously. What if—?' asked Anna.

'It's no use thinking about what one should or shouldn't've. After all, what would you have said to the police? From what you told your mother and I, he didn't ask about a specific person, did he?'

'Eddie occasionally suggests I'm naive about certain things. This time, I fear you're the one who won't face up to reality. Dad, I don't mean to hurt you, but…'

The conversation fizzled out as both adults withdrew into their own thoughts.

Anna suddenly let out a cry, 'What have I done?'

'What's the matter?' The vicar crossed the few feet between them and pulled his daughter into him. 'Now, now. What's all this about?'

Anna buried her head into the vicar's shoulder. 'There's something else, I can't tell you about it, but—'

'I don't understand. You're not making any sense,' replied her father as he gently stroked his daughter's hair.

Anna pulled away from her father. 'Its... oh, Dad, I can't—'

'Anna, stop. You're making no sense at all. Come, sit with me.' Her father guided his distraught daughter to the kitchen table and finished making the tea. 'We've hardly seen you for a week. Yes, you've mentioned bits and pieces about what you, Tom and the lieutenant have been up to, but you're trying to join dots that do not, perhaps, connect.'

Anna took a china cup and saucer from her father. 'The thing is... you know, Eddie vanishing, and, well... the vicarage being watched. And then there's the man asking questions in the thrift shop... Oh, and not forgetting an anonymous letter from someone saying they saw a pastor arguing with Sidney Langham, making him get in a car and driving him away quickly, well—'

'A letter? What do you mean?'

Anna told her father about her meeting with Inspector Spillers.

'My goodness, what is the world coming to? There is one thing though, you said you couldn't tell me anything. Well, if you meant to, you have, so you'd better tell me the rest. What's going on, Anna?'

What have I done? All I'll do now is worry my father even more.

Realising she had little choice, Anna spent the next ten minutes telling her father everything she'd been up to since the previous Sunday.

Why do I feel better for that, knowing I'll have worried Dad to death?

'Did someone promise me a cup of tea?' said Helen as she entered the kitchen, her tears dried and handkerchief nowhere to be seen. 'A person could die of thirst waiting for you two.'

'Ah, my dear, apologies, we got talking, you know, dad and daughter stuff. Why don't you take the weight off your feet, and I'll bring you your tea?'

She sat opposite and shook her head at Anna. 'You're a terrible liar, like most vicars, Charles Grix. I didn't catch everything you said from the vestibule, but I heard enough. The question is, what are we to do about it?'

Adding milk to his wife's tea, the vicar ambled to the table and placed a brightly decorated cup and saucer in front of Helen. 'We shall speak to the police. *You'll* rest here.'

'Oh no, you don't. I've felt sorry for myself for long enough today. It's time we got on with things.'

How would we manage without you? So strong for everyone else.

Before Anna could respond, the telephone rang. The kitchen's occupants swapped anxious looks. Anna was the first to move.

Running into the vestibule, she stood motionless in front of the telephone for a moment.

I want to know, but I'm frightened.

Summoning the courage to lift the receiver, she waited for whoever had rung to speak. 'Oh, Tom, it's you? Any news?'

Anna hung on his every word, then placed the handset back on its cradle.

She had hardly walked five feet back towards the kitchen when the telephone rang for a second time. Retracing her steps, Anna had no hesitation in answering this time.

'News, Tom?' Anna's mood rapidly changed as she realised it wasn't

Tom after all. The voice was vaguely familiar, yet she couldn't place it. The man introduced himself. 'Dr Janson, how can I help?'

What does he want?

'You want to meet? Why?' Anna tried to concentrate, but her thoughts were still on Tom and any news of Vinny as Janson continued to talk. 'Why there?' Now he had her full attention. 'But it's already pitch black?' She listened keenly to his last request. 'Very well, seven o'clock.'

Anna replaced the handset for the second time in as many minutes.

What was all that about—and do I trust him?

As Anna re-entered the kitchen, she saw her mother and father talking quietly as they sat side-by-side at the table, although she couldn't make out what they were saying.

'Someone's popular,' said Charles, breaking off eye contact with his wife. 'Any news?'

They both look shell-shocked.

'The first call was from Tom. He said he'd put a call in to Norwich and King's Lynn headquarters. They're getting officers to the major train stations and putting checkpoints on the primary routes out of both counties, while Tom is setting up a search party more locally.'

Neither mother nor father commented. A nod was the only sign either parent understood what their daughter was saying.

I feel so helpless.

'And the other call?' asked Charles.

She hesitated.

Do I tell him the truth, or lie to my father?

'Anna… the second call?'

'It was Dr Janson from the college Sidney Langham attended. He wants to meet me… tonight. Seven o'clock in Three-Mile-Bottom.'

I hope I've done the right thing.

She saw the shocked look on both her parents' faces. 'I know, I know, it'd be stupid to go, but say whatever Janson's mixed up in has something to do with Vinny? Of course, it might be about Eddie. Either way, I have to find out.'

'And what if he simply wants to get you on your own and do you harm? Have you thought about that?' responded Charles.

I knew I shouldn't have told him.

'… And don't look at me like that, Anna. I know you too well. I imagine you pondered whether to tell us. Well, you did the right thing, but I cannot allow you to go to that meeting alone. Such a thing is a preposterous risk I won't permit you to take, grown woman or not.'

Why do parents always make you feel five years old?

'Dad, I'll be fine. Besides, Tom is busy helping to find Vinny. I'd much prefer he do that than hold my hand.'

'Who said anything about Thomas? I shall come with you. But before we go anywhere, you're having a hot meal.'

I love you both so much.

'You're a rubbish driver, Dad,' said Anna as her father brought the borrowed Austin seven to a stuttering halt by the public telephone box. The hamlet of Three-Mile Bottom looked deserted in the blackout, save for one or two local men making their way to the pub, hands in pockets to offer some protection against the chill evening air.

'Well, it has been quite a while since I sat behind a steering wheel. I'll give you that, but we made it, didn't we?'

Anna couldn't help giggling. 'If you mean we only drove into one farmer's field, yes. It's a good job the gate was open. When exactly *did* you last drive a car, father?'

'Oh, it's "Father", now, is it? I must be in trouble. 1932.'

'What?'

'Nineteen thirty-two. You asked when I last drove a vehicle. So, there you have it.'

Anna gave the vicar a suspicious glance. 'I said a car, not a vehicle. I know you, you're a stickler for language. Go on, tell me. What precisely was it you drove in 1932?'

Her father fidgeted, a sure sign in Anna's eye that she'd caught him out.

'Bill Lancelot's tractor. I drove it during the village fete parade.'

'Bill's old tractor? I remember that fete. The men had to push you half the way. That tractor was a museum piece even back then. What was it you said? "I shall never drive a mechanical device again." Didn't the brakes fail and—'

'Yes, yes, very well. A mere detail. We're here now, so keep your eyes peeled for this Janson fellow.'

You are funny, Dad.

Ten minutes passed, leaving Anna little to do but watch the moon ascending into a cloudless sky. The sound of a car approaching breeched the otherwise silent hamlet.

'That must be him,' said Anna as she caught sight of some dimmed headlights approaching. 'It's got to be him.'

A few seconds later, Anna could make out the shape of a car with gleaming black paintwork that glistened in the soft evening light.

It makes an easy target for enemy bombers shining like that.

The car continued its journey; the driver not bothering to look at Anna before passing and coming to a stop fifty feet behind them. Anna waited to see what its occupant would do. At first, all remained silent before she heard a car door banging shut. She looked around to see a lone figure, his tall torso leaning at a slight angle against the car.

'Time for me to go, Dad. Please, you stay here.'

She could see the hesitancy in her father's face.

'On condition that you don't get in that car, or leave my line of sight - will you promise me?'

Anna nodded, gave her father a kiss on his cheek and got out of the Austin.

Thank heavens he's looking the other way; Janson doesn't know I got out of the passenger-side.

She strolled towards the man, who seemed to be distracted by two men talking outside the pub entrance.

'Good evening, Dr Janson.'

I frightened the life out of him.

'Oh, Miss Grix. I... I didn't hear you approach.'

I enjoyed that too much. Dad would not approve.

'Thank you for meeting me at such brief notice, I—'

'Why now? You did your best earlier today to get Sergeant Bradshaw suspended and me in a heap of trouble with his superior. What's changed?'

Janson toyed with a delicate silver cross and chain, which he'd strung around the fingers of his left hand. 'I can only apologise for my actions. Once I had spoken to the Cambridgeshire police, I reflected on my actions, and—'

'You don't mean to tell me you've driven almost eighty-miles and dragged me out on a cold evening to apologise?'

Janson held up his open palms. 'I quite see why you're angry. All I ask is that you allow me to... you brought someone with you?' Janson turned his head to his left as Anna's father neared.

Oh, Dad, I asked you to stay back.

'Are you alright, my dear? This gentleman seemed to become agitated. I thought you might need my help?'

How can I be angry at him for looking after me?

'I'm fine, Dad. Dr Janson is about to tell me why he wished to meet me, isn't that correct?'

Janson concentrated his gaze on the vicar.

Here we go again. Don't even think about ignoring me now that another man has arrived.

'I've heard a great deal about you, Reverend Grix. So nice to meet you. The vicar of St Paul's was most complimentary.'

Don't fall for it, Dad.

'Well, that's nice to hear, Dr Janson. However, I'm here entirely in a supporting role. It is to my daughter you must explain yourself to.'

Thank you, Dad.

'Yes,' spluttered Janson. 'Of course, I shall do that. I thought that two men of the cloth might share—'

'We have nothing to share apart from our love in God. Dr Janson. Now that I know my daughter is safe, I shall withdraw and allow you to speak directly to Anna.'

Dad is such a clever man.

Charles sauntered back to the car, leaving Anna in total control of the situation. 'Now, Dr Janson, you were about to tell me what all this is about.'

Janson pulled his coat collar up against the stiffening breeze. 'I'm sure you know I argued with Sidney quite near this spot?'

Keep digging, Dr Janson.

'Well, I need you to understand I was trying to protect the man, not harm him.'

'Protect?' said Anna, trying not to show her surprise.

'Yes, protect. You worked out I didn't take that lecture and I knew it wouldn't be long before the sergeant or you'd be back demanding an explanation. Well, in truth, I did travel to Norfolk by car that day, but not for the reason you think.'

'And what is it you assume I'm thinking, Dr Janson?'

He paused as if to gather his thoughts. 'I apologise, I cannot know, but based on our conversation in my office this morning, it's not too far a leap of logic for you to conclude that I killed Mr Langham.'

Where's this going?

'And did you?'

Janson looked horrified. 'No. A thousand times, no. My intention, although clumsy, was to protect him. On that I failed miserably, which is something I shall regret for the rest of my life.'

Anna noticed Janson had started to shake and wasn't sure if it was through fear, or the chill of a December evening.

'Shall we take shelter out of the wind?' asked Anna.

Janson nodded, turned and opened the rear passenger door of his car. In an instant, her father shouted, which led Anna to put a hand up. 'No, Dr Janson. Not yours. Follow me.'

She pointed to the tiny Austin. By the time both reached the car, her father had the passenger door open, and the front seat tipped forward to allow Janson to climb into the rear bench seat of the two-door vehicle, grunting as he did so.

He sounds as if he's in pain.

Although the small Austin car didn't benefit from a heater, the combined body heat of its three occupants provided at least some relief from the dropping temperature outside, although it came at the cost of the windows rapidly steaming up.

'Now, where were we, Dr Janson?' said Anna as she adjusted the rear-view mirror to get a better view of him without the need to twist in her chair.

He's keen to talk, I think.

'I admit I drove to Aylsham train station. Sidney was more than surprised to see me when he left the building and began looking for a taxi.'

Anna didn't take her eyes off Janson. 'If what you say is true, why not tell Sidney that you had to stay at the college instead of rushing over sixty miles hot on the heels of a train?'

'I knew he had to change trains at Ely and there'd be a wait for his Norfolk connection, so it wasn't so much of a rush.'

'That's beside the point, Dr Janson, but thank you for clearing that little conundrum up. But why the car journey in the first place?'

He hasn't taken his eyes off me.

'The argument we had that day, that was the latest of several heated exchanges with Sidney over the months preceding his death. At first, he listened calmly to what I had to say, then not so much, until he wouldn't discuss it at all.'

'Discuss what, Dr Janson?' said Anna.

Janson slumped his seat.

Don't clam up on me now.

Silence fell as Janson looked at the bare metal floor of the car, while Anna and her father exchanges exasperated glances.

'Create in me a clean heart, O God, and renew a steadfast spirit within me.'

Anna watched Janson as her father's calming tone worked its magic.

'Ah, Psalm 51:10. Such a great comfort, Reverend Grix.'

I suppose only ecclesiastical folk can talk to each other like that without feeling the slightest bit self-conscious.

'Well, now is the time for that clean heart, Dr Janson,' said Charles.

Janson nodded. Anna wasn't sure who the acknowledgement focused on, her father, or the man himself.

'Miss Grix, I know you have spoken to Walter several times. However, I don't know if he mentioned a certain person who visited Sidney some months ago? You may wonder why I do not name this person. Well, it's because no one saw them. The only evidence they were at the college was an odd note left in the visitor's book — we encourage all our visitors to leave a comment.'

You didn't ask me to write in it, thought Anna.

'Although Sidney told me he'd had a visitor, and on what date, he didn't reveal further details about the person. By matching the comment in the book with what Sidney told me, I have a name, or at least I think I have.'

What is the man talking about?

'Dr Janson, you've lost me.'

Janson leaned forward in his seat, 'The note read, O lykos—'

'Erchetai... the wolf comes,' interrupted Anna.

She watched Janson's astonished expression as she finished his sentence.

'But... how... how did you know? Have you seen the visitors' book?'

Anna shook her head. Interrogator and interrogated locked eyes without physically seeing each other face-to-face courtesy of the car mirror.

'Anna?' said her father. 'Is there something we should know?'

She hesitated for several seconds, pondering what to do before throwing the question back to Janson to test exactly how much he knew.

'Is there, Dr Janson?'

'All I know is that this person had a hold over Sidney and the only person in the world that the man had a deep attachment to was his aunt. I suppose you know about her, Miss Grix?'

This time Anna thought it better to lay her cards on the table.

'Yes, I do. The question is, can we trust you with what I know? As things stand, I'm not sure because one piece of information remains absent from the explanation about your argument here in Three-Mile-Bottom with Sidney Langham.'

'But I've told you all I know.'

'Stop it,' barked Anna. 'I've had enough. Let's assume you had Sidney's wellbeing foremost on your mind the day you rushed to Aylsham. I know how long the change of trains takes at Ely and believe me, from where you started your journey, you'd have had to drive like the wind, so no more nonsense, please.'

'Anna, my dear.' Her father's gentle censure corrected Anna's abrasive tone.

'OK, let's start again,' she said. 'I have two further questions for you. Whether I telephone the police to come and arrest you or ask for their help to find Sidney's true killer will depend on how you answer them.'

'Miss Grix, I assure—'

'I'm past that. Now, my questions: One, why did you drive him all the way from Aylsham to Three-Mile-Bottom? It's miles from St Paul's where the vicar was waiting to greet him. Two, You forced him into your car and drove him off at speed from just down the road. Where were you going? Think carefully, because we know how Sidney Langham's journey ended.'

Janson's head dropped for the second time.

'Let's have none of that. I want answers,' said Anna.

Janson toyed with his cross and chain as he raised his head and met Anna's gaze in the mirror. 'Once Sidney got over the shock of seeing me, he calmed down but said he wouldn't talk about "that subject", as he put it. He said he'd only stay in the car if I brought him here to Three-Mile-Bottom. When I asked him why, he said he had someone important to meet. I'd never been here before we arrived. The place is so small, and I got suspicious.'

'What happened when you arrived?' asked Anna.

'He jumped out of the car almost before I'd stopped. Once I caught up with him — he was down there by the pub—we argued.

231

I asked him to get back into the car and tell me what was going on, but he refused.'

'But you forced him into your car?' said Anna.

'I did not force him. He said he'd left something on the seat and needed to get it. I admit, I followed him back to the car, and yes, I shut the car door behind him while he scrambled for whatever he was looking for. It must have slipped behind his seat. I jumped in and raced off, hoping he'd see sense, but he went berserk and began hitting me. I still have the bruises on my shoulders and chest. Eventually, he tricked me into stopping. He seemed calmer and said he wanted to talk after all but needed some fresh air. We got out of the car and walked. It was then he hit me again and knocked me over. I'm not a young man, Miss Grix. By the time I got to my feet, Sidney was in the car and racing off.'

'But he couldn't drive?' exclaimed Anna.

'That's what I thought, but someone had clearly taught him. He knew exactly what to do.'

Anna shook her head, 'But what about you? How did you get back to the college?'

'I hitchhiked. People are always nice about stopping for a pastor. A military wagon pulled over; they were heading for their barracks in Norwich. From there I caught a train back to Cambridge.'

A last question occurred to Anna. 'But why did you remove the number plates?'

'What are you talking about? Why would I remove them from my car? I always record the plate on the inside of the glove box in case I ever get pulled over by the police. You wouldn't think the police would do that, would you? But they do. I think they like to offload some stresses they face. So, in case they ask for my index number and I'm sat in the car, I can flip the glove box open as if I'm looking for something and reel off the number to them. If you look in my new car, you'll find I've done the same thing.'

If that's true, we'll see whether Inspector Spillers found it, but some of his story still sounds farfetched.

She glanced at her father.

'Dr Janson, we shared a psalm a few minutes ago. In the spirit of renewing your spirit, is everything you have told my daughter the truth?'

'Yes, so help me, God.'

Chapter Eighteen: Going Dark

Anna had hardly crossed the threshold of the vicarage than she called out to her mother, 'Any news about Vinny?'

Helen appeared from the kitchen within seconds, her demeanour delivering her daughter the unwelcome answer. 'Tom rang. There's no trace of the young one, but they're doing everything they can.'

I should be out there looking for Vinny, not messing about on some stupid investigation, thought Anna.

'Who do we have here?' said Helen.

'Mum, this is Dr Filip Janson,' said Anna as she stood aside to allow her father and Janson to step inside the house. 'He was the spiritual adviser to—'

'Yes, that poor man who died last Sunday. Well, by the looks of it, you could all do with a cup of tea. Let's go into the lounge and I'll sort it out.'

Anna could see her mother had been crying again but disguised her upset by avoiding her glance and moving the contents of her heavy wool cardigan from one pocket to the other.

'On second thoughts,' said Helen, 'Why don't you help me make the tea while the men go through to the lounge?'

Mum wants to talk.

'The house is so quiet without Vinny, Mum. He'd normally be in bed by now. Even so, the place is different… empty.' Anna responded to the comforting hand of her mother on her shoulder as they entered the kitchen. 'Do you think it was that man who came into the thrift shop that took him?'

Helen sighed as she filled the kettle and placed it onto the AGA, while Anna busied herself fetching the cups and saucers from a large dresser that stood against one wall of the large Victorian space.

'To be truthful, there's no way of knowing. My gut feeling says yes, because there's no way Vinny would've left of his own accord, and I'm certain Eddie didn't take him. I suppose I'm…' Helen hesitated for a second as she gave her daughter a concerned look. 'It's just that…'

Say it, Mum, say it.

Helen turned to watch the kettle on the AGA and fiddled with a blue and white tea towel, ready to wrap around the iron handle once the kettle boiled.

'You think someone who's involved in that man's death has taken him, don't you?'

Helen continued to stand with her back to Anna.

Mum's crying.

The rapid raising and lowering of her mother's shoulders gave Anna all the notice she needed to detect her mother's true mood. She covered the few yards to her mother at a snail's pace, not sure what to do, other than return her mother's caring gesture of a moment ago.

What have I done?

Helen whipped around as soon as her daughter's open hand settled on her shoulder. 'Why do you have to involve yourself in these things, Anna? Isn't looking after evacuees and helping in the thrift shop enough for you?'

Both women began to tear-up.

'But, Mum, I—'

'But nothing, Anna. First you rush off from church, then you disappear day after day chasing some nonsense or other and now you bring a stranger back, having dragged your father into whatever mess you've got yourself into. It's not only your mess, is it, Anna? What if Vinny's been taken by someone you or Eddie's upset? What if this is about a warped act of revenge to get back at you? For Heaven's sake, Anna, isn't it enough for you that people… civilians are being killed all the time because of this horrible war, yet all you can do is play Sherlock Holmes? And now we've lost Vinny.'

The haunting whistle of the kettle boiling distracted both women for a second as Helen whipped around to move it from the heat, forgetting to pick up the tea towel and instead burning her hand on the hot metal of the handle. She let out a sharp scream of pain as she let go of the kettle, sending it skidding across the AGA until it collided with a heating ring and tipped some of its boiling contents onto the tiled floor and sending a column of steam into the air.

'Mum, are you hurt? Here, let me have a look,' said Anna as she inspected an injury to her mother's right palm, Anna could see the flesh was already reddening. 'We must run it under the tap.' Helping Helen to the sink, Anna turned on the cold water to allow a stream of ice-cold liquid to calm her mother's angry skin.

'I'm sorry, Mum. I didn't mean to—'

'No need, I… oh, that's better,' replied Helen as the coolness of the water took effect. 'I shouldn't have shouted at you, this isn't your—'

'But it is, Mum,' replied Anna, her tears flowing. 'You're right. If I hadn't insisted on getting involved last Sunday, none of this would've happened. Vinny would be tucked up in bed… but more than that, oh… to be truthful, I don't know why I chase around the place with Eddie and Tom. My job should be enough, but—'

Helen took hold of her tearful daughter and squeezed tightly. 'But it's not, because you are what you are, Anna, that's why. It's wrong of me to blame all this on you. I'm an old softie who let her emotions get the better of her.'

'Is everything alright in here?' The vicar's calming tone filled the kitchen, catching both women by surprise.

'Oh, daft me, burning my hand on the kettle. Cold water's done the trick. Now, you go back through, and we'll bring the tea in two shakes of a cat's tail.'

Dad knows there's something wrong.

'Helen Grix, If I know anything about you, it's—'

'Two minutes, Charles, now go back to our guest.'

And he knows when not to argue.

The vicar turned on his heels and, after giving his wife a last, knowing look, left the kitchen and made his way back to Dr Janson.

'Your palm is blistering, Mum. You'll need to see the doctor tomorrow... oh, it's Sunday tomorrow, what will you—'

'I won't fuss, that's what I'll do. Now come on, let's pull ourselves together and make this tea. You never know, Tom might call at any minute with good news.'

Please ring.

'The telephone, I almost forgot. Mum, I'll be back in a minute. There's someone I have to ring.'

Anna felt her mother's eyes on her as she hurried into the vestibule and picked up the telephone handset and dialled a familiar number.

Yes, he's answering.

'Inspector Spiller, thank goodness you're back. I have some news for you... What, you found it? ... Tell me, was it in the glove compartment? ... But how? ... I think you ought to call in at the vicarage, Inspector, there's someone here you might wish to talk to.'

As Anna put the handset down and turned back to the kitchen, she froze. Her mother was in the vestibule holding a tray of tea ready to take through to the lounge.

'The time is coming when you'll have to make some hard choices. I mean not only between your war work and catching criminals. Change is coming, Anna. I feel it in my bones. You have a lot of thinking to do.'

What does she mean, not *only*? thought Anna as her mother turned away and strolled towards the lounge.

Lieutenant Elsner sat on a heavy wooden chair with his hands behind his back, held firm in a set of handcuffs. Alone in an upstairs room without furnishings, he pondered what his next step might be.

This is what happens when you let yourself get too close to someone. I've been a fool.

The sound of an occasional car passing by and people wishing each other a pleasant day, which he could hear through the single window that punched an otherwise featureless room, made his confinement more bizarre in his eyes.

Falling for the oldest trick in the world is one thing. Getting myself handcuffed makes me feel like a jerk.

Eddie spent what felt like hours to him tracing the cracks in the lath and plaster ceiling, combined with counting how many roses there were per row on the cheap faded wallpaper. As he mulled over whether one pattern of cracks in the ceiling resembled a side profile of his old English teacher, Eddie heard a key turning in the door lock behind him.

Perhaps I'll finally see who got the better of me.

Come on, let me see you.

'Lieutenant Edward Elsner of the American Army Airforce Special

Reconnaissance Division. How nice that we finally meet, although I must confess, I'd hoped others might fulfil their task to avoid any need for our paths to cross. As it is, well... good afternoon... No, what am I thinking? It's dark now? Good evening.'

Is it a man or woman? thought Eddie as he listened closely to the cut-glass deep voice of his invisible captor and pondered how they'd opened the door and walk to within a hair's breadth of him without making the slightest noise.

'That's a neat trick.'

The stranger let out a short, throaty laugh. 'In my profession, lieutenant, it pays to remain silent. As you see... oh, of course, you can't see me, can you? I'm good at it, don't you think?'

And overconfidence will be your downfall.

'Talking of which, what precisely *is* your business?'

'So many questions, lieutenant.'

*They've moved to my left. It's like being a mouse in a tra*p.

'No, just the one. Who are you?' said Eddie.

'That makes two, Edward, or should I call you Eddie like Miss Grix does?'

'What have you done with her? You said if I met you, she'd be safe. Show her to me.' Eddie sensed air movement in the room's stillness.

They're moving again, now to my right. I'm getting the hang of you, cowboy.

'Believe me, you'll be reunited before too long, but first you must tell me why General Bob Murphy sent you to this forsaken piece of England full of old peat diggings and windmills that sticks out into the North Sea like a boil on ones back.'

To be reunited isn't necessarily the same thing as seeing one another, thought Eddie.

'Tell me who you are and what this is about. We'll see where the conversation takes us. I assume the fact I'm still alive means I'm still of some use to you, so let's please stop all this horsing around.'

They're moving towards me. Perfume?

'So, I'll call you, Miss, instead of Mr, shall I? I thought you said you liked to stay silent. The perfume is a bit of a giveaway, isn't it?'

'Be quiet,' barked his captor.

Vain and easily rattled, too. That's useful, thought Eddie.

'You may think of me as a… yes, I have it, a pack animal who likes to forage alone. As for what I do, well, let me see… Yes, I have it. I'm a collector. I gather seemingly random bits and pieces together and make them more valuable by making connections others cannot see.'

Eddie allowed the exchange to falter while he did some rearranging of information himself.

A woman, well-bred, overconfident, vain. Yet something is driving her to get up to who knows what — spying?

'Oh, I do like puzzles. A pack animal who likes to forage alone, you say. Perhaps like a sheep… or a lemming?'

Her breath is on my neck.

Eddie spontaneously threw his head back, hoping to catch his assailant.

'So predictable, lieutenant.'

A sudden, excruciating pain in the nape of his neck overwhelmed his senses.

What the…

'I've already put you into unconsciousness once today, lieutenant. Take the pain you felt as a warning. Maybe next time you won't wake up. Now tell me the locations you've earmarked for military airfields. Tell me what I want to know, and you can go. Stay silent and… well, I simply say your reunion with Miss Anna may be delayed.'

'If you lay a finger on—'

'You'll do what, lieutenant? Attempt to attack me with the back of your head again? Please, don't be preposterous. As for being a sheep or lemming, they're herd, not pack animals. Try something with sharp teeth who enjoys the chase, no matter how long it takes.'

The woman is talking nonsense.

Eddie looked out into the blackness of the early evening through a thick layer of dust on the room's sole window as he thought of a suitable riposte. 'Ah, I've got it. You think of yourself as a vulture, although technically, they have a sharp beak. However, you smell like one.'

He felt cold metal pressing on the nape of his neck.

'Don't provoke me, lieutenant. Whether you live or die rests in my hand.'

It took Eddie a couple of seconds to realise his captor had some sort of weapon that could, in an instant, render its victim unconscious, or kill.

Let's see if she'll admit who she is.

'What if I said for all that upper class accent, you share a certain connection with Greece?'

'Ah, what a wonderful country. The giver of democracy to the world; the wise words of Aristotle, Plato, and Archimedes. To say nothing of its wonderful language. So rich, descriptive, yet to the point.'

'Then we can agree your code name is Lykos?' said Eddie.

She repeated her throaty laugh. 'Be careful what you say, my friend. Do nothing to prejudice your chance of survival, since you're aware of what I'm capable of doing to people I have no further use of.'

If only I could get my hands on you.

'You mean like murdering an innocent man and staging a car accident to throw the authorities off the scent? What type of human being does that?' He again noticed her breath on the back of his neck.

'One who does her duty to the Fatherland, whatever the cost. He had his chance to assist the cause. He failed. The Fuhrer does not accept failure. It cannot be permitted, so Mr Langham paid the price for his incompetence.'

'Then the missing number plates; removing the man's ring. That was all to—'

'To make the police investigation I knew would follow a little more difficult, yes. My original intention was to make sure it turned up in Filip Janson's office, but things are going so well that I decided not to bother making the trip to Cambridge. For good measure, I took Langham's collar stud off and dropped it under the car. I knew the police would carry out a fingertip search of the crash scene and provide a further link back to the church. I've no idea if it was found but thought it a nice touch to add complexity to their lives.' For the first time, his captor allowed herself to be seen by Eddie as she moved stealthily around his shackled body.

She's tiny. Maybe 5' 1", thirty-years-old or so, a sharp dresser. And that cut-glass English accent, what a class act.

'Yes, most people who cross me wear the same expression as you once they understand I have no compunction about killing to get what I want. You have experienced a little of what I can do.'

Eddie raised his head as he stared at the ceiling and the familiar crazed pattern of cracks that he'd spent so much time examining earlier. 'Where's Anna?'

His gaoler laughed. 'I expect her to be where she normally is at this time on a Saturday evening. In fact, you're in a far better position to answer your question than I am.'

'What, you mean…'

I've been played. She's a real pro and I'm the sucker.

'Lieutenant, you fell for the oldest trick in the book. I know how much you care for the dear vicar's daughter. Men are so stupid when it comes to women. You think you're the ones in charge. Men are so entertaining to watch as you dance to our tune.'

There's that overconfidence thing again, lady.

'So, let's get this straight,' said Eddie. 'You somehow got the telephone number of my billet, rang to say if I didn't get to Lipton St Faith's old coachworks within twenty-minutes, you'd kill Anna, only to leave a note in the place to say I had a further twenty-minutes to get here or you'd kill Anna, and it was all lies? Why make me go to the village first? You must have known I might have gone straight to the vicarage to check first?'

She moved towards Eddie, staying out of range of his feet. 'Lieutenant, all men are the same. You see yourselves as knights in shining armour set on rescuing the imprisoned maiden. When the truth is, you're all as thick as two short planks. Besides which, you're a military officer used to complying with orders. Yes, you might have called in at the vicarage, but in the few days I've come to know you, I knew if your lady-friend's life was at stake, you would do exactly as ordered — and you did!'

Time to put this lady on the back foot.

'Does that go for your beloved Fuhrer? You know that stuff you said about men being predicable and stupid. He's a man, isn't he, or have I misunderstood his great friend, Dr Goebbels?'

Eddie's captor flew into a rage. It was then he noticed a slim metal object like a torch in the woman's right hand.

What's that?

Lykos moved around her prisoner and pressed the cold metal onto his neck. In an instant, Eddie lapsed into unconscious.

By the time the lieutenant came around, he was alone in the room.

What is that thing? He thought as he rotated his head in a failed attempt to provide relief to his aching neck. *She must be able to adjust the strength of whatever that weapon delivers. That's why she twisted the case.*

Later, although he was unsure how long he'd been unconscious, Eddie heard the key turning in its lock. This time his gaoler didn't bother disguising her movement. To his surprise, she held a small tray with a beaker of water and a bread crust on which a greyish-yellow topping had been applied.

'Let's start again, shall we?' Lykos' voice returned to its former low, silky-smooth tone. 'Comply with my rules and we shall get on with each other like good chums. First, you will not insult the Fuhrer. If you do, I shall kill you. Second, in exchange for something to eat and drink, you shall tell me the locations of the military airfields your president is planning to build in Norfolk.' She held out the tray. 'Now, shall we be friends?'

Eddie smiled. 'And how do you expect me to eat that with these on?'

He moved his head from side to side to draw attention to the handcuffs.

Lykos smiled and laid the tray on the rubbish-strewn floor.

'Fortunately, I'm not too hungry right now. However, seeing as you'll kill me whatever happens, why not humour your victim a little?'

Lykos looked at Eddie, then at the tray of bread and water resting on the floor. 'Let me guess, why is an upper-middle-class English woman like me serving the Fatherland?'

'Something like that,' responded Eddie, the intensity of his glare matching hers.

'Fools, weak fools lead this country. The Fuhrer has offered generous peace terms on several occasions, only for his benevolence to be thrown back in his face.'

'By peace terms, don't you mean surrender? Also, does his benevolence include bombing innocent people?'

Lykos's calm exterior changed in an instant. 'It may have escaped your memory, but the British bombed Germany first. Their air force could not have known whether they killed civilians when they bombed our ports. Drop a bomb on a civilian by mistake and they're still dead. It makes no difference to them whether it was intended, so please, lieutenant, let us at least be clear on the facts.'

Where is the bitterness coming from?

'Don't Polish civilians count? They had done nothing to Germany. If we are, as you say, to be clear on the facts, if memory serves, your Fatherland invaded without warning and unleashed... now, what do you call it? Yes, a Blitzkrieg. Isn't that so?'

Lykos kicked the tin tray to one side, causing the beaker to tip and spill its contents and the bread to act as an unwilling sponge.

'Enough of this nonsense. You'll tell me what I want to know or—'

'Or what?' shouted Eddie. 'Oh yes, you'll kill me. That'll go down well with your superiors, I'm sure. What was it you said earlier, the curate had to die because he failed in his mission? Well, you'll have failed if I don't tell you what you want to know... that is, if I have anything to tell you in the first place. Currently, your prospects aren't looking too good, are they? By the way, as we're talking about failure, what hold did you have over Sidney Langham that ultimately cost him his life?'

Come on, take the bait.

Lykos shrugged her shoulders. 'He was weak. We told him his only living relative in Belgium was to be executed for colluding with the enemy if he didn't help us. He did everything we told him, except—'

'Except get to me.' *This is all making sense.* 'So, you blackmailed an innocent young man to do your dirty work?'

'I told you, all men are stupid,' sneered Lykos.

It's now or never.

245

'I'll be sure to tell Adolf that when I next see him,' said Eddie as he attempted to stand. Half-bent because of his arms being behind his back and manacled, he lunged forwards to knock his captor off her feet. For all her slight frame, she neatly sidestepped his move, meaning Eddie tumbled forward, coming to a stop on his side as he hit the floor with a clatter. He caught sight of the pen-like object as she moved and dreaded what might be coming.

'No.'

Hurting… dark.

Ugh.

Chapter Nineteen: A Top Bloke

'Dr Janson, what I still don't understand is why you called me?' Anna studied Sidney Langham's spiritual adviser closely as her parents looked on in the spacious lounge of the vicarage.

The pastor toyed with his cup of tea and shuffled his feet nervously as he sat on one of two armchairs forming a pair on either side of a roaring, open fire. 'Once I'd calmed down after ringing the Cambridgeshire Police about your most recent visit, I realised all I'd done was to bring more attention to myself. I guessed you'd trace the car Sidney died in back to me. 'People watched me argue with Mr Langham, and as you yourself commented, I didn't deliver the lecture the day he left for Aylsham. I suddenly realised everything pointed back to me and here am I, a foreigner in time of war up to no good. It isn't a great leap of logic from murder to spying for someone in my position, is it?'

Perhaps we forget the pressure some feel in war.

A tap on the door interrupted Janson's explanation. Helen glanced at the carriage clock on the mantle shelf. 'Who's knocking at ten-thirty on a Saturday night?'

'It has to be Tom,' said Anna as she sprang to her feet and ran down the vestibule. 'He must have news of Vinny.' She grabbed for the lock to release the catch, flinging the door open without a thought for anything other than the young boy who had become such an intimate part of their lives.

'Any news?' said Anna.

'May I at least get out of the cold? It's freezing out here,' replied Tom as he removed his police helmet and rushed past Anna into the warm interior of the vicarage.

'Yes, come in, I wasn't thinking,' replied Anna, closing the front entrance, seemingly unaffected by the bitter chill.

'Have you found Vinny? I mean, he's not—'

'He's fine. At least we think he is.'

'You *think*?'

'Vinny's been sighted twice in Norwich with a man, in St Stephens Street and on the Prince of Wales Road. It seems they're making for the train station.'

'I'll come, too,' blustered Anna as her parents came out of the lounge to investigate what all the fuss was about.

'Is it true?' said the vicar.

Tom nodded. 'It's too much of a coincidence. Norwich Police said the lad was giving the man a right earful… in a Liverpudlian accent. It has to be Vinny.'

'There'll be no more trains out of Norwich tonight, will there?'

'I'm afraid there will,' replied her husband. 'Freight trains run overnight, as do the mail trains. If someone wants to get Vinny out of Norfolk tonight, they'll have several opportunities.'

A solemn quiet fell over the vestibule as the vicar's words sank in. *Why would anyone want to take Vinny, unless…?*

'What if an uncle snatched Vinny to take him back to Liverpool?'

The vicar shook his head. 'But that makes little sense. Liverpool is suffering as much bombing now as they ever have. Why would anyone take a young boy back into those conditions?'

'Homesickness,' said a voice from the lounge doorway. 'I know what it's like to be forced from one's home. The longing to get back never fades, even if going back might entail danger. Family means everything, especially in times of war.'

Dr Janson's words resonated around the vestibule.

We forget how lucky we are to have family around us.

Tom glanced at his wristwatch. 'If you're coming, we have to leave now Anna.'

Helen rushed forward. 'Yes, you must go with Tom. Bring Vinny back to us… but be careful, promise me.'

Anna moved towards her mother's open arms as they hugged each other.

'Come back safe to us,' added her father.

As Tom opened the front door, he turned back to the vicar. 'Inspector Spillers will be along first thing in the morning to speak to Dr Janson. Can he stay here tonight? Otherwise I'll have to put him in a cell.'

Janson gave the vicar an anxious glance as Charles nodded. 'I'll take responsibility for delivering him to the Inspector. You have my word on it. Isn't that so, Dr Janson?'

The pastor mouthed a silent, "Thank you" to the vicar and offered a gentle smile.

That's the first time I've seen Janson smile.

The quiet interlude didn't last long.

'Thank you reverend, I hoped you'd offer. OK, Anna, let's get going.'

The sudden blast of cold air which met Anna as she ran to the police car made her thankful she'd grabbed her heavy coat from the clothes rack as Tom pulled her out of the front door. 'How long will it take?'

'Forty minutes with the wind behind us,' replied Tom as he slipped the clutch and encouraged the heavy vehicle to speed up out of the village by pressing his right foot to the floor.

Driver and passenger were each immersed in their own world as the Norfolk countryside opened up, its rural landscape bathed in the gentle light of a full moon.

'A bomber's evening,' said Tom as he cleared the condensation from the windscreen with his handkerchief.

Anna hesitated for a few seconds as she took in the tranquillity of their surroundings. 'They fly over here to bomb us, and we pass them going the other way to bomb them. Each morning, families count their dead and pray for bad weather to stop the enemy from coming back. What's the sense in it all, Tom?'

Tom shrugged his shoulders, 'But what's the alternative? We can't let them bombard us out of existence?'

'No. I get that, but in the end, the politicians will get around a table and agree to end it like last time.'

'Oh, yes,' replied Tom, his tone edged with cynicism. 'That went well, didn't it?'

Heaven forbid, it's all too depressing, thought Anna.

Ten minutes passed without conversation as the police car made steady progress towards Norwich.

'You're not still thinking about politicians, are you?' said Tom as he headed for the thrusting spire of Norwich Cathedral, which had pierced the landscape for over 800 years.

'You're joking,' replied Anna. 'I've been pondering about Eddie, you know, what's happened to him. Oh, he'd tell me he's a military man and can look after himself, but all the same…' Anna's voice tailed off.

Tom gave the windscreen another wipe, this time with the cuff of his coat in the continuing battle to keep the windscreen clear. 'You've become close, the two of you, haven't you?'

Anna shuffled in her chair. 'I'm not sure about that. We're mates. A bit like you and me, I suppose.'

Am I being honest with myself?

She noticed Tom looking at her instead of the road.

I'm confused. Not sure how I'm feeling about the two of them. What's happening to me? Better change the subject.

'Never mind Eddie, what about Fanny? Have you rearranged your date yet?'

Tom sighed. 'I'd intended to do it tonight, but young Vinny put paid to that.'

Perhaps he's keen on her after all, thought Anna.

'Oh, I've something to tell you,' said Tom.

Now he's the one changing the subject.

'We asked the hospital to look for signs of damage to the back of Langham's neck.'

'Bruising?'

'Yes, and catastrophic damage to his spinal cord made by something that penetrated his neck.'

'You mean like Herbert Trethel?'

'Exactly like Herbert. Whoever killed him also murdered Langham. They thought at first the car crash had snapped his neck until they discovered what they called "mechanical damage."'

What a waste of a life.

'What's up?' said Anna as she watched Tom turn his attention to the horizon.

He leaned into the windscreen, rubbing the glass furiously to get a better view. 'It's a plane.'

'One of ours?'

'Can't tell, too far away, but I doubt it at this time of night. I think it's too small for a bomber. My guess is it's a German fighter returning from protecting their bombers on a night raid to Liverpool or one of the other northern cities.'

Tom slowed the police car to a crawl as he attempted to identify the plane, which descended as it approached at lightning speed.

'It's firing at us. We've got to get off the road or we've had it,' shouted Tom as tracer bullets drew a menacing line from the airplane towards the car. He pressed the accelerator and waited for the old car to respond. 'Come on, you old jalopy.'

'He's heading straight for us, Tom,' said Anna as she intuitively curled into the smallest size she could and buried her head in her hands.

At last, the car responded as Tom violently swung the steering wheel to the right, causing the car to pitch to the left as it skidded into a narrow lane with a high bank nearest the oncoming attacker. Within a few seconds, it was all over. The fighter plane swooped low behind the police car and thundered to the south-east with a deafening roar of its angry engine.

The pair sat in silence for what seemed like an age.

'Will he come back for a second go?' asked Anna.

Tom wiped his forehead. 'We'll know in about thirty-seconds, but I doubt it. I suspect he'll be running low on fuel and he was chancing his arm for an easy kill. He won't waste fuel doubling back to try again.'

It was only at that point Anna felt an icy breeze. 'Wind your window up, will you? It's freezing in here.'

Tom gave Anna a confused look. 'It's already closed.'

They both investigated the back of the police car.

'It's gone,' said Anna. 'The window, it's shattered.'

'That's not all,' said Tom. He pointed to a tear in the roof lining. A jagged hole almost an inch in diameter pierced its mild-steel shell. 'He hit us at least once.'

Anna looked up at the damage in wonder. 'He came within inches of killing us both.'

Tom smiled at his passenger, 'Coming within inches isn't the same as hitting us. It could well have been miles. The important thing is he missed.'

Tom has changed these last few months. He's so calm. What a brave man he is.

With no time to lose, the two friends buttoned their coats and drew up their collars to defend themselves again against the howling gale coming through the broken window. They spent the next twenty-minutes with their eyes fixed on the reassuring sight of the cathedral spire. Moving cautiously through the deserted city streets, Tom eventually brought the damaged car to a halt next to Bethel Street police headquarters for Norwich.

'You two look as though you've lost a shilling and found a sixpence,' said a cheery desk sergeant of the spacious police station.

'The other way around,' responded Tom, to the confusion of his colleague.

'He's waiting for you, go through.' The officer lifted a hinged portion of the desk counter that gave access to the staff area of the station.

'Ah, there you are, Tom. Have a good run in from the sticks, did you?'

'Something like that, Derek,' said Tom as he exchanged weary looks with his companion. 'Anyway, this is Anna. Young Vincent billets at her place. Speaking of which, any news of the lad?'

His opposite number shook his head. 'Other than the earlier sightings, no. Except to say we now know they'll be staying somewhere in Norwich overnight.'

'But you can't be certain,' said Anna, her tone sharp. 'What about the freight and mail trains?'

Tom's opposite number was already shaking his head before Anna had finished speaking. 'Track damage because of enemy action way down the line. Nothing is moving until they've repaired the tracks.'

That's something, at least.

'That means they'll be in a B&B, and I bet it'll be somewhere near the train station,' said Tom.

'I agree,' responded Derek.

Tom scratched his head. 'From what I remember of that area, there are dozens of B&Bs down there. Any chance of help?'

Derek frowned. 'We'll do our best, Tom… got our hands full tonight, what with all the dance halls tipping out. I'll put a call through to the nearest police box to see if there's a bobby nearby who can help out.'

Tom thanked his colleague as they turned to leave. Within a minute they stood on the street, the quiet broken only by a police van disgorging a full load of drunken servicemen off to spend the night sobering up in a police cell, or await the military police to cart them off to a detention centre.

'Let's take the car. Walking would take us a good ten minutes.'

Anna required no further invitation to avoid more drunken men impeding their progress.

'We've been lucky so far, haven't we?' said Anna.

'What, you mean Norwich?' replied Tom as he looked out of the side window of the police car. 'I suppose so, but I doubt it'll stay that way.'

Anna paused for a moment. 'The Nazis invented a new name for what they did to Coventry, they called it being "Coventrated." They could as easily do the same here.'

Tom released his left hand from the steering wheel and rested it on Anna's shoulder.

That's the first time he's done that since we were children.

'All we can do is fight back as and when we can. They won't beat us. I know it in my bones. We won't lose.'

Why do I enjoy being with Tom so much lately?

'Now, on to more pressing matters,' said Tom. 'I'll park up at the bottom of Kett's Hill and suggest we make our way along the main road towards the railway station. There has to be at least a dozen B&Bs along this road.'

Within minutes, the pair began their quest by knocking on the first guest accommodation they came across. A movement of the blackout curtains to a ground floor front room told Anna the landlady was still up. An elderly lady opened the door a few inches and asked what the police wanted so late in the evening. Tom explained the situation, to which the woman responded by pointing to a sign in the window stating, "No Vacancies".

The same scenario played out on four further occasions as the pair worked their way along the road.

'Here we go again,' said Anna. As before, a twitch of the curtains preceded the front door being opened a few inches.

'It's funny you should ask that; I took in a man and young boy earlier this evening. The child was in a right strop, but he must be asleep now, because it's all quiet up there.'

Anna couldn't believe their luck. *We've found him.*

'May we come in?' asked Tom.

'Of course, dear. Take the first door on your left. I'll lock up.'

Anna followed Tom into a sizeable lounge filled with mementos of the woman's life set against the dim glow of a gas lamp and dying embers of the coal fire.

'What's he been up to?' asked the landlady as she entered the room, closing the door quietly behind her.

'I'm not at liberty to say,' said Tom. 'It's especially important I get access to whichever room they're staying in without alerting them to our presence.'

The landlady gave Tom an affectionate smile. She pointed at a photograph on a side cupboard. 'Same as my Peter, you are, sergeant.'

The photo showed a tall man in a police uniform standing outside the guildhall in the centre of Norwich.

'That one is outside the old guildhall before Bethel Street opened in 1936.'

'Your husband?' asked Anna.

'Was,' the woman replied. 'He's been gone these past ten years. He drowned saving a young lad from the river Wensum - down the road, in fact. I say a prayer whenever I go by. It brings me comfort if you know what I mean.'

Anna approached the photo. 'May I?'

The landlady smiled as she encouraged her visitor to pick up the silver photo frame.

'A handsome chap, Mrs...?'

'Oh, forgive me. The name's Chapel. He was a powerful man, too. He wouldn't hurt a fly though, not unless you broke the law, then he didn't stand for any nonsense.'

She took the photo from Anna and admired her dead husband's image for several seconds before replacing it on the cupboard. 'So, if that man upstairs has been up into no good, you have my blessing to punch him on the nose if he resists arrest.' Mrs Chapel gave an impression of a boxer to reinforce her point.

'I'm sure it won't come to that; however, we'll see. Which room are they in, Mrs Chapel?'

The landlady strolled across the room to a small mahogany bureau.

She opened the roller-shutter. Next, she withdrew a long, delicate gold chain with a key attached to her blouse, bent forward, and unlocked a small metal case that rested within the bureau.

'This is my pass key; it opens them all. You want room eight on the top floor. It's a climb, but you two are young enough to cope with the stairs, I'm sure.'

Tom took the pass key from Mrs Chapel and signalled for Anna to follow. Any hope of a quiet ascent lapsed as each step creaked more than the one before.

'Someone is bound to poke their head out the door,' said Tom.

'What, in a B&B? I don't think so,' replied Anna.

Finally, the pair reached the top step, which led to a small, narrow space with two doors leading off it.

'I wouldn't like to fall over the bannister,' said Anna as she pointed to an eighteen-inch gap between flights of stairs, meaning it was possible to fall between them from the top of the house all the way to the ground floor.

Tom didn't respond. Instead, he concentrated on listening for any movement from within room eight. 'It's as quiet as a churchyard.'

Anna watched on pensively as Tom slid the passkey into the door lock as silently as possible. He turned to Anna and smiled. 'I've got it, ready?'

The sergeant had the door opened in a split second. 'Police, stand still.' Tom had his right hand raised, in which he held tight hold of his police-issue truncheon.

Crikey, I wouldn't like to get on the wrong side of Tom, thought Anna.

A man stood inside the sparsely furnished room. Vinny was nowhere to be seen. Behind the startled adult, who held his hands above his head, lay an open window, its threadbare curtains swaying in the cold December breeze.

'Wait a minute, I've met him before,' said Anna. 'He's—'

The man bolted for the door. Tom swung his truncheon at the fleeing man, catching him square on his upper right arm.

As he continued his flight for freedom, Anna brought his attempt to an abrupt end by sticking her foot out, over which the man promptly tripped and fell headlong into the landing bannisters, breaking several as he came to a stop with the upper third of his body precariously hanging over the edge of the landing.

'That's Lindsay Fox-Marsden.'

'Who?' asked Tom.

'Oh, it doesn't matter for now, I'll tell you when things calm down, suffice to say a certain Mr Grey will be interested to speak with him.'

Tom shook his head as he attempted to place handcuffs on his prisoner. 'Don't resist me. You won't like the result if you try. Give me your hands and relax and you'll be safe. Struggle and, well, let's say it's a long way down to the hallway.'

Anna gave Tom a shocked look. *He wouldn't, would he?* she thought.

'Where's the boy?' barked Tom.

Fox-Marsden kept his counsel.

'I said, where is the boy. I won't ask again.' Tom made as if to push his prisoner over the edge of the landing.

'Tom, no, what are you doing?'

'OK, OK, I'll tell you, now get me off this floor.'

Would he have done it? Perhaps I don't know Tom as well as I thought I did.

'You'll stay down there until you tell me where the boy is.'

A moment's hesitation by his prisoner led Tom to nudge Fox-Marsden's prone torso further over the landing.

'He's gone. That boy is mad. He kicked me in the shin and

head-butted me in the stomach before opening the window and making off. That's the truth.'

'I'm not sure you'd recognise the truth if it bit you on the nose, now, get up.' Tom pulled the man back onto the landing, rolled him over and helped his prisoner sit against the door of room seven.

Meanwhile, Anna had run to the open window to scan the city's dark streetscape. 'Why did you take him from the village...' she shouted.

At first, Fox-Marsden didn't respond. Only Anna's lunge made him change his mind. 'I was told to. They made me.'

'Made you,' shouted Anna, 'Who made you?'

'I can't say... she'll kill me.'

She? Who's he talking about? thought Anna.

Tom gave Fox-Marsden a dig with the end of his truncheon. 'Believe me, you'll tell us eventually, but that can wait. How long ago did the boy leave? and why didn't you go after him?'

'Uh,' the prisoner cried out in pain. 'Thirty-minutes, no more. He was too quick for me. Go after him? Have you seen how far it is down that drainpipe?'

Anna looked forlornly out of the window. 'He could be anywhere by now, Tom.'

'Do you know what, Anna? I've an idea. What is it that Vinny likes above anything else?'

Anna turned. 'You mean aside from the Hershey chocolate Eddie gives him? Well, football, I suppose.'

'Exactly,' said Tom. 'And whose ground is around the corner?'

Anna's eyes lit up. 'Norwich City.'

The pair exchanged hopeful smiles.

'Let's get this weasel to Bethel Street station. After that, we'll shoot down to the football ground,' said Tom.

Anna looked pensive. 'That Mr Grey I mentioned, he will want to speak to Fox-Marsden. I'll tell you all about it later, but I don't think either of us has a choice but to get him back to Lipton St Faith. Will the local force release him back to your custody later?'

Tom nodded. 'The governor at Bethel Street and Inspector Spillers are best mates. It shouldn't be a problem.'

Luck was with Tom and Anna as they left Mrs Chapel's B&B in the form of two police officers on their beat. A two-minute briefing from Tom brought the constables up to speed.

'OK, thanks for doing that, and remember any problems, get the station to ring my governor, yes?'

After watching his two colleagues march their prisoner smartly away toward Bethel Street, Tom turned to Anna. 'We might as well walk. It's not too far.'

Oh, if only.

As the pair strode quickly down one street after another, the sheer height of the football stadium announced its presence as they neared the monolith.

'I know a shortcut,' said Tom, pointing to a narrow alleyway to their right. As they exited the narrow space, the air glowed bright orange. 'Someone's not too worried about German bombers,' said Tom, before catching sight of a small group of people. 'Well, I never. Look at this, Anna.'

Following hard on Tom's heels, she left the alleyway behind and focused on a small shape sitting on a plank of wood between several men.

'Vinny, is that you?'

In an instant, the youngster sprang from his makeshift seat and hurtled over to Anna. 'I knew you'd come. I gave soft lad a kickin' 'e won't forget in a hurry.' 'E told me you were with me Ma and she was sick after the train journey from Liverpool. Said it was a surprise visit. 'E said you said I should go with 'im, so I did.'

The pair gave each other a long, tight hug as the boy hung onto Anna's lower body as if his life depended on it.

'He's alright for a Scouser I suppose,' shouted one of the poorly dressed men with their palms held out towards the warming fire.

'Them's alright, them lot,' said Vinny. 'That one is Fred, and that one, Jimmy… and the one with no hair or teeth. That's Cyril. They're my mates now. I owe 'em one and said if ever they come up my way, I'll get me Uncle Jack to take 'em for a few bevvies down the Dog and Sparrow. 'E's not my real uncle, but me Ma says I should call 'im that, I don't know why but 'e's always bringing me sherbet dabs, so that makes 'im a top bloke.'

Anna planted a kiss on the top of Vinny's head. 'Time to get you home, young man.'

Chapter Twenty: An Awful Reality

The morning began quietly enough with the vicar walking Dr Janson to the police station for his appointment with Inspector Spillers.

Once Charles returned to the vicarage, matters descended into chaos as he frantically searched for his sermon as the church bells heralded Sunday Worship's imminent commencement. 'I put it on my office desk, and now it's gone. What shall I do?'

Helen let out a sigh. 'We go through this palaver at least once a month, and where do you always find your sermon? In your cassock. Have you looked?'

The vicar huffed as he dismissed his wife's words of advice with the flick of his hand as he continued to open and close cupboard drawers in what was proving to be a futile search.

'Don't you dismiss me with your hand like that, Charles Grix. Vicar or not, do that again and you'll be spending the rest of Sunday locked in my pantry. Now, look inside your cassock before I do it for you.'

'You'd better do as Mum says, Dad. She's called you by your full name; you know what that means.'

Anna's advice did the trick.

'I apologise. Yes, I'm being a pig-headed old man, but I can tell you for sure that—'

The vicar cut his sentence short as he felt an inside pocket of his cassock. 'Ah, I wonder how that got there?'

The two women burst out laughing as Charles mumbled incoherently and dashed from the room, making for the church.

'Honestly, that man. Almost forty-five years married, and he's never altered.'

Anna smiled. 'Would you want him to change after all that time?'

Helen had a twinkle in her eyes. 'Oh, no. I have your father where I want him. You'll understand when you get married.'

Fine chance of that, thought Anna.

Before she could plan a suitable response, a sharp rat-tat-tat-tat from the front door knocker reverberated around the vestibule.

'I bet your father's forgotten something.' Helen rushed to the door. 'Charles Grix, what is it... Ah, Tom, it's you. That thing I said about Anna's father. It's nothing.'

Tom smiled. 'Then I'm only glad I'm not in Charles's shoes this morning.'

'You don't know how right you are,' said Anna as she joined her mother at the front door. 'Are you coming to church with us? We're about to leave, aren't we Mum?'

Helen smiled as she grabbed for her winter coat from an oak coatrack on the wall beside her.

'No, I can't. Believe it or not, Inspector Spillers has insisted I talk to that woman at Winterton-on-Sea again. It seems she's still complaining about strangers roaming around the place. Fancy a run out with me.'

'You're a coward, Tom Bradshaw. You only want me to come with you because she got the better of you the other day,' replied Anna.

'Not at all, I—'

'Well,' said Helen, 'if you don't mind, I'll be on my way. The state your father's in means he'll probably forget the order of service like last time. Beatrice Flowers will love that. Be safe, you two, and don't be late for lunch. I've got a nice cut of beef for once. Tom, you're welcome to join us.' With that, Helen rushed between Tom and her daughter before disappearing with Vinny across the churchyard and through the east entrance of the church.

'How can a man turn down the offer of a free Sunday roast?' said Tom.

'Never mind the beef and two veg for now. What's all this about Winterton?' replied Anna.

The sergeant helped Anna with her coat before both faced the cold December drizzle. 'Like I said before that woman who shouted at me the other day is at it again and the Inspector wants it stopped once and for all. As if I didn't have enough to do with the murders of Sidney Langham and Herbert. We'll make this short and sweet and tell her it's got to stop, or I'll have her for wasting police time.'

'There speaks a brave policeman,' giggled Anna.

Tom smiled as he held the car passenger door open for his companion. 'I've got protection with me, so it'll be fine.'

The journey to Winterton-on-Sea passed without incident as the pair went back over the murder cases and mused about Eddie's whereabouts.

'What I don't understand,' said Tom, 'is why he hasn't been in touch. It's all so secretive. Then again, perhaps he's in trouble?'

Anna shook her head. 'He's big enough to take care of himself, so I don't reckon he's in any real danger, but we both know he's been acting funny since he recognised Langham's corpse. I can't help pondering if our curious Mr Grey and Eddie's superior are pulling his strings. If I'm correct, Inspector Spillers knows more than he's letting on,' said Anna.

'What you're saying is, you don't have a clue?' responded Tom.

Anna glanced at her companion, 'To the point, as usual, Thomas. Anyway, we're about to arrive in Winter—'

'What's up?' said Tom.

'That's his car.'

'Who's?'

'Eddie's. Look over there. The back end of Eddie's is sticking out of that boat shed.'

Tom slowed the police car. 'You're right,' he replied. 'But it makes no sense?'

Anna shrugged her shoulders. 'That about sums the last week up. The question is, why is his car here? He loves it to bits, so I can't see him being far away.'

'How about this for a plan of action,' said Tom. 'As soon as we've dealt with our serial complainer, we'll have a good mooch around to track him down, OK?'

Anna nodded as she took a last glance over her shoulder at the distinctive red sports car as Tom stopped the car several yards back from the Victorian train station.

'She lives in one of them; number six, apparently,' said the sergeant, pointing out of his side window at two detached stone cottages that stood separate from several other nearby buildings.

'It's the left-hand one, then,' said Anna as she waited for Tom to lock the car and join her for the short walk to the front door.

Other than the two of them, the only other person around was a station porter loading several boxes into a small van.

'I suppose everyone's at church,' said Tom.

'Which is where we should be. I'll have to say some extra prayers tonight to make up for missing dad's service,' replied Anna, trying not to make her cheeky grin too obvious.

Tom opened the wrought iron garden gate and held it for Anna.

'I'd have thought our busybody would've been among the first to have donated her gate and fencing to the war effort. Dad hated cutting our fence up, but he said it was the right thing to do.'

Anna glanced at the ornate iron work as she led the way to the quaint cottage's tongue-and-grooved front door. 'Is she expecting you?' said Anna as she knocked on the door for the second time.

Tom stood back to check for anyone standing at a window. 'I imagine so. The Inspector told me to be here for ten-fifteen sharp.' He glanced at his wristwatch. 'We're bang on time. Here, let me give it a knock.'

The sergeant pounded on the door with the side of a clenched fist. Several seconds passed as the pair waited for an answer.

'Are you sure the Inspector said number six, not seven?' said Anna, pointing to the house next door.

Tom took out his police notebook and opened the black leather cover. 'Definitely number six,' he replied. 'I'll look around the back. Give me a shout if she opens the door in the meantime.' The sergeant sauntered around the side of the house and out of Anna's line of sight.

Two minutes later, he reappeared. 'Quiet as a graveyard. She isn't in and that's all there is to it, which means I'll have to come back yet again… such a waste of my time. If this woman costs me my roast dinner, I won't be happy, I can tell you.'

Anna gave the door a last knock in the forlorn hope that it might solicit a response. 'Nope, she's not here,' she said. 'I tell you what, why don't we nip next door to see if they know where she might be?'

'My last hope of salvaging my dinner, come on,' said Tom as he led Anna through the garden gate.

'This place looks just as deserted,' said Anna as she approached the front door and lightly tapped on the leaded glass panel, which decorated the top quarter of the door.

'It can't be that everyone is at church, surely,' said the sergeant as he looked through one of several small glass panes that made up the lounge window. 'To be honest, it looks empty. Perhaps no one lives here?'

Anna joined Tom at the window, peered through the dust covered glass and was about to agree with her companion when she thought she saw something. 'I'm sure the door from the lounge to whatever's behind it moved, Tom.'

The sergeant took a second look. 'I can't see anything. Why don't we go around the back?'

What are we getting ourselves into? thought Anna.

'Come on, and mind the rubbish, it looks like a builder's yard,' said Tom as he led the way down the side of the property and picked his way through a selection of old floorboards, broken house-bricks, and various bits of broken furniture.

The overgrown rear garden reflected the properties' general state of disrepair as Tom stepped gingerly through a patchwork of tall grass and faded summer wildflowers. 'Nope, can't see a thing,'

Anna stepped towards the rear door. 'It's open.'

Tom took a last look up at the bedroom windows before confirming Anna's discovery. 'I bet kids have wrecked the place.' He pushed on the rickety door, which moved freely enough to allow access. 'You wait here, I'll take a quick look.'

You're welcome, thought Anna as she watched her companion vanish into the building's dishevelled interior.

'What on earth's the matter?' said Anna as she watched Tom re-emerge, his face drawn and pale.

'She's dead.'

What's he talking about? thought Anna.

'The woman I came to interview, at least it looks like her… she's stone cold.'

Anna entered the semi-derelict building, squeezing past Tom after giving his arm a reassuring rub. A familiar sight met her as she walked the few yards to where the body lay. 'She's in the same position as we found Herbert Trethel. That's spooky.' The corpse looked as though it had collapsed in on itself and lay in a crouched position similar to an Inca mummy, except the body's head had slumped forward onto its still chest.

'That's not the only similarity,' said Tom as he pointed to the back of the woman's head. 'Look at the neck.'

Anna neared the corpse. 'The same bruising... and look, a slight penetration wound in its centre. Exactly like Herbert.'

'And I bet it did the same sort of damage to her spinal cord the pathologists said caused Sidney Langham's death,' said Tom as he touched the corpse's exposed arm with the back of his hand. 'Cold.'

The pair stood over the woman's still frame as they took in the tragic scene.

'Three people murdered in different locations by the same means. What kind of human being does that?' said Anna.

Tom scattered several discarded magazines along the floor with the side of his foot. 'Are they human? I've seen some awful things as a policeman, but the planned brutality of these murders is some-thing else. It's the work of a professional. Look,' said Tom, pointing to the dead woman. 'No struggle, just dispatched in cold-blood... for what reason?'

Anna shook her head, unable to respond with any kind of answer that might explain the awfulness of what lay at their feet. Then she caught sight of something shining on the floor. 'Look at that?'

'What?' replied Tom.

'There, it must have been under that clutter of paper you moved aside with your foot.' Bending down to retrieve the object, she froze.

'What is it?' asked Tom.

Anna held up a small silver military pin. 'Eddie wears one like this. He must have been here.'

What am I saying? thought Anna.

Both looked back at the dead woman.

'No… not… Eddie—' muttered Tom.

'He can't of… but?' replied Anna, the colour draining from her face.

Tom scratched his chin. 'Let's face it, Eddie was nowhere to be seen when we found Herbert; he's still missing and here we have another body… and evidence he's at least been in this room.'

Anna shook her head, unable to process the turmoil. 'But what about the cottage hospital? It was Eddie that spotted the scar on Sidney's ear.'

'Yes,' said Tom, 'but he only explained that to you days later. And from what you say, he was in a heck of a state. What if—'

'Stop, Tom. I can't bear it.'

'Perhaps you can't, but it's my job to follow the evidence. That pin got here in only one of three ways; one, an American serviceman other than Eddie has been in here; two, someone else dropped it here, or three—'

'Eddie.'

'Yes, Anna, Eddie's—'

'No, you've misunderstood. Eddie, he's in the next room.'

'What?' exclaimed Tom as Anna pointed to a door, open just enough to see a figure seated with his back to the far wall.

The pair exchanged shocked glances.

Please, don't let him be dead, thought Anna.

Tom approached the panelled pine door, which had lost most of its brown paint covering. What remained hung from the timber surface in various states of bubbling and peeling. He touched at the door to reveal a little more of the space beyond.

'He seems to be asleep, or unconscious,' said Tom.

Anna moved position so she could take a better look. *What's happened to him? Please let him be innocent.* She moved forward.

'No, Anna. Let me,' said Tom as he gave the door another push. As it swung back on its hinges and Tom passed through the opening, Eddie suddenly came to life.

'Tom, no. Don't let her get you with—'

The sergeant followed his instinct to fling the door fully open to get a full view of what might await him. As he did so, a shocking thud pervaded the air as a steel prong half-an-inch in diameter penetrated the door panel nearest Tom's neckline.

'Behind it!' screamed Eddie.

Tom pulled the door back to him before once again slamming it back as far as he could make it. This time a cry of pain rang out as he rushed through the door opening, yelling for Anna to stay where she was.

The sergeant stood well clear of the door, to see the shape of a slight figure grasping at a metal object to free it from the door panel.

'Leave it,' shouted Tom as he withdrew the truncheon from his belt. 'I said, leave it.' He held the dense wooden restraint above his head, ready to strike. The woman ignored his orders.

Anna ran through the door and over to where Eddie sat before turning to view the insidious sight before her.

She looks insane, thought Anna as she watched the contorted facial features of the woman snarl as she fought to release her weapon.

'Don't let her touch you with that, Tom. It'll kill you,' shouted Eddie in a weary voice.

Tom restrained the woman with a single sharp crack of his truncheon to her shoulder. This time it was she who crumpled to the floor.

'Get her away from it,' said Eddie, his voice becoming weaker with each intervention.

Anna leapt into action by running across the room and slamming the door shut, so keeping the impaled weapon well away from its warped owner.

'You're under arrest for the murder of Sidney Langham, Mr Herbert Trethel, and persons unknown within this property...'

As Tom completed cautioning the woman, Anna retraced her steps to Eddie. She knelt in front of him and caressed his tired cheeks. 'What happened here? You frightened me to death when you vanished again.'

Eddie offered the beginnings of a smile before almost lapsing into unconsciousness.

'Never mind, it can wait. Now let's get you up.' She saw a set of handcuffs held Eddie tight to the chair. Looking over her shoulder at Tom, she saw he'd restrained the woman with little effort. 'Are all police handcuffs the same... you know, the lock?'

'No,' replied Tom, 'but I bet she's still got the key.' The sergeant went through each of the woman's pockets, against which she put up little resistance, until he found the key. 'We got lucky, here it is.'

Anna caught the small metal object mid-flight as Tom threw it across the room. Seconds later, she'd freed Eddie, yet his hands remained in a fixed position behind his chair.

Poor man, he must have been sitting like that for who knows how long, she thought. As Anna attempted to move his arms, Eddie let out a cry of pain.

'Leave him be, Anna, he'll move them when he's ready. I expect his circulation needs to kick in before he can do anything. In the meantime, let's see what we have here.'

Tom manoeuvred the woman against the wall with her legs stretched out on the untidy floor and walked the few steps back to the door. Taking a handkerchief from his pocket, he took a firm hold of the metal object stuck in the old timbers and turned it from side to side. After one failed attempt to dislodge the implement, he tried a second time. A sharp tug freed the item. 'It reminds me of something I've seen farmers and vets use, but it's heavily modified.'

'May I look?' said Anna.

Tom glanced at his prisoner to make sure she hadn't moved before stepping across to Anna.

'I've no idea what it is?'

Tom pressed the bolt-like projection of the weapon back into the casing and primed the weapon for use by pulling on a lever on the underside of the metal body. Next, he moved back to the door. 'Watch this.' A light touch on the trigger sent the bolt shooting into the door. Again, it penetrated the wood and stuck out the reverse side.

'Imagine the damage that will do to the soft tissue of someone's neck before it smashed into their spinal cord. It's evil.'

Anna checked the back of Eddie's neck. Sure enough, the tell-tale signs of bruising were present. 'So how come Eddie is still alive?'

Once Tom had withdrawn the weapon from the door, he showed Anna how to moderate the power of the captive bolt mechanism. 'Do you see the rachet setting above the trigger? Well, by altering the setting, she could choose whether to stun or kill her victim. Eddie was lucky, she must have needed him for something.'

Anna refused Tom's offer to hold the insidious weapon, instead she looked back at her frail friend. 'And I think I know what it was she wanted.'

'Is that what this is all about... all the murders. Has Eddie something to do with their deaths after all?'

Anna shook her head. 'No... at least not in the way I think you mean, but in one sense, you're correct. If it were not for the job Eddie does, none of this would've happened.'

'I don't understand.'

'Why don't you call the station to get Lykos safely behind bars, then we'll get Eddie back to the vicarage and I'll explain everything.'

'Lykos? Who's Lykos?' exclaimed Tom.

By the time Tom's colleagues collected his prisoner, Eddie had regained a greater presence of mind, though not back to his old self, he still had the presence of mind to enquire about his sports car.

'Yes, it's fine,' said Anna. 'At least the back end is, because that's all we saw of it when we came into the village. But before you say anything, don't think for one second you're in any state to drive it. I've had a word with Tom. He'll take you to the vicarage and I'll drive your car back.'

'You?' exclaimed Eddie in a tired tone.

'Yes, me, and you're in no position to argue, so that's that.'

By the time the mini convoy got back to Lipton St Faith, Sunday lunch was in full swing. Instead of taking Eddie into the busy kitchen, Anna and Tom quietly led him through the vestibule without alerting the others to their presence and made him comfortable on the lounge sofa. Anna watched as the lieutenant curled up holding a cushion between his arms, which rested across his chest and raise his head to the roaring fire. Within seconds, he'd lapsed into a deep sleep.

Tom and Anna's arrival in the kitchen met with a riot of cheerful voices and smiling faces. Among the throng were Inspector Spillers and Mr Grey.

That man looks almost normal, thought Anna.

'I assumed you two were going to miss Sunday lunch again,' said Helen. 'What was it in Winterton-on-Sea that kept you so long?'

'Oh, nothing,' said Anna, looking at Vinny.

'Ah, I see,' replied her mother as the youngster, oblivious to the conversation, fought with a troublesome Brussels sprout.

273

'Perhaps we might have a word after lunch, sergeant?' said Inspector Spillers.

'Of course, sir,' replied Tom, relief spreading across his face as it dawned that he might enjoy a Sunday roast after all.

The next hour passed with genial conversation as Vinny did his usual job of entertaining everyone.

Why do we have to grow up? thought Anna as she delighted in the youngster's perspective on everyday things.

Eventually, Helen made a move to gather the dishes in the sink.

'I'll help you with those, Mum,' said Anna.

'Thank you,' replied Helen. 'Oh, and by the way, the shopkeepers were as good as their word in donating supplies for Mrs Flotman. I'm told she was overcome, so your instincts were correct.'

I'm so glad she accepted the gifts, thought Anna.

'Thank you for organising that, Helen, and you for suggesting it in the first place, Anna,' said the vicar. She and her late husband did so much for the village in the past. It's nice to give something back, isn't it? Anyway, I'll leave you two to it and look in on the lieutenant to see how he's doing.'

Meanwhile Inspector Spillers motioned to Tom and Mr Grey that they should retire to the police station for a debrief, before turning back to Helen. 'Perhaps we might all meet back here at say seven o'clock, if that's OK with you, Mrs Grix?' said the Inspector.

'Of course, it is… and please, remember, it's Helen.'

'And I'll make my way back to Cambridge,' said Dr Janson.

Inspector Spillers checked his progress from the room. 'Ah, I wonder, Dr Janson, whether you might stay a little longer, it may surprise you what you'll learn later and I'm sure one of my officers will drive you back to the college. In the meantime, you may wish to join us at the station… er, no cell this time, I promise.'

Spillers' disarming smile was enough for Janson to accept the invitation without further comment.

The kitchen's remaining occupants, Anna and Helen busied themselves washing and drying the dishes. The only intrusion was the vicar's dulcet tone quietly floating down the hallway into the kitchen, advising that Eddie had fallen into a deep sleep.

'He's had quite a day of it, poor man,' said Helen.

'I can't imagine what he's been through these past few days.'

Helen looked at her daughter. 'I hoped you might help me answer that question.'

I knew that question was coming, thought Anna.

'There's a lot I can't tell you, Mum, although I hope we'll both learn the full story this evening. Let's you, dad and me talk in his office after we've finished here. I'll tell you as much as I know.'

Anna proved to be as good as her word as she spent the best part of an hour explaining all that had happened between Tom, Eddie, and herself over the previous seven days.

'Now it makes sense,' said her father. 'You're saying Vinny's abductor knew the woman you call Lykos?'

'Again, we'll know more tonight,' replied Anna, 'but my guess is that Fox-Marsden, or whatever his real name is, has been used every bit as much as Sidney Langham. My guess is that Lykos did her homework. Perhaps she knew he was desperate to prove his claim to the baronetcy and used it as leverage to get him involved. After all, he's connected to the fascists, so what better fall guy than a naive fantasist who wanted to be accepted by the upper class?'

'And Herbert Trethel?' asked the vicar.

Anna sighed. 'That's perhaps the saddest thing about all that's gone on. He was in the wrong place at the wrong time, and all because he agreed to do Tom a favour. Lykos had to be certain the car bore no trace of her, not if her plan to implicate Dr Janson was to succeed. And her anonymous letter almost worked - you saw what a state the man was in when we confronted him at Three-Mile-Bottom. Lucky for him, he was in the habit of always making a record of his number plate in the car. Without that, I doubt he'd have had a leg to stand on, because until that point, everything seemed to point to him. After all, who'd swallow a story of secret agents and pretend baronets?'

'Don't forget the woman you found this morning, Anna,' said Helen.

Anna thought for a moment. 'You know, I feel terribly guilty about her. See, I never even bothered to find out her name. I assumed she was just another busy body with too much time on her hands. I guess she was, but that was no reason for her to be murdered. Perhaps she called around to the house to satisfy her own curiosity. In Lykos' warped head, she presumably couldn't take the risk of a nosy neighbour exposing her to the authorities and certain execution as a spy.'

Anna yawned as she slumped back into her father's favourite leather chair.

'It seems the lieutenant isn't the only one who needs sleep,' said her father. 'There's nothing more to do until the Inspector and the others return this evening. Why don't you go upstairs for a couple of hours?'

Anna hesitated.

'Come along, my girl. Bed for you,' said Helen.

I don't have the energy to argue.

By seven o'clock, the vicarage lounge resembled a doctor's waiting room, with every chair taken by an individual waiting to tell their story. The house's regular residents, plus Fanny, Tom, Inspector Spillers, Mr Grey and Eddie, sat ready for events to unfold as Helen busied herself distributing tea and the contents of a tin of biscuits she'd been holding back for months.

'It's a good job Vinny's in bed,' said Helen, 'he'd be in this tin like a ferret chasing rabbits.'

A quiet murmur of laughter rippled around the room as some declined Helen's offer, while others eagerly accepted the rare sugary treat. Minutes passed as the trickle of conversation between individuals petered out until only the sound of bone-china cups contacting their saucers broke the silence.

'Well, I guess we should finish what began just over a week ago by Mr Grey and I updating you all,' said Inspector Spillers as he rose from his chair to stand on one side of the blazing open fire.

'I can confirm that we have charged a 38-year-old woman for the murders of Sidney Langham, Herbert Trethel and Violet Hudson.'

So that's who the poor woman was, thought Anna.

'I have also charged her with the attempted murder of Lieutenant Eddie Elsner and Sergeant Tom Bradshaw.'

Both my special men had a lucky escape from that monster, thought Anna.

The Inspector glanced at Mr Grey, who accepted his invitation to take up the narrative.

'Perhaps I should begin by reminding you all that anything you hear in this room is to be treated as confidential and subject to the Official Secrets Act, announced Grey in a solemn tone. 'The reason you're being briefed at all is that each of you has been directly involved, or come into close contact, with the murder suspects we'll discuss this evening. I cannot rule out other "strangers" contacting some of you in the future and who appear to know your background. If this happens, you must contact me immediately. I shall leave my number with the Inspector so that you may do this.'

'Do you think that likely?' said the vicar.

Grey clasped his hands together as if praying. 'No, I don't, but it would be remiss of me not to point the danger out, no matter how remote. It is naive to think we know the full extent of the enemy's spy network and so we must be alert to the danger. Now, to business. Perhaps the most important thing to inform you of is that we now know the real name of the woman known as "Lykos" is, in fact, a lady called Mrs Felicity Stanhope.'

A murmur of surprise rumbled through the room.

'An archetypal English name,' commented Anna. 'Did she work for you, Mr Grey?'

'As ever, Miss Grix, a most perceptive observation. No, she did not, at least not directly. Sadly, Mrs Stanhope was, until recently, a trusted member of another department that falls within my sphere of operations.'

The occupants of the room, except for Inspector Spillers, looked at Grey with a communal display of confusion.

'I don't understand?' said the vicar.

Grey wore a faint smile. 'A spy, Reverend. Felicity Stanhope was a British spy specialising in counterintelligence, which gave her ready access to all we had on Oswald Mosley and his fascist followers, as well as certain other information being received by our operatives across Europe. Stanhope is also something of a linguist and speaks German and French to perfection.'

Eddie let out a muffled moan as he rubbed the back of his neck before gathering his thoughts. 'A double agent?'

Grey shook his head. 'Alas, no. Had she been one, we'd probably have picked up on her activities sooner. No, the woman is a traitor, and will pay the price for her duplicity. Perhaps we'll never know how many brave men and women she condemned to death after we dropped them into France by betraying their presence to the Nazis.'

'That's too horrible,' said Fanny as she moved nearer to Tom and linked his arm. 'Why did she do such a nasty thing?'

Did Tom just shy away from Fanny? thought Anna.

'An intriguing question, Miss Coulson. That's what we couldn't understand. We knew someone within the intelligence service was leaking crucial information to the Germans, but couldn't get close to who it was. Then we picked up a report about Lindsay Fox-Marsden making a nuisance of himself asking certain establishment figures about this gentleman.' Grey pointed at Eddie.

All eyes fell upon the American, who concentrated his gaze on the oak herringbone flooring.

'This was known when you kidnapped us?' said Anna, her voice tinged with anger.

Again, Grey smiled. 'Invited you both in for a brandy, not kidnapped, Miss Grix. However, to answer your question, yes. It was the lieutenant's sudden request to visit Bletchley Park that alerted us to something unusual happening, so—'

'Wait a minute,' said Eddie as he raised his head to look at Grey, causing a second painful neck spasm. 'General Murphy passed on my request to visit Bletchley to you?'

Grey shook his head. 'No, lieutenant, at least not directly. Let us be clear, you above all others in this room — and that probably includes me, know how closely our governments are cooperating to defeat the Nazis and their Axis "friends", so it shouldn't be a shock to you that your superior shared his concerns with my superior. From that moment on you, and anyone you consorted with became of interest to us.'

'Concerns,' replied Eddie, the already deep furrows on his forehead becoming more prominent.

'Indeed, lieutenant. Your superior alerted us to the fact you'd spent some time at that establishment previously, which to be clear to the rest of you, I cannot divulge. Indeed, you will forget any reference to that place, which is mentioned this evening. Do I make myself clear?'

Heads nodded without a word being said.

'So, you set us up to meet Fox-Marsden. You even suggested how we might reel him in?' Anna kept Grey firmly in her sights as she spoke.

'Yes, I guess that was clumsy of me,' replied Grey, 'but we had to get close to him. We knew you contacting him would set several hares running. We maintained a close watch, and it did.'

'You mean the thug that was with him in Newmarket that day?' said Eddie.

'No, no,' responded Grey, 'He was not one of ours, but I'm certain it must have crossed your mind that the heavy was present as much to report back to Lykos... er, I mean Felicity Stanhope, as he was to "protect" Fox-Marsden?'

Anna nodded. 'Even so, Mr Grey, those "hares" you mention led to the deaths of two further innocent people. How do you live with yourself?'

'Miss Grix,' began Grey, 'contrary to popular belief and American movies... Apologies, lieutenant, I mean no offence, but intelligence officers are not all cold-blooded killers.'

'You killed Herbert Trethel and that woman this morning as sure as if you'd pulled the trigger yourself,' shouted Anna.

'I did what had to be done,' replied Grey in a staccato tone devoid of emotion.

'And if that had involved seeing the lieutenant murdered, as he almost was; that counts as "duty", also?'

'Yes,' replied Grey, as the two combatants stared each other out.

'... And me?' said Anna in a quiet tone.

'And you, Miss Grix.' Grey mirrored Anna's tone as they continued to glare at each other.

Anna was the first to break eye contact.

Eddie hasn't moved a muscle to defend me. They're all as bad as each other, she thought.

The room fell silent as Anna took her seat and Grey lit a half-finished cigar with a long taper from a glazed container on the fire hearth.

Taking his time to light his cigar, Grey inhaled before blowing a cloud of dense bluish smoke into the still air, which released the pungent aroma of the Havana leaf.

'I will not apologise for telling the truth, Miss Grix. If I survive this war, I'm certain that in the years to come I'll reflect on my actions, lawful as they are, and struggle to come to terms with the loss of lives, guilty and innocent, my action caused.' He turned to Anna's father. 'Perhaps the church will grant me a measure of redemption. I do hope so. This country continues to fight for its very existence and I'll continue to do my duty, no matter what the price.

The room again fell into silence until, at length, Fanny spoke. 'I don't understand what turned this Lykos lady from one of ours into a spy?'

Grey puffed on his cigar again before resting it by his side while removing a spot of tobacco from his lower lip. 'I asked the same question of my superiors as soon as we learned her identity earlier today. The awful truth is all that has happened comes down to matters of the heart.'

'What do you mean?' asked Helen.

'Felicity Stanhope's husband was found dead in a bombed-out London town house. Nothing unusual about that these days, you might say. Her reaction seems to have been to contact us to ask how she could help fight back against an enemy that had murdered her husband of over twenty years standing. Once we learned of her language skills, we snapped her up. However, the coroner asked questions long after the inquest when a witness came forward to say they had heard a shot fired earlier that evening. An autopsy found a bullet wound hidden above his hairline.'

The vicar shuffled in his chair, 'Why did the autopsy not discover the wound? Obscured it may have been, but surely any half-diligent pathologist would have found it?'

Grey frowned. 'You don't understand, vicar. After the air raid, they discovered him in the cellar of the collapsed town house. You can imagine what state it was in, and he was just one of over 250 that night. I imagine that if the house hadn't been bombed, his body may have remained undiscovered for months, perhaps years, now that so many of the finer London properties are shut up for the duration.'

'You're forgetting the man had a loving wife, Mr Grey. Don't you think she may have noticed his absence?' asked Anna, her tone edged with sarcasm, a trait she rarely displayed.

'I suppose I deserved that, Miss Grix, but it turns out he worked in one of many Whitehall departments set up specially to destabilise the enemy. Again, I cannot go into the details. Suffice to say that his wife would have been quite used to not seeing her husband for months on end. She herself lived in a small property outside London and would have had no reason to visit their town house after closing it up at the outbreak of the war.'

'Until the authorities got in touch to say the house had been bombed and…'

'And requested she provide certain personal details of her husband so that he might be formally identified, if you understand what I'm getting at,' interrupted Grey.

Anna fired back, 'Yes, I do, Mr Grey, but you can't expect us to believe that it's possible for a distraught widow to pick up a telephone and ring the British intelligence service and ask to be a spy to get back at her husband's killer's?'

All eyes fell on Grey as he gave himself breathing space by sucking on the remnants of his cigar, before carefully flicking ash into the open fire. 'As I say, Miss Grix, there are things it is not possible for you to know. What I can say is...'

'That's not good enough and don't patronise me, Mr Grey. There's more to Felicity Stanhope's background than you're telling us. Three murders and the near deaths of two men I love trumps your little game.'

Anna felt a collective gaze rest on her.

What? she thought, before noticing the shocked look Eddie and Tom were giving her, and each other. Anna also noted Fanny's less than supportive glance.

I don't care what anyone thinks anymore, thought Anna.

Grey looked at the remaining stump of his cigar before tossing the unburnt tobacco into the hissing coals as pockets of methane escaped. 'Love is a dangerous thing, is it not, Miss Grix? It draws us into events we are not experienced at dealing with, yet we ignore our natural instincts to run away. In fact, when someone, or something we hold dear, is in danger, some people have an unerring tendency to run towards danger to save the very thing that's dear to them.'

'I don't understand?' replied Anna.

Grey smiled, 'Oh, I think you do, Miss Grix,' he replied, making his passing glance at Tom and Eddie obvious to the room. 'And so it was with Felicity Stanhope. What I am prepared to tell you is that she convinced herself British intelligence murdered her husband.'

Grey's admission sent a shock wave through the room.

'Yes, it's fantastic, isn't it?' said Grey as he scanned the faces of his bewildered audience. 'You see, her husband, a most successful businessman by all accounts, had several business interests in Germany before the hostilities broke out. We can only assume she thought the British establishment was purging anyone who had helped the Nazis in the run up to the war.'

'And are they?' asked Anna pointedly.

'No, Miss Grix, it is not. Again, perhaps you watch too many movies on the subject.'

Anna shook her head, 'So all this stemmed from a wife's mistaken belief that the English murdered her husband?'

'When you put it like that, Miss Grix, yes. Certain dispatches were, let us say, intercepted, which first alerted us to the code name, "Lykos". However, we didn't know who the operative was.'

He's looking at Eddie to warn him not to say anything about Bletchley Park, I bet, thought Anna.

'Joining up the dots,' continued Mr Grey, 'we now know Lykos, and Felicity Stanhope are the same person.'

Anna sat ramrod straight in her chair as if struck by a bolt of lightning. It *was her; she was the one staring at me when Beatrice Flowers was giving me a dressing down in the high street... and it was her who stood opposite the kitchen window staring at the house.*

'But that still doesn't explain this awful woman's link to Sidney Langham, or that would-be baronet chap... what's his name? I have it, Fox-Marsden,' said the vicar.

Grey picked up, then replaced a framed photograph of the Grix family that held pride of place on the fireplace overmantel. 'Family is a powerful force, is it not, vicar?'

'The essence of our being, I would say,' replied Charles, unsure why the question had been put to him.

'Perhaps we should take a step back,' said Grey. 'In Felicity Stanhope, we have the wife of a successful businessman and the lifestyle that goes with it. Yet on hearing about the death of her husband, that lifestyle is threatened—worse than that, what if her husband's links to Germany were to surface? Might that not threaten her own social standing... something upper middle-class men and women are paranoid about.

After all, their type exists in a world where success is very much based on who, rather than what you know.'

The vicar once again fidgeted in his chair. 'You're not seriously suggesting she became a spy to...'

'Maintain her place in polite society? No, Reverend Grix, I'm not,' interrupted Grey. 'However, the world as she knew it died with her husband. We can but guess at her true motives... and I do not hold out much hope that the interrogation she is about to undergo in the Tower of London will leave us knowing much more that we know now. If found guilty of murder and treason, which I have no doubt she will, the last face that woman will see on earth will be that of Albert Pierrepoint as he places the noose and a canvas hood over her head before she is consigned to oblivion.'

'Please, Mr Grey, I...'

'I appreciate your care for all souls, no matter how damaged, but that's the truth of it, reverend. She will hang. As for why she contacted both the British establishment and the Germans, I can only conjecture that she truly believed that her husband had been targeted by us and saw an opportunity to exact revenge on his killers, no matter how fanciful the idea–and earn money from the Nazis. Don't forget, through her dead husband's contacts, she'd have had little trouble getting through to the higher echelons of the German military. I know they'd have carried out a background check and snapped her up once convinced of her motive. Once vetted and cleared, they'd have assigned a special agent to act as her handler... then allocated her a mission.'

'Sidney Langham?' asked Tom.

'Precisely,' replied Grey. 'Once they had their clutches on his aunt, they had a direct means to join a few of their own dots up.' Turning to Eddie, Grey continued, 'Like it or not, lieutenant, the Nazis know you're here. What they didn't know... and hopefully still don't, is why.

So, getting a vulnerable curate to find out what you were up to was too good an opportunity to miss.'

Eddie rubbed his eyes, his fatigue obvious to the rest of the guests. 'But I first came across him months…'

'Be careful what you say, lieutenant,' interjected Grey. 'Yes, it was, and that was the start of this sorry saga. How he knew you were there, we'll never know. However, we can be thankful nothing got back to his handler… or if it did, he sent no communication on the matter to Germany.'

'How can you be sure of that?' asked Anna.

'We are,' replied Grey in a tone brooking no further enquiry on the subject.

'And Fox-Marsden?' said Tom.

Grey smiled. 'A useful idiot. I'm sure the Germans told Lykos… I mean Felicity Stanhope to promise him he'd be made a baronet with his own lands once they'd overrun the country. All spies are good at playing to the vanities of others, Miss Grix, and from that standpoint, her target would have been easy to recruit. There's no doubt in my mind that the Nazis realised she might be useful to them, allocated her a code name and, after making sure she wasn't a double agent, trained her in novel ways to kill silently, as she has so ably proven over recent weeks.'

'I still don't…'

'Don't get why British intelligence took her seriously?' said Grey. 'Believe me, we get cranks, and well-meaning members of the public telephoning Whitehall every day, wanting to "do their" bit by becoming a spy. They're all checked out, so we understand why they rang; you know, for good or ill, that sort of thing. 99.99% turn out to be fools or innocent, if somewhat deluded, men and women. Occasionally we'll hit upon someone with a special skill we can make use of… and sometimes we get taken in, as when Mrs Stanhope made contact.

In fact, she wrote in at first, then telephoned. Of course, she didn't know which department to write to, or telephone number to ring, but we cross-check all contact. Her tenacity and language skills made us prick our ears up… and before anyone asks, yes, vetting took place. She was brilliant and has made fools of us.'

'And cost people their lives, Mr Grey,' said Anna.

Grey fell quiet for a few seconds. 'Yes, you're correct, Miss Grix, but then the courage of several people in this room, not least yourself, plus any intelligence that we had, limited the damage Lykos could inflict.'

Anna shrugged her shoulders, 'Is that supposed to make me… or any of us feel better?'

Grey sat on the arm of a nearby chair. 'It's not for me to say how any of you should feel, except whether you know it, you have done your duty… yet it is something no one outside of this room must ever find out about.'

What a waste of life, thought Anna as she glanced around a room full of decent people who, she felt, had been unwitting bit-part players in a bigger game none of them truly understood.

Eventually, Helen broke the reflective silence. 'I think we could all do with a cup of tea.'

'Just the thing,' said Charles. 'And why don't we listen to the wireless to cheer us up?' He looked at the carriage clock on the mantle shelf. 'Ah, excellent, we should just catch the last half of "It's That Man Again". I love ITMA… it's so funny.'

'It's best when Colonel Chinstrap says, "I don't mind if I do,"' said Tom.

'What about when Mrs Mopp's catchphrase, "Can I do you now, sir?"' added Fanny.

As the vicar's guests waited for the wireless valves to warm up and begin broadcasting the sound, the mood in the room lifted in anticipation of a few minutes of radio comedy as a distraction from the upsetting events of recent days and intensity of the previous hour.

'I've listened to it several times. I don't get it,' said Eddie.

'That's because you're—'

The vicar interrupted Anna as he listened to the first scratchy words coming from the wireless as it warmed up. He looked at his wristwatch before checking the carriage clock again. 'Oh, dear, the clock must need winding up. It's stopped. I'm afraid we've missed ITMA.' Charles was about to switch the machine off when a familiar voice filled the room.

"This is the BBC Home Service. Here is the news, and this is Alvar Lidell reading it. Japan's long threatened aggression in the Far East began tonight with air attacks on United States naval bases in the Pacific. Fresh reports are coming in every minute. The latest facts of the situation are these. Messages from Tokyo say that Japan has announced a formal declaration of war against both the United States and Britain. Japan's attack on American naval bases in the Pacific were announced by President Roosevelt in a statement from the White House tonight.

The first statement said that the naval base of Pearl Harbor and other naval and military targets in the chief Hawaiian island of Oahu had been attacked from the air. Almost immediately after came the announcement that Manilla in the Philippines had also been raided. A little while ago, Mr Stephen Early, Whitehouse Press Secretary, said that as far as was known at the moment, the attacks were still going on. "In other words," he said, "we do not know if the Japanese have bombed and left." Acting on his executive authority, President Roosevelt has ordered the mobilisation of the United States Army and given instructions to both the army and navy to carry out undisclosed orders prepared for the defence of the United States.

So much for the official news, press messages and radio observers on Oahu said that the attacks on the island began early in the morning and it seems a hundred or more planes took part. Some reports say that an oil tank was set on fire and an airfield hit. As soon as the planes appeared overhead, American anti-aircraft guns opened fire and American fighter aircraft also went up.

A number of planes are said to have been brought down. Naval and military units soon cleared citizens from the streets with the aid of volunteers. Many people went up to the hill to watch the raid. A radio observer said some damage has been done to Pearl Harbor, and that the United States battleship, Oklahoma, built in 1914, has been hit and a fire started."[iv]

The sullen atmosphere in the lounge hung like a threatening storm cloud as its inhabitants took in the enormity of the emerging situation.

Grey broke the sombre silence. 'That announcement puts a rather different emphasis on the telephone call I told you about the other night, Miss Grix, lieutenant. I imagine certain important persons are discussing much graver matters, rather than a breach of information about clandestine American operations in Norfolk.'

'I've no idea to what you refer regarding my daughter and Lieutenant Elsner, Mr Grey. What I can tell you is that tonight's news detailed a crime against the entire world. It has immense implications for us all,' said Charles, as he rested his elbows on his knees, intertwined his fingers and placed his forehead on his clasped hands, his eyes shut tight.

Anna glanced around the room. The others seemed, like her, not to know what to say or do.

After a moment's silent prayer, the vicar stood, ambled over to the wireless set and switched the machine off. No one spoke.

Epilogue

Tom turned to Fanny, who was in tears. He held her close yet concentrated his gaze on Anna.

He's a good man. I was wrong to be jealous of him with Fanny, yet he's looking at me? thought Anna as she divided her attention equally between the sergeant and lieutenant.

Next, she watched her mother comfort her father.

What must go through their minds after 1914 and 1938?

A telephone rang, causing everyone except the American to jump at the sudden intrusion.

'I guess it'll be for me,' said Eddie as he quietly left the room. Within thirty-seconds he appeared at the entrance to the kitchen and caught Anna's eye.

Am I losing him, too? through Anna as she silently withdrew so that the two of them stood close to one another in the privacy of the vestibule.

No, I don't want to hear it.

Eddie placed a finger beneath Anna's chin and tenderly raised her head until their eyes met. The tears flowed as she waited to hear the words she'd been dreading for months.

'That was General Murphy. He wants me in London within four hours.'

'But that means…'

Eddie took hold of Anna and laid a kiss on her forehead. 'I have to leave now. Driving the car will be slow with the blackout, but I have no choice, I have my orders.'

Anna's tears flowed freely as the implications of Eddie's news sank in. 'When will I see you?'

The lieutenant didn't answer at first, instead; he stared blankly into space. Gathering himself, he placed a kiss on Anna's cheek. 'I don't want to lie to you. It's not a case of when, but, if. I doubt they'll send me back now that most of my work is done. Remember what I told you when we first met about needing to do my bit to honour my father? Well, I'm a fighter pilot. That's what they trained me to do, and Pearl Harbor, well, the Japanese won't stop there. It's time for me to do my proper job, my beautiful Anna.'

Beautiful?

Anna pulled back from Eddie a few inches to gauge body language.

He means it.

There was only time for the briefest of kisses to cement their new understanding before Eddie released his gentle hold and moved towards the front door. 'Say goodbye to them, will you, and say I was just passin' through.'

I don't want him to go. It's not fair.

Anna tried to smile as she rushed over to Eddie, the freezing wind making little inroad to halt their tight embrace.

'Youse will have to marry 'er, now you've kissed. That's what me Ma says blokes have to do.'

The pair broke their embrace to see Vinny halfway down the staircase leaning against the bannister rail.

Eddie gestured for the boy to join them. 'Will you do something for me, young man?' said Eddie

Vinny looked suspicious. 'Am I still in trouble for kickin' that no-mark?'

Eddie smiled. 'No, you're not in any trouble. It's just that I've got to leave for a while. Will you look after Anna for me?'

Vinny looked puzzled. 'What, you mean until you come back, like?'

Anna turned from the young boy as her tears flowed.

'Something like that, Vinny. So will you do it?' said Eddie as he half-closed the front door to keep the bitter wind from flooding into the house.

'What's in it for me?' Vinny's cheeky demand lifted the spirits of both adults.

'I thought Anna was as good as your sister?' said Eddie.

Vinny nodded. 'She is, but what's that got to do with doin' a bit of business?'

Eddie's smile widened as he dug into his uniform pocket and withdrew an unopened Hershey bar. 'This will have to do as a down payment. You'll get the rest when—'

'When you come back, right?' said Vinny, as he relieved Eddie of his offering.

'You look after this precious lady for me; deal?'

Vinny looked at the bar of chocolate, then at Anna. 'She'll be alright with me.' The boy took hold of Anna's hand as Eddie opened the front door wide enough for him to pass through.

'I...' whispered Eddie.

'I love...' mouthed Anna, but not before she watched the door close behind the lieutenant.

Vinny strained his neck to look up at Anna as he held tight on to his unofficial sister. 'It's no use crying 'cos that won't get the spuds peeled, that's what me ma always says.'

i   Daily Express Newspaper, 3 December 1941 [online]
Available through ukpressonline.co.uk
[Accessed on 20 April 2021]

ii   Daily Express Newspaper, 3 December 1941 [online]
Available through ukpressonline.co.uk, 3 December 1941
[Accessed on 21 April 2021]

iii   Daily Express Newspaper, 6 December 1941 [online]
Available through ukpressonline.co.uk
[Accessed 23 April 2021]

iv   BBC news bulletin, 7 December 1941 [online]
Available through @BBCArchive
[Accessed on 30 April 2021]

English (UK) to US Glossary

Albert Pierrepoint: Official executioner, whose tenure covered the period of WWII.

(Car) bonnet: Hood.

(Car) boot: Trunk.

Apples and pears: London 'cockney' rhyming slang for 'stairs'.

ARP warden: Volunteer tasked with alerting the local population of an impending bombing raid and subsequently giving the 'all clear' signal, often by blowing a whistle while riding a bicycle.

Bevvies: British colloquialism for pints of beer.

Biff: A British slang term for hitting someone. This is always said in jest and often used in old children's comic books.

Bletchley Park: Significant base for British intelligence operations during WWII.

Bobby: Slang term used for uniformed police. Derived from the short form of its Victorian founder, Sir Robert Peel.

Brylcreem: A male hair grooming product still popular today.

Bubble and squeak: Traditional British dish made with beef and cabbage fried together. The names derive from the sound made by the ingredients when cooking. In WWII, any leftovers from previous meals substituted for the beef, which was in short supply because of rationing.

Camp coffee: A product invented in Scotland in 1876. The product typically comprises chicory and dry coffee extract, water and sugar, which mix to form a dark brown syrup.

Chipper: Old-fashioned term for someone who is happy/ sees the bright side of things.

Chum: Friend.

Fibber: Colloquialism for lying - always said in jest or when teasing a person

Film: Movie.

Five Bob: Five shillings - there were twenty shillings to the British pound before decimalisation in 1971.

Grafton Rooms: A famous night club, dance hall in Liverpool.

Hobson's Choice: Having to take what is offered or leave it. Said to have originated from 16c Englishman, Thomas Hobson.

Hoity-toity: Old-fashioned term used in the UK to describe someone who thinks themselves 'posh' or above themselves.

Hot Pot: A traditional British dish. A type of stew often served with a pastry crust.

Jalopy: Old-fashioned term to describe a vehicle in a terrible state of repair or unreliable.

Knock your block off: Colloquial saying for hitting someone around the head. Usually said in jest.

Land Girls: Colloquial name for the Woman's Land Army. They carried out a range of jobs on the land left vacant by agrucultural workers and other men working the land conscripted to the armed forces. The women could be directed by the government to work anywhere in the country.

Lorry: Truck for hauling produce and goods, e.g., a small version of the modern American 'rig'.

MG: Trading name of the Morris Garage vehicle manufacturer.

No-mark: Liverpool slang for a person of no consequence.

Old Money: Refers to the traditional landed gentry of the British aristocracy as a group, as opposed to 'new money' through which wealth is attained from being in 'trade'.

Pavement: Sidewalk.

Peat Diggings: Origins of the Norfolk Broads, a network of inland waterways that were originally excavated for peat. When the sea levels rose, the excavations filled with water.

Pint of Twos: A pint of beer comprising a half-pint of brown, 'mild' beer (a little like Guinness) and half a pint of light coloured 'bitter', e.g., like Budweiser.

Pop your clogs: British colloquialism for dying.

Public House: Long form description for a British Pub.

Quisling: A person who collaborates with enemy occupying forces. The name originates from Norwegian officer who nominally headed the government during the WWII German occupation.

Regicide: The purposeful killing of a monarch.

Robert Kett: Norfolk landowner who sided with the people in objecting to the enclosure of farmland on July 8th, 1549.

Roasties: Nick-name for roasted potatoes.

Scallywag: British slang term for a likeable rouge. 'You're a little scallywag, you are'.

Scamp: Affectionate term for a mischievous youngster.

Scouser: British slang for a person from Liverpool, England.

Sherbet Dabs: Candy = A card tube filled with sherbet, along with a liquorish stick with which to 'suck' the sherbet from its container.

Sixpence: A pre-decimal (1971) British coin. 40 sixpences added up to one British pound.

Tap: Faucet.

Tea cake: A light, sweet, yeast-based bun containing dried fruits.

The Speaking Clock: First used in the UK in July 1936. Telephone customers rang a free number to hear the precise time announced every ten seconds.

Trolly: Gurney.

Tuppence: Two pennies - There were 240 'pennies' in a British pound.

Windscreen: Windshield.

Workhouse: An austere establishment used to house the destitute in former times.

WRVS: Women's Royal Voluntary Service fulfilled several volunteer roles in WWII. Now called the RVS - Royal Voluntary Service.

Wymondham: Norfolk Market town, pronounced Wind-am.

www.ingramcontent.com/pod-product-compliance
Lightning Source LLC
Chambersburg PA
CBHW031122210626
46816CB00016B/1764